To Emma Ingram (the real Emma) and her mother

There's Something about Christmas

DEBBIE MACOMBER

First Published in Great Britain 2016
By Harlequin Mira, an imprint of HarperCollins*Publishers*
1 London Bridge Street, London, SE1 9GF

There's Something About Christmas © 2005 Debbie Macomber

Includes bonus story *Shirley, Goodness and Me* © 1999 Debbie Macomber

ISBN 978-1-848-45447-7

1116

Chapter One

On that cold day I was born, in February 1955, my great-aunt gave me a classic fruitcake for the celebration of the occasion of my birth. Every year during the holidays I pull it out of the attic and take a look at it and it still looks great, and every year I try to get up the nerve to take a slice and try it.

—Dean Fearing,
chef of The Mansion on Turtle Creek

This job was going to kill her yet.

Emma Collins stared at the daredevil pilot who was urging her toward his plane. She'd come to Thun Field to drum up advertising dollars for her employer, *The Puyallup Examiner,* and wasn't interested in taking a spin around southeast Puget Sound.

"Thank you, but no," she insisted for the third time.

Oliver Hamilton seemed to have a hearing problem. However, Emma was doing her best to maintain a professional facade, despite her pounding heart. No way would she go for a ride with Flyboy.

The truth was, Emma was terrified of flying. Okay, she white-knuckled it in a Boeing 747, but nothing on God's green earth would get her inside a small plane with this man—and his dog. Oliver Hamilton had a devil-may-care glint in his dark blue eyes and wore a distressed brown leather jacket that resembled something a World War Two bomber pilot might wear. All he needed was the white scarf. She suspected that if he ever got her in the air, he'd start making loops and circles with the express purpose of frightening her to death. He looked just the type.

Placing the advertising-rate sheet on his desk, she turned resolutely away from the window and the sight of Hamilton's little bitty plane—a Cessna Caravan 675, he'd called it. "As I was explaining earlier, *The Examiner* has a circulation of over forty-five thousand. As you'll see—" she gestured at the sheet "—we have special introductory rates in December. We serve four communities and, dollar for advertising dollar, you can't do better than what we're offering."

"Yes, yes, I understand all that," Oliver Hamilton said, stepping around his desk. "Now, what I can offer *you* is the experience of a lifetime...."

Instinctively Emma backed away. She had an aversion to attractive men whose promises slid so easily off their tongues. Her father had been one of them. He'd flitted in and out of her life during her childhood and teen years. Every so often, he'd arrived bearing gifts and making promises, none of which he'd kept. Still, her mother had loved Bret Collins until the end. Pamela had died after a brief illness when Emma was a sophomore at the University of Oregon. To his credit, her father had paid her college expenses, but Emma refused to have anything to do with him. She was on her own in the world and determined to make a success of her career as a journalist. When she'd hired on at *The Examiner* earlier that year, she hadn't objected to starting at the bottom. She'd expected that. What she *hadn't* expected was spending half her time trying to sell advertising.

The Examiner was a family-owned business, one of a vanishing breed. The newspaper had been in the Berwald family for three generations. Walt Berwald II had held on through the corporate buyouts and survived the competition from the big-city newspapers coming out of Tacoma and Seattle. It hadn't been easy. Now his thirty-year-old son had taken over after his father's recent heart attack. Walt the third, the new editor-in-chief, was doing everything he could to keep the newspaper financially solvent, which Emma knew was a challenge.

"Hey, Oscar," Oliver said, bending to pet his dog. "I think the lady's afraid of flying."

Emma bristled, irritated that he'd pegged her so quickly. "Don't be ridiculous."

He ignored her and continued to pet the dog. She couldn't readily identify his breed, possibly some kind of terrier. The dog was mostly white with one large black spot surrounding his left eye. Right out of that 1930s show *Spanky and Our Gang*. Wasn't that the name? She shook off her momentary distraction.

"I'm here to sell you advertising in *The Examiner*," she explained again. "I hope you'll reconsider."

Oliver straightened, crossing his arms, and leaned against his desk. "As I said, I'm just getting my business started. At this point I don't have a lot of discretionary funds for advertising. So for now I'll stick with the word-of-mouth method. That seems to be working."

It couldn't be working that well, since he appeared to have a lot of time on his hands. "Exactly what is it you do?" she asked.

"I give flying lessons and I've recently begun an airfreight business."

"Oh."

"Oscar and I haven't crashed even once."

He was obviously making fun of her, and she didn't appreciate it. Nor did she take his alleged safety record as an incentive to leap into the passenger seat.

"But then," he added, "there's always a first time."

"Exactly what I was going to say," Emma muttered. "Well, I'll leave the information with you," she said more pleasantly. "I hope you'll think about our proposal when it's financially feasible."

Retrieving her briefcase and purse, she headed toward the door—which Oliver suddenly blocked with his arm. His smile was as lazy as it was sexy. Hmm, funny how often *lazy* and *sexy* went together. Considering all that boyish charm, plenty of other women had probably melted at his feet. She wouldn't.

She met his gaze without flinching.

"Are you sure I can't take you up for a spin?" he asked.

"Absolutely, positively sure."

"There's nothing to fear except fear itself."

"Uh-uh. Now if you'll excuse me, I have other calls to make."

He moved aside. "It's a shame. You're kinda cute in an uptight sort of way."

Unable to resist, she rolled her eyes.

Oliver chuckled and walked her out to her car, his dog trotting behind him. Normally Emma would've taken time to pet the terrier, but Oliver Hamilton would inevitably read that as a sign she was interested in him. She was fond of animals, especially dogs, and hoped to get one herself. Unfortunately, her apartment complex didn't allow pets; not only that, the landlord was a real piece of work. As soon as she had the chance, Emma planned to find somewhere else to live.

Using her remote, she unlocked her car door, which Oliver promptly opened for her. She smiled her thanks, eager to leave, and climbed into the driver's side.

"So I can't change your mind?"

She shook her head. The one thing a ladies' man could never resist, Emma had learned from her father, was a woman who said no. Somehow, she'd have to get Oliver to accept her at her word.

She reached for the door and closed it. Hard.

Oliver stepped back.

After she'd started the ignition and pulled away, he smiled at her—a mysterious smile—as if he knew something she didn't.

As far as Emma was concerned, she'd made a lucky escape.

Her irritation had just begun to fade when she returned to the office and walked down to her cubicle in the basement, shared with half a dozen other staff. The area was affectionately—and sometimes not so affectionately—termed The Dungeon. Phoebe Wilkinson, who sat opposite her, glanced up when Emma tossed her purse onto her desk.

"That bad?" Phoebe asked, rolling her chair across the narrow aisle. She was one of the other reporters, a few years older than Emma. She was short where Emma was tall, with dark hair worn in a pixie cut while

Emma's was long and blond. Most of the time, anyway. Occasionally Emma was a redhead or a brunette.

"You wouldn't believe my afternoon."

"Did you sell any ads?" Phoebe asked. It'd been her turn the day before and she'd come back with three brand-new accounts.

Emma nodded. She'd managed to get the local pizza parlor to place an ad in the Wednesday edition with a dollar-off coupon for any large pizza. That way, the restaurant could figure out how well the advertising had worked. Emma just hoped everyone in town would go racing into the parlor with that coupon. Badda Bing, Badda Boom Pizza had been her only sale.

"That's great," Phoebe said with real enthusiasm.

"Yes, at least our payroll checks won't bounce." She couldn't restrain her sarcasm.

Phoebe frowned, shaking her head. "Walt would never let that happen."

Her friend and co-worker had a crush on the owner. Phoebe was the strongest personality she knew, yet when it came to Walt, she seemed downright timid—far from her usual assertive self.

Emma sighed. Her own feelings about men had grown cynical. Her father was mostly responsible for that. Her one serious college romance hadn't helped, either; it ended when her mother became ill. Emma hadn't been around to help Neal with his assignments, so he'd dropped her for another journalism student.

Pulling out her chair, Emma sat down. She hadn't worked so hard to get her college degree for *this*. Her feet hurt, she had a run in her panty hose and no one was going to give her a Pulitzer prize when she spent half her time pounding the pavement and the other half writing obituaries.

Yes, obituaries. Walt's big coup had been getting a contract to write obituaries for the large Tacoma newspaper, and that had been her job and Phoebe's for the past eight months. Emma had gotten quite good at summarizing someone else's life—but that hardly made a smudge on the page of her own.

She hadn't obtained a journalism degree in order to persuade the local department store to place mattress sale ads in the Sunday paper, either. She was a reporter! A darn good one…if only someone would give her a chance to prove herself. Emma longed to write a piece worthy of her education and her skills, and frankly, preparing obituaries wasn't it.

"I don't think I can do this much longer," she confessed sadly. "Either Walt lets me write a real story or…" She didn't know what.

Phoebe gasped. "You aren't thinking of quitting, are you?"

Emma looked at her friend. She'd been hired the same week as Phoebe. The difference was, Phoebe seemed content to do whatever was asked of her. She loved writing obituaries and set the perfect tone with each one. Not Emma. She hated it, struggling with them all. The result was always adequate or better because Emma took pride in her work, but it just wasn't what she wanted to be doing. She had ambition and dreamed that one day she'd write feature articles. Eventually, she hoped to have her own column.

"I don't *want* to quit. I've been waiting six months for Walt to offer me something more than funeral home notices."

"Sleep on it," Phoebe advised. "You've had a rough day. Everything will seem better in the morning."

"You're right," she murmured. An ultimatum shouldn't be made on the spur of the moment. Besides, it wasn't the obituaries or even drumming up advertising dollars that depressed her the most.

It was Christmas.

Everywhere she went, there was holiday cheer. But not everyone in the world loved Christmas. She, for example, didn't enjoy it at all. Christmas was for families and she didn't have one. Yes, her father was alive, but that was of little comfort. Since her mother's death, he always invited Emma to his house in California and she always took a certain grim satisfaction in refusing him.

Almost everyone she knew had family and shared the holidays with them. Emma was alone. But she'd rather be by herself than spend it with her father and his new wife. Last year she'd ignored the season entirely. On

Christmas Day she'd gone to a movie and had buttered popcorn for dinner and that had suited her perfectly.

"You don't want to quit just before Christmas," Phoebe told her.

Emma sighed again. "No, you're right. I don't." But she said it mostly to avoid upsetting Phoebe.

"You're actually going to confront Walt?" Phoebe peered at Emma across The Dungeon aisle the next morning.

"Yes," Emma murmured. She'd decided that after almost a year, she wasn't any closer to writing feature articles than the day she was hired. It was time to face reality. She'd reached her limit; she was finished with working in the bowels of the drafty building, tired of spending half her week traipsing around Bonny Lake, Sumner and Puyallup searching for advertising dollars.

"What are you going to say to him?" Phoebe's brown eyes regarded her carefully.

She didn't know what she could say that she hadn't already said a hundred times. If Walt refused to listen, she would simply hand in her notice. She wouldn't leave until after Christmas; that was for strictly financial reasons. Where she'd apply next, however, was the question.

"Walt won't want to lose you," Phoebe said confidently.

"You mean when he isn't yelling?"

"He has a lot on his mind."

Emma narrowed her eyes. Phoebe's infatuation with Walt blinded her to the truth.

It was now or never. Emma stood, squaring her shoulders. "Okay, I'm going to talk to Walt." She motioned at the stairwell. "Do I have the *look?*" The one that said she was serious.

"Oh, yes!" Phoebe was nothing if not encouraging.

"You'll be stuck writing all the obituaries," Emma cautioned.

"I don't mind," her friend said.

"Okay, here goes."

Emma marched up the stairs and toward the back of the first floor, where Walt's luxurious office was situated. Well, perhaps it wasn't as luxurious as all that, except when compared to the dank basement where Emma and Phoebe were relegated.

Walt glanced up, frowning, as she planted herself in the threshold to his office.

"Do you have a minute?" she asked politely.

His frown slowly transformed itself into a smile, and for the first time Emma noticed her employer had company. She opened her mouth to apologize, but Walt didn't let her finish.

"I was just going to ask you to step into my office." He waved her inside. "I believe you've met Oliver Hamilton."

It was all she could do not to ask why he was here.

"Hello again," Emma managed to say as her stomach lurched. She should've known; Oliver wasn't a man who took no for an answer.

He stood when Emma came into the office and extended his hand. "Good to see you again, too."

Emma reluctantly exchanged handshakes, not fooled by his friendly demeanor, and avoided eye contact. A weary sensation came over her. The man was up to no good. At this point she didn't know *what* he wanted, but she had a feeling she was about to find out—a sinking feeling, which was one of those clichés she'd learned to excise in journalism school.

"Sit down," Walt instructed when she remained frozen to the spot.

She did, perching on the chair parallel to Oliver's.

Walt leaned back in his seat and studied her. Despite the free and easy style typical of the office, Emma chose to dress as a professional, since that was the way she wanted to be perceived. Her hair was secured at the base of her neck with a gold clip. The impression she hoped to create was that of a working reporter with an edge. Today's outfit was a classy black pinstripe suit with a straight skirt and formfitting jacket.

"You've been saying for some time that you'd be interested in writing something other than obituaries," Walt began.

"Yes, I feel—"

"You say you want to write what you refer to as a 'real story.'"

Emma nodded. She glanced out of the corner of her eye at Oliver. "However, if the story's about planes and such, I don't think—"

"It isn't." Her employer didn't allow her to finish.

Emma relaxed. Not completely but enough so she could breathe normally.

"It's about fruitcake."

Emma was dying to write a human interest story and after months of pleading, Walt was finally giving her an assignment. He wanted her to write about *fruitcake*. Surely there was some mistake.

"Fruitcake?" she repeated just to be sure she'd heard him correctly. Emma didn't even like fruitcake; in fact, she hated the stuff. She firmly believed that there were two kinds of people in the world—those who liked fruitcake and those who didn't.

She'd once heard an anecdote about a fruitcake that was passed around a family for years. It was hard as a brick and the fruitcake shuffle finally ended when someone used it as an anchor for a fishing boat.

"*Good Homemaking* magazine ran a national fruitcake contest last month," he went on to explain. "Amazingly, three of the twelve finalists are from the state of Washington."

He paused—waiting for her to show awe or appreciation, she supposed.

"That's quite a statistic, don't you think?" Oliver inserted.

Still leery, Emma slowly nodded once more.

Walt smiled as if he'd gotten the response he wanted. "I'd like you to interview the three finalists and write an article about each of them."

Okay, so maybe these articles weren't going to put her in the running for a major writing award, but this *was* the chance she'd been hoping for. There had to be more to these three women than their interest in fruitcake. She'd write about their lives, about who they were. She had her first big break and she was grabbing hold of it with both hands.

The professional in her took over. "When would you like me to start?" she asked, trying not to sound too eager.

"As soon as you want," Walt told her, grinning. Judging by the gleam in his eyes, he knew he had her. "The magazine's going to announce the winner on their website in three weeks, and then do a feature on her in their next issue. It could be one of our ladies. Flatter them," Walt advised, "and get permission to print their recipes."

"All right," Emma said, although she had the feeling this might be no small task. A niggling doubt took root and she shot a look at the pilot. "I assume all three finalists live in the Puget Sound area?" Oliver was in the newspaper office for a reason; she could only pray it had nothing to do with fruitcake.

Walt shrugged. "Unfortunately, only one lives in the area." He picked up a piece of paper. "Peggy Lucas is from Friday Harbor in the San Juan Islands," he said, reading the name at the top of the list.

A ferry ride away, Emma thought. Not a problem. It would mean a whole day, but she'd always enjoyed being on the water. And a ferry trip was definitely less dangerous than a plane ride.

"Earleen Williams lives in Yakima," Walt continued. "And Sophie McKay is from Colville. That's why I brought in Mr. Hamilton."

Emma peered over her shoulder at the flyboy with his faded leather jacket.

He winked at her, and she remembered his smile yesterday at the small airport. That I-know-something-you-don't smile. Now she understood.

A panicky feeling attacked her stomach. "I can drive to Yakima. Colville, too..." Emma choked out. She wasn't sure where Colville was. Someplace near Spokane, part of the Inland Empire, she guessed. She wanted to make it clear that she had no objection to traveling by car. It would be a piece of cake. Fruitcake.

"A woman alone on the road in the middle of winter is asking for trouble," Oliver said solemnly, shaking his head. "I don't think that's a good idea, do you?" While the question was directed at Walt, he looked at Emma.

His cocky grin was almost more than she could bear. He *knew*. He'd known from the moment she'd refused to fly with him, and now he was purposely placing her in an impossible position.

Emma glared at him. Hamilton made it sound as if she were risking certain death by driving across the state. Okay, so she'd need to travel over Snoqualmie Pass, which could be tricky in winter. The pass was sometimes closed because of avalanche danger. And snow posed a minor problem. She'd have to put chains on her tires. Well, she'd face that if the need arose. In all likelihood it wouldn't. The interstate was kept as hazard-free as possible; the roads were salted and plowed at frequent intervals.

"I wouldn't want to see you in that kind of situation," Walt agreed with Oliver. "In addition to the risk of traveling alone, there's the added expense of putting you up in hotel rooms for a couple of nights, plus meals and mileage. This works out better."

"What works out?" Emma turned from one man to the other. It was as if she'd missed part of the conversation.

"We're giving advertising space to Hamilton Air Service and in return, he'll fly you out to interview these three women."

For one crazy moment Emma couldn't talk at all. "You...want me to fly in that...little plane...with him?" she finally stammered. The last two words were more breath than sound. If she started to think about being stuck in a small plane, she might hyperventilate right then and there.

Walt nodded. He seemed to think it was a perfectly reasonable idea.

"I—"

"I've got a flight scheduled for Yakima first thing tomorrow morning," Oliver told her matter-of-factly. "That won't be a problem, will it?" His smile seemed to taunt her.

"Ah…"

"You *have* been saying you wanted to write something other than obituaries, haven't you?" This was from Walt.

"Y-yes."

"Then what's the problem?"

"No problem," she said, her throat tightening and nearly choking off the words. "No problem whatso-ever."

"Good."

Oliver stood. "Be down at the airstrip tomorrow morning at seven."

"I'll be there." Her legs had apparently turned to pudding, but she managed to stand, too. Smiling shak-ily, she left the office. As she headed down to her desk, Emma looked over her shoulder to see Walt and Oli-ver shaking hands.

Phoebe was waiting for her in The Dungeon. "What happened?" she asked eagerly.

Emma ignored the question and walked directly over to her chair, where she collapsed. Life had taken on a sense of unreality. She felt as if she were watching a silent movie flicker across a screen, the actors' movements jerky and abrupt.

"Aren't you going to tell me?" Phoebe stared at Emma and gasped. "You quit, didn't you?"

Emma shook her head. "I got an assignment."

Phoebe hesitated. "That's great. Isn't it?"

"I...think so. Only..."

"Only what?"

"Only it looks like you're going to be writing the obituaries on your own for a while."

Phoebe gave her a puzzled smile. "That's all right. I already told you I don't mind."

"Maybe not, but I have a feeling that the next one you write just might be mine."

Chapter Two

The first thing Emma did when she got home from the newspaper office that evening was check her medicine cabinet. Her relief knew no bounds when she found six tablets rattling around in the dark-brown prescription bottle. A few months earlier, she'd twisted her knee playing volleyball. Phoebe had conned her into joining a league, but that was another story entirely. The attending physician in the urgent-care facility had given her a powerful muscle relaxant. Her knee had continued to hurt, as Emma vividly recalled, but thirty minutes after she'd swallowed the capsule, she couldn't have cared less. All was right with the world—for a couple of hours, anyway.

Knowing how potent those pills were, she'd hoarded them for a situation such as the one she now faced with Oliver Hamilton. For the sake of her career she'd accompany him in his scary little plane, but it went without saying that Emma would need help of the medicinal variety. If she was going to be flying with Oliver Hamilton she had to have something to numb her overwhelming fear at the prospect of getting into that plane. She clutched the bottle and took a deep breath. For the sake of her craft and her career, she'd do it.

Emma simply couldn't survive the trip without those pills. One tablet to get her to Yakima and another to get her home. That left four, exactly the number she needed for the two additional trips.

Thankfully, Phoebe had agreed to drive her to the airport and then pick her up at the end of the day. Emma was grateful—more than grateful. Once she'd taken the muscle relaxant, she'd be in no condition to drive.

At six-thirty the next morning, Phoebe pulled up in front of the apartment complex. Carrying her traveling coffee mug, along with her leather briefcase, Emma hurried out her door to meet her friend.

"Don't you look nice," her landlord said, startling her. She was sure that was a smirk on his face.

Under normal circumstances Emma would've taken offense, but in her present state of mind all she could do was smile wanly.

Mr. Scott leaned against his door, this morning's *Examiner* in his hand. He was middle-aged with a beer belly and a slovenly manner, and frankly, Emma was surprised to find him awake this early in the day. After moving into the apartment, she'd stayed clear of her landlord, who seemed to be…well, the word *sleazy* came to mind. He didn't like animals, especially cats and dogs, and in her opinion that said a lot about his personality, all of it negative.

"Good morning, Mr. Scott," Emma greeted him, making a determined effort not to slur her words. The pill had already started to take effect and, despite the presence of the loathsome Bud Scott, the world had never seemed a brighter or more pleasant place.

"It's a bit nippy this morning, isn't it?" he asked.

Emma nodded, although if it was chilly she hadn't noticed. In her current haze nothing seemed hot or cold. From experience she knew that in three or four hours the pill would have lost most of its effect and she'd be clear-headed enough for what she hoped would be an intelligent interview.

"I don't suppose you know anyone who needs an apartment," Bud Scott muttered. He narrowed his gaze as if he suspected she wasn't sober—which was a bit much considering she rarely saw him without a can of Milwaukee's finest.

"I thought every unit in the complex was rented," Emma said.

"The lady in 12B had a cat." He scowled as he spoke. He'd underlined the *No Pets* clause a number of times when Emma signed her rental agreement. Any infraction, he'd informed her, would result in a one-week notice of eviction.

"Mrs. Murphy?" Emma cried when she realized who lived in 12B, two doors down from her. The sweet older lady was a recent widow and missed her husband dreadfully. "You couldn't have made an exception?" she asked. "Mrs. Murphy is so lonely and—"

"No exceptions," Mr. Scott growled. He shoved open his door and disappeared inside, grumbling under his breath.

"What was all that about?" Phoebe asked when Emma got into the car.

"He is truly a lower life-form," she declared righteously. "Doesn't possess an ounce of compassion." She stumbled a bit on the last word.

Phoebe gave her an odd look. "Are you all right?"

Emma smothered a yawn and then giggled.

"What did you do?" Phoebe asked, eyeing her suspiciously.

"Remember the pain pills I got last August?"

"The ones that made you so…weird?"

"I wasn't weird. I was happy."

"Don't tell me you took one this morning!"

In response Emma giggled again. "Just one. I need it for the plane ride. Can't leave home without it."

"Emma, you're supposed to be doing an interview."

"I know… The pill will wear off by then."

"But…"

"Don't worry, I'm fine. Really, I am."

Phoebe didn't look as if she believed her. When she stopped at a traffic signal, she cast Emma another worried glance. "You're *sure* you're doing the right thing?"

Emma nodded. All at once she felt incredibly tired. Closing her eyes, she leaned her head against the passenger window. In her dreamlike state, she viewed a long line of circus animals parading down to Bud Scott's office and protesting on behalf of Mrs. Murphy. The vision of elephants carrying placards and lions ready to rip out his throat faded and Emma worked hard to focus her thoughts on the upcoming interview. Fruitcake. Good grief, she hated fruitcake. She wanted nothing to do with it.

Yesterday, once she'd received her assignment, Emma had phoned Earleen Williams, the Yakima finalist, who was a retired bartender. Earleen had seemed flustered but pleased at the attention. Emma had made an appointment to talk with her late this morning. She'd spent much of the night reviewing her questions when she should've been sleeping. No wonder she was exhausted.

"We're at the airport," Phoebe announced.

Emma stirred. It required tremendous effort to lift her head from the passenger window. Stretching her arms, she yawned loudly. The temptation to sleep was almost irresistible, especially when she realized that all too soon she'd be suspended thousands of feet above the ground.

"Flying isn't so bad, you know," Phoebe said in a blatant effort to encourage her.

"Have you ever flown in a small plane?"

"No, but..."

"Then I don't want to hear it. See you back here tonight," Emma murmured, hoping to boost her own confidence. People went up in small planes every day. It *couldn't* be as terrifying as she believed. But this wasn't necessarily a rational fear—or not completely, anyway. It didn't matter, though; fear was still fear, whatever its cause. She reminded herself that in a few days she'd be able to laugh about this. Besides, writers across the centuries had made sacrifices for their art, and being bounced around in a tin can with wings would be hers. By the end of this fruitcake series, she might even have conquered her terror. Even if she hadn't, she'd never let Hamilton know.

Oliver and his dog were walking around the outside of the aircraft, inspecting it, when she approached, briefcase in hand.

"You ready?" he asked, barely looking in her direction.

"Ah...don't you want to wait until the sun is up?" she asked. She hoped to delay this as long as possible. The pill needed to be at the height of its effectiveness before she'd find the courage to actually climb inside the aircraft.

"Light, dark, it doesn't make any difference." He walked toward the wing and tested the flap by manually moving it up and down.

"There hasn't been a problem with the flaps, has there?" she asked, following close behind him. Too bad he was so attractive, Emma mused. In another time and place... She halted her thoughts immediately. This man was dangerous and in more ways than the obvious. First, he was intent on putting her at mortal risk, and second... Well, she couldn't think of a second reason, but the first one was enough.

No, wait—now she remembered. Since he was a good-looking, bad-boy type, she probably wasn't the only woman attracted to him. Tall, dark, handsome and reckless, to boot. Men like Oliver Hamilton drew women in droves and always had. He was far too reminiscent of her father, and she wasn't interested. Emma preferred quiet, serious men over the flamboyant ones who thought nothing of attempting ridiculous, hazardous stunts like flying small rattletrap planes.

"You're worried about the flaps?" he asked, and seemed to find humor in her question.

"Haven't they been working properly?" While Emma actually had no idea what function the flaps played in keeping an airplane aloft, she was sure it must be significant.

Something in her voice—perhaps a slight drawl she could hear herself—must have betrayed her because Oliver turned and gave her his full attention. Frowning, he asked, "Have you been drinking?"

"This early in the morning?"

"You didn't answer my question."

"No," she returned with an edge of defiance. "I don't drink."

"Ever?" His eyebrows rose as if he doubted her.

She shrugged. "I do on occasion, but I don't make a habit of it."

His dog sneezed, spraying her pant leg. This was her best pair of wool pants and she wasn't keen on showing up for the interview with one leg peppered with dubious-looking stains. Oscar sneezed again and again in quick succession, but at least she had the wherewithal to leap back. "Yuck!" she muttered. "Oh, yuck."

"You wouldn't happen to be wearing perfume, would you?" Oliver demanded in a voice that suggested she was attempting to carry an illegal weapon on board.

"Yes, of course I am. Most women do."

He grumbled some remark she didn't hear, then added, "Oscar's allergic to perfume."

"You might've told me that before now," she said, wiping her pant leg a second time. Thank goodness she'd brought gloves. And thank goodness they were washable.

He raised his shoulder in a nonchalant fashion. "Probably should have. It slipped my mind." He continued his outside inspection of the plane. "Oh, yeah," he said, testing the flap on the opposite wing, "I need to know how much you weigh."

"I beg your pardon?" There were certain things a man didn't ask a woman and this was one of them.

"Your weight," he said matter-of-factly.

Despite her drug-induced state of relaxation, Emma stiffened. "I'm not telling you."

"Listen, Emma, it's important. I'm loaded to the gills with furnace parts. I have to know how much you weigh in order to calculate the amount of fuel we're going to need."

She scowled. "You expect me just to blurt it out?" A woman didn't tell a man anything that personal, especially a man she barely knew and had no intention of knowing further.

"If I miscalculate, we'll crash and burn," Oliver said, apparently assuming this would persuade her to confess.

She glared at him in an effort to come up with a compromise. With her mind this fuzzy, it was difficult. "I'll write it down."

He didn't seem to care. "Whatever."

Emma set her briefcase on the floor inside the plane and extracted a pencil and small pad. The only time she weighed herself was when she suspected her weight had fallen. She certainly wasn't overweight, but a desk job had done little to help her maintain the figure she'd been proud of back in college. A few pounds had crept on over the last five years. She penciled in her most recent known weight, according to a doctor's visit last year, and then quickly erased it. After a moment's hesitation, she subtracted ten pounds. At one point in the not-so-distant past, she'd weighed exactly that and she would again, once she got started with an exercise program.

Tearing the sheet from the pad, she folded it in fourths and then eighths until it was about the size of her thumbnail.

Oliver was waiting for her when she'd finished. He held out his hand.

Emma was about to give him the folded-up paper, but paused. "Swear to me you'll never divulge this number."

He grinned, increasing his cuteness a hundredfold. "This is a joke, right?"

"No," she countered, "I'm totally serious."

He grunted yet another comment she didn't understand and grabbed what now resembled a paper pellet. "I can see this is going to be a hell of a flight."

Oliver stepped away, and Emma didn't see where he went, but he came back a few moments later. He casually told her it was time to board. She stood outside the aircraft as long as she dared, summoning her courage. Maybe she should've swallowed two tablets for this first flight.

Oscar was already aboard, curled up in his dog bed behind the passenger seat. He cocked his head as if to say he couldn't understand what she was waiting for.

"You got lead in your butt or what?" Oliver said from behind her.

With no excuse to delay the inevitable, she hoisted herself into the plane and then, doubling over, worked her way forward into the cramped passenger seat. Her knees shook and her hands trembled as she reached for the safety belt and snapped it in place, pulling at the strap until it was so tight she could scarcely breathe.

Oscar poked his head between Oliver's seat and Emma's, and she was left with the distinct impression that she'd taken the dog's place. Great, just great. She'd arrive for her first interview with her backside covered in dog hair.

Oliver handed her an extra set of earphones and pantomimed that she should put them on. "You ready?" he asked.

She forced herself to nod.

He spoke to someone over the radio in a language she didn't understand, one that consisted solely of letters and numbers. A couple of minutes later, he taxied to the end of the runway. And stopped there.

Emma didn't know what that was about but regardless of the reason, she was grateful for a moment's reprieve. Her head pounded and her heart felt like it was going to explode inside her chest.

Oliver revved the engine, which fired to life with an ear-splitting noise. The plane bucked as if straining against invisible ropes.

Despite her relaxation pill, Emma gasped and grabbed hold of the bar across the top of the passenger door. She clutched it so hard she was convinced her fingerprints would be embedded in the steel.

Without showing a bit of concern for her well-being, Oliver released the brake and the plane leaped forward, roaring down the runway. Emma slammed her eyes shut, preferring not to look. She held her breath, awaiting the sensation of the wheels lifting off the tarmac.

For the longest time nothing happened. She opened her eyes just enough to peek and realized they were almost at the end of the runway. Despite the speed of the aircraft they remained on the ground. In a few seconds of sheer terror, Emma realized why.

She'd lied about her weight.

Hamilton had miscalculated the weight on board. In her vanity, she'd shaved ten pounds—well, maybe fifteen—off the truth. Because of that, she was about to kill them both.

Unable to restrain herself, Emma dragged in a deep breath and screamed out in panic, "I lied! I lied!"

No sooner had the words left her mouth than the plane sailed effortlessly into the sky.

Chapter Three

Fruitcakes are like in-laws. They show up at the holidays. You have no idea who sent them, how old they are, or how long they'll be hanging around your kitchen.

—Josh Sens, freelance writer in Oakland, California, and food critic for *San Francisco* magazine

The fear dissipated after takeoff. Emma kept her eyes focused directly in front of her, gazing out at the cloud-streaked sky. For the first while her heart seemed intent on beating its way out of her body, but after a few minutes the tension began to leave.

It wasn't long before the loud roar of the single engine lulled her into a sense of peace. No doubt that was due to the pill, which was exactly the reason she'd taken it. When she did find the courage to turn her head and look out the side window, she found herself staring Mt. Rainier in the face. She was so close that it was possible to see a crevasse, a giant crack in a glacier. Had there been hikers, she would've been able to wave.

Gasping, she shut her eyes and silently repeated the Lord's Prayer. Talk about spiritual renewal! All that was necessary to get her nearer to God was a short flight with Oliver Hamilton.

Forty minutes later as they approached the Yakima airport, Oliver made a wide sweeping turn with a gradual drop in altitude. Emma felt the plane descend and nearly swallowed her tongue as she reached for the bar above the side window again, holding on for dear life.

"You okay?" Oliver asked when he noticed how she clung to the bar with both hands.

How kind of him to inquire now. These were the first words he'd spoken to her during the entire flight. He'd glanced at her a number of times, as if to check up on her, and whenever he did, he started to laugh. She failed to understand what was so funny.

"I'm okay," she said with as much dignity as she could. A little the worse for wear, but okay, she mentally assured herself. Her head was beginning to clear.

She felt every air pocket and bump as the plane drew closer to the long runway. When the wheels bounced against the tarmac, Emma was ready for the solid thump of the tires hitting concrete, but the landing was surprisingly smooth. She slowly released a sigh of pent-up tension; she'd lied about her weight and lived to tell the tale. Now all she had to do was make it through this interview and find something noteworthy about Earleen Williams and her fruitcake recipe.

Oliver taxied the plane off the runway. He cut the engine and as the blades slowed, he unbuckled his seat belt and picked up his clipboard.

Emma was just starting to breathe normally again when Oscar sneezed.

"You might want to leave the perfume behind for the next flight," Oliver said matter-of-factly.

Emma wiped her cheek although most of the spray had been directed elsewhere. She resisted the urge to tell Oliver he could leave his dog behind, too. At this point, she didn't want to risk offending the pilot—or his dog. And, she supposed, it wasn't really Oscar's fault....

Crawling behind her, Oliver opened the door and climbed onto the airfield. Emma followed, bent double as she made her way out of the aircraft, feeling a sense of great relief. He offered her his hand as she hopped down. She was hit by a blast of cold air, which she ignored. Staring down at the ground, she was tempted to fall on all fours and kiss the tarmac.

A white van bearing the name of a local furnace company pulled up to the plane. Oliver spoke briefly with the driver, then walked over to where Emma stood.

"How long do you think the interview will take?"

"Ah…" Emma didn't know what to tell him. "I'm not sure."

He stared out toward the Cascade Mountains, only partially visible in the distance. "We've got bad weather rolling in."

"Bad weather? How bad?"

"Don't worry about it."

"I…" How could he say such a thing and then expect her not to worry? She was already half-panicked about the return flight and he'd just added to her fears.

"Do what you have to do and then get back here. I want to take off as soon as I can."

"All right." She glanced around and felt a sense of dread.

"What's wrong?"

"I…I don't have any way of getting to Earleen's house."

"Not a problem," Hamilton said, walking to the other side of the plane.

Emma assumed he was going to ask the guy in the van to give her a ride, but that turned out not to be the case. He climbed back inside the Cessna and returned a moment later with a large leather satchel.

"What's that?"

"A foldable bike."

Emma watched as he unzipped the bag and produced the smallest bicycle she'd ever seen. "You don't honestly expect me to ride this…thing, do you?" The wheels were no more than twelve inches around. She'd look utterly ridiculous. Nervous as she was about this first interview, she hoped to make up in professionalism what she lacked in experience.

"What's wrong?" he asked, frowning.

"I'll phone for a taxi." It went without saying that the newspaper wouldn't reimburse her, but she absolutely refused to arrive pedaling a bicycle Oliver Hamilton must have purchased from a Barnum and Bailey rummage sale.

"Hold on," Oliver barked, clearly upset. He walked over to the van this time and spoke to the driver. The two had a short conversation before Oliver glanced over his shoulder. "What's the address you have to get to?" he shouted.

Fumbling to find the slip of paper inside her briefcase, Emma read off the street name.

"She can tag along with me," the driver said.

"Great." Oliver flashed the other man an easy smile.

"Thank you so much," Emma murmured, grateful to have saved the taxi fare. She hurried around to the passenger side and opened the door. One look inside, and Emma nearly changed her mind. The van, which must've been at least ten years old, had obviously never been cleaned. The passenger seat was badly stained and littered with leftover fast-food containers, plus half-eaten burgers and rock-hard French fries. A clipboard was attached by a magnet to the dashboard and several papers had fallen to the floor.

"You getting in or not?" the driver asked.

"In." Emma made her decision quickly and hopped inside the van. She could just imagine what Walt would say if she announced that she'd missed the interview because she refused to get inside a messy vehicle.

Earleen Williams lived on a street called Garden Park in a brick duplex. The van dropped Emma off and drove away before she had time to thank the driver. He was apparently glad to be rid of her and she was equally thankful to have survived the ride. She'd worry later about getting back to the airfield.

Straightening her shoulders, Emma did a quick mental survey of her questions. She'd reviewed her class notes about interviews and remembered that the most important thing to do was engage Earleen in conversation and establish a rapport. It would be detrimental to the interview if Emma gave even the slightest appearance of nervousness.

Emma so much wanted this to go well. She didn't have a slant for the story yet and wouldn't until she'd met Earleen. If she tried to think about what she could possibly write on the subject of fruitcake, it would only traumatize her.

Knowing Oliver was probably pacing the pilots' lounge, Emma walked onto the porch and pressed the doorbell. She stepped back and waited.

"Oh, hi." The petite brunette who answered the door couldn't have been more than five feet tall, if that, and seemed to be around sixty. It was difficult to tell. One thing Emma did conclude—Earleen wasn't at all what she'd expected. She wore a turquoise blazer and black pleated pants with a large gold belt and rings on every finger. Big rings.

"You're Earleen?"

"I am." She unlatched the screen door and held it open for Emma. "You must be that Seattle reporter who phoned."

"Emma Collins," she said and held out her hand. "Actually, I'm from Puyallup, which is outside Seattle." There was a difference of at least a quarter-million readers between the *Seattle Times* and *The Examiner*—maybe more. The *Seattle Times* hadn't sent her a circulation report lately.

"Come on inside. I've got coffee brewing," Earleen said, smiling self-consciously. "This is the first time anyone's ever wanted to interview me."

They had a lot in common, because this was Emma's first interview, too, although she wasn't about to mention that.

Earleen looked past her. "You didn't bring a photographer with you?"

Actually she had. Emma would be performing both roles. "If it's all right, I'll take your picture later."

"Oh, sure, that's fine." Earleen touched the side of

her head with her palm as if to be sure every hair was neatly in place, which it was. She smelled wonderful, too. Estée Lauder's Beautiful, if Emma guessed correctly. Just as well Oscar wasn't around or he'd be sneezing on her pant leg.

"I thought we'd talk in the kitchen, if you don't mind," Earleen said as she led the way. "Most folks like my kitchen best."

"Wherever you're most comfortable," Emma murmured, following the older woman. She gazed around as she walked through the house and noticed a small collection of owl figurines lined up on the fireplace mantel, among the boughs of greenery. The Christmas tree in the corner was enormous, and it had an owl— yes, an owl—on top.

The kitchen was bright and roomy. There was a square table next to a window that overlooked the backyard, where a circular clothesline sat off to one side and a toolshed on the other. A six-foot redwood fence separated her yard from the neighbors'.

"Sit down," Earleen said and motioned to the table and chairs. "Coffee?"

"None for me, thanks." After the pill she'd taken earlier, Emma didn't think she should add caffeine, afraid of the effect on her stomach—and her brain. She took out her reporter's pad and flipped it open. "When did you first hear the news that your recipe had been chosen as a national finalist?"

Earleen poured herself a mug of coffee and carried it to the table, then pulled out a chair and sat across from Emma. "Three weeks ago. The notification came by mail."

"Were you surprised?"

"Not really."

"Any reason you weren't surprised?"

Earleen blushed. "I know I make a good fruitcake. I've been baking them for a lot of years now."

Emma could see this wasn't going to be as easy as she'd hoped. Earleen wasn't much of a talker.

"Do you have a secret ingredient?"

"Well, yes. I have two."

Emma made a notation just so Earleen would recognize that she was paying attention. "Would you be willing to divulge them to our readers?"

Earleen rested her elbows on the table and held the mug with both hands. "I don't mind telling you, but maybe it'd be better if I showed you."

Emma frowned slightly when the other woman rose from the table. She dragged out a step stool, placed it in front of the refrigerator and climbed the two steps. Then she stretched until she could reach the cupboard above the fridge and opened it. Standing on the tips of her toes, Earleen brought down a bottle of rum and a bottle of brandy.

"Your secret is...alcohol?"

Earleen climbed off the step stool and nodded.

"One of my secrets. I didn't work all those years at The Drunken Owl for nothing. I serve a mighty fine mincemeat pie, too. That recipe came from my mother, God rest her soul. Mom always started with fresh suet. She got it from Kloster's Butcher Shop. When I was in high school, I had the biggest crush on Tim Kloster. My friends used to say I had Klosterphobia." She giggled nervously.

Emma didn't think it was a good idea to point out that "phobia" was technically the wrong term. She hesitated, unsure how this interview had gotten away from her so quickly. "About the fruitcake... Did that recipe come from your mother, too?"

"Sort of. Mom was raised during the Great Depression, and her recipe didn't call for much more than the basics. Over the years I started adding to it, and being from Yakima, I naturally included apples."

"Apples," Emma repeated and jotted that down.

"Actually, I cook them until it's more like applesauce."

"Of course." Having lived in Washington for only the last eight months, Emma wasn't all that familiar with the state. She knew more about the western half because she lived in that area. Most of the eastern side remained a complete mystery.

Come to think of it, as Oliver landed she'd noticed that there seemed to be orchards near the airport. Distracted as she'd been, it was nothing short of astounding that she'd remembered.

"Yakima is known for apples, right?" she ventured.

"Definitely. More than half of all the apples grown in the United States come from orchards in Yakima and Wenatchee."

Emma made a note. "I didn't know that."

"The most popular variety is the Red Delicious. Personally, I prefer Golden Delicious. They're the kind I use in my fruitcake."

Emma held her breath. "I hope you'll agree to share the recipe with *The Examiner's* readers."

Earleen beamed proudly. "It would be my honor."

"So the liquor and the apples are your two secret ingredients."

"That's right," Earleen said in a solemn voice. "But far more important is using only the freshest of ingredients. It took me several tries to figure that out."

Emma was tempted to remind her that one of the main ingredients in fruitcake was dried fruit. There wasn't anything fresh about that. But again she managed to keep her mouth shut.

"How long have you been baking fruitcakes?" Emma asked next.

"Quite a few years. I started in—way back now. You see, I was going through a rough patch at the time."

"What happened?" Emma hated to pry, but she was

a reporter and she had a feeling she'd hit upon the key element of her article.

"Larry and I had just split, and I have to tell you I took it hard."

"And Larry is?"

"My ex-husband."

Emma couldn't help observing that Earleen seemed more of a conversationalist when she stood on the other side of the kitchen counter. The closer she got to the table, the briefer her answers were. Emma speculated that was because of Earleen's many years behind a bar. She'd always heard that bartenders spent a lot of time listening and advising—like paid friends. Or psychiatrists.

"The first time I ever tried Mom's fruitcake recipe was after Larry moved out."

"I'm sorry."

"Me, too. Have you ever been married?" Earleen asked.

"No…" The sorry state of her love life was not a subject Emma wanted to discuss.

"Larry and I were high-school sweethearts. He went to fight in Vietnam and when he got back, we had a big wedding. It was the type of wedding girls dream about. Wait here a minute," she said and bustled out of the kitchen.

In a couple of minutes, she returned with her wedding photograph. A radiantly happy bride smiled into the camera, her white dress fashioned in layers of taffeta and lace. The young soldier at her side was more difficult to read.

"Unfortunately, Larry had a weakness for other women," Earleen said sadly.

"How long have you been divorced?"

"From Larry? Since 1984."

"You've been married more than once?"

"Three times."

"Oh."

"All my husbands were versions of Larry."

"I see."

"I didn't learn from my mistakes." Earleen turned away. Then, obviously changing the subject, she said, "I imagine you'll want to sample my fruitcake." She slid open the bread box and took out an aluminum-foil-wrapped loaf. "Have you noticed that people either love fruitcake or hate it?" she said companionably. "There doesn't seem to be any middle ground."

"That...seems to be true," Emma agreed.

"Like I said, I started baking after Larry left," she said, busily peeling away the cheesecloth from the loaf-size fruitcake. "I'd never suffered that kind of pain before. I figured if you've ever been divorced you'd know what I mean."

Emma was confused. "I don't exactly think of fruitcake as comfort food."

Earleen shook her head. "I didn't eat it. I baked it.

Loaf after loaf for weeks on end. I was determined to bake the perfect fruitcake and I didn't care how long it took. I must've changed that recipe a hundred times."

"Why fruitcake?"

She paused as if she'd never put it into words. "I'm not sure. I guess I was looking for the happiness I always felt as a kid at Christmastime."

There it was again, Emma mused. Christmas. It did people in emotionally, and she wasn't going to allow that to happen, not to her. She found it easy enough to ignore Christmas; other people should give it a try. She might even see if Walt would let her write an article about her feelings. Emma believed she wasn't alone in disliking all the hype that surrounded Christmas.

"When I was with Larry and my two other husbands, I felt there must be something lacking in me," Earleen continued. "Now I don't think so anymore. Time will do that, you know?" She glanced at Emma. "As young as you are, you probably don't have that much perspective." Earleen paused and drew in a deep breath.

Emma stopped taking notes. She suspected this was it; she was about to get to the real core of the interview.

"By the time Larry and I split up, both my parents were gone, so I was pretty much on my own. I realize now that I was searching for a way to deal with the pain, although God knows the marriage was dead. That's where the fruitcake came in."

"The comfort factor," Emma said with a nod. "How long were you and Larry together?" she asked.

"Sixteen years. It's a shame, you know. We never had kids and it was real lonely after he left."

"What happened to him?" Secretly Emma hoped he was miserable. In some ways Earleen reminded Emma of her mother.

The woman sighed. "Larry married the floozy he'd taken up with, and the two of them got drunk every night. It only took him a few years to drink himself to death."

"How sad," Emma said, and she meant it.

Earleen shrugged. "I was single for nearly ten years. I thought I'd learned my lesson about marrying the wrong man, but obviously I hadn't."

"What about the other two husbands?"

"Morrie courted me for a long time before I agreed to marry him. He didn't have a roving eye so much as he did a weakness for the bottle." She paused. "Of course, Larry had both. The thing is, and you remember this, young lady, you don't meet the cream of the eligible bachelor crop working in a tavern."

Emma scribbled that down so Earleen would think she'd given due consideration to her words.

"Morrie died of cancer a couple of years after we were married." She shook her head. "I never should've married Paul after that."

"What happened with Paul?"

A dreamy expression came over her. "Paul looked so much like Larry they could've been brothers. Unfortunately, looks weren't the only trait they shared. We were married only a year when he suffered a massive stroke. He had a girlfriend on the side but he really loved my fruitcake. I think if Larry had lived, he would have, too."

"Do you have anyone to share your good news with?" Emma asked. "About being a finalist?"

Earleen shrugged again. "Not really, but it doesn't matter."

"Of course it matters," Emma insisted. "Your recipe was one of only twelve chosen from across the entire United States. You should be kicking up your heels and celebrating."

"I will with friends, I suppose." Earleen opened her cutlery drawer for a knife and sliced through the loaf. "It's time I started baking again," she said. "This close to Christmas, I'll bake my mincemeat pies. People are already asking about them."

"When do you bake your fruitcakes?"

Earleen sipped her coffee, her fingers sparkling in the light. All ten of them. "I usually bake up a batch every October and let it set a good two months before I serve it. The longer I give the alcohol to work, the better. Then, before Easter, I bake another version that's similar but without the dried fruit." Earleen moved the slice onto a plate and brought it over for Emma to taste.

Although she wasn't a fan of fruitcake, Emma decided it would be impolite to refuse. Earleen watched and waited.

Emma used her fork to break off a small piece and saw that it was chock-full of the dried fruit to which she objected most. She glanced up at the older woman with a quick smile. Then she carefully put the fruitcake in her mouth—and was shocked by how good it tasted. The cake was flavorful, moist and pungent with the scent of liquor. The blend of fruit, nuts, applesauce and alcohol was *divine*. There was no other word to describe Earleen's fruitcake.

"You like it, don't you?"

"I do," Emma assured her, trying not to sound shocked. "It's excellent."

"I'm sure Larry would've thought so, too," Earleen said wistfully. "Even if he's the reason I started baking it."

"You still love him, don't you?" It seemed so obvious to Emma. Although she'd married twice more, Earleen Williams's heart belonged to a man who hadn't valued her. Her mother had been the same; Pamela Collins had loved her ex-husband to her dying day. Emma's father had never appreciated what a wonderful woman she was. For that sin alone, Emma wanted nothing more to do with him. He'd been a token husband the same way he'd been a token father.

When she spoke, Earleen's voice was resigned. "I've

been over Larry for a long time," she explained. "Much as I loved him, all I can say is that it's a good thing he left when he did. Larry was trouble. More trouble than I knew what to do with."

More trouble than Earleen deserved, Emma reflected.

"Is there anything else I can tell you?" Earleen asked. She seemed eager to finish the interview. "I didn't mean to talk so much about my past. I never could figure out men—but I know a whole lot about fruitcake."

Emma scanned her notes. "I think I've got everything I need for now."

After snapping a picture of Earleen and collecting the recipe, she asked, "Can I call you later if I have any questions?"

"Oh, sure. Since I retired from The Drunken Owl, I'm here most of the time."

"Would you mind if I used your phone book?" Emma stood and gathered up her things. "I want to call a taxi to take me back to the airport."

"You don't need to do that." Earleen shook her head. "I'll drive you. It's not far and I have errands I need to run, anyway."

"Are you sure?"

"Of course I am. It's my pleasure."

Emma smiled her gratitude. She already knew that Walt wasn't going to reimburse her for any taxi fare, and it was too close to the end of the month for un-necessary spending on her part.

Earleen backed her twenty-year-old Subaru out of the garage and Emma got inside. The contrast between the interior of Earleen's vehicle and the furnace com-pany van was noteworthy in itself.

Ten minutes later, Earleen dropped Emma at the air-port and after a few words of farewell, drove off.

As soon as Emma climbed out of the Subaru, Oliver came from the building next to the hangar, with Oscar trotting behind him.

"You done?"

Emma nodded absently, wondering how to struc-ture her article on Earleen. Start with her childhood or her wedding or—

"How'd it go?" he asked, interrupting her thoughts.

She stared at him, eyes narrowed. "In case you didn't know it, men can be real scum."

To her surprise, Oliver grinned. "You're going to have even more reason to think so when you hear what I've got to say."

This didn't sound promising. "You'd better tell me," she said.

Oliver buried his hands in his pockets. "Blame me if you want, but it won't make any difference. We're grounded."

"Grounded?" She blinked. "What does that mean?"

"We're grounded," he repeated. "Because of the weather. We're stuck in Yakima."

Earleen's Masterpiece Fruitcake

2 cups sugar
1 cup butter
2 ½ cups applesauce
2 eggs, beaten
2 cups raisins
2 cups walnuts, chopped
4 cups flour
1 tsp. salt
1 tbsp. soda
1 tsp. baking powder
1 tsp. cloves
1 tsp. nutmeg
2 tsp. cinnamon
2 pounds candied dried fruit mix
1 ½ cups chopped dates

Cream sugar and butter. Add beaten eggs and applesauce. Mix flour, salt, spices, soda and baking powder, then gradually add to other ingredients. Mix well. Blend in candied fruit, dates, raisins and nuts. Mixture will be stiff. Bake in 325-degree oven in two loaf pans for one hour.

Cool and remove fruitcake from pans. Cut a piece of cheesecloth to fit and soak in ½ cup rum or brandy. Pour any remaining alcohol over the fruitcake. Wrap fruitcake in cheesecloth and then cellophane, followed by aluminum foil. Store in refrigerator for up to three months.

Chapter Four

"This is a bad joke—isn't it?" Emma cried. "Oh, please tell me it's a joke."

"Sorry."

From his darkening scowl, Emma could see he wasn't pleased about this turn of events, either. He'd obviously enjoyed giving her the bad news but he wasn't grinning anymore. A delay probably affected his bottom line. Oscar sat down next to Oliver and stared up at him confidently. She'd heard somewhere that a man was always a hero to his dog; that was certainly the case with poor deluded Oscar.

"I mentioned the weather earlier, remember?" Hamilton said.

Emma had forgotten that. Her afternoon muscle relaxant was ready to be swallowed, and she was glad she hadn't taken it yet. "What are we supposed to do now?"

"Wait it out. We could find ways to entertain ourselves."

This was exactly the kind of comment she expected from Flyboy. And was that a wink? "In your dreams," she snapped.

"Do you have any other brilliant suggestions?"

Emma wished she did.

"We might be able to get out late this afternoon, but I wouldn't count on it." He raised his eyes to study the heavily clouded sky. "There's a snowstorm in the mountains and it's heading in our direction. The clouds don't concern me as much as the problem with icing."

Emma wasn't sure what that meant; she had her own problems. "I've got an article to write," she murmured, biting her lower lip. Walt had wanted the first piece written as quickly as possible. Earleen Williams had been a great interview, but Emma still hadn't decided exactly what slant she should take. She needed time to study her notes and think over their conversation.

Oliver nodded glumly. "To tell you the truth, I'm not thrilled about sitting around here all day, twiddling my thumbs."

Emma realized he could've left after making his delivery if he hadn't been waiting for her. She felt bad about that. She'd been less than gracious. "Are you hungry?" she asked.

"Why?" His voice was suspicious.

"I was being friendly." She glanced across the street at a café. Several letters in the neon sign had burned out. It'd once read MINNIE'S PLACE but now said MI...CE. This wasn't exactly an enticement, but Emma's stomach was growling. It was past noon and all she'd had to eat was a small slice of liquor-drenched—and quite delicious—fruitcake..

"Are you offering to buy me lunch?"

Emma mentally calculated how much cash she had with her. "All right, as long as you don't order anything over five dollars."

Oliver grinned. "You've got yourself a date."

"This *isn't* a date."

"Sure it is," he said. "One day I'll tell our children you asked me out first."

"One more remark like that, and you can buy your own lunch."

Oliver chuckled. "I wasn't trying to be funny."

"Yeah, right."

"You're half in love with me already."

Emma didn't dignify that with a reply. They started walking toward the café; Oscar trotted obediently beside them and seemed to know to wait by the restaurant door. Oliver patted his head and assured the terrier he'd get any leftovers.

Emma resisted reminding Oliver that it wasn't a good idea to feed people food to a dog, but she doubted he'd listen. If she had a dog, she'd feed him only the highest-quality, veterinarian–approved dog food.

Once inside the café, they slid into a red vinyl booth, facing each other. Emma reached for the menu, which was tucked behind the napkin dispenser, and quickly decided on the ham-and-cheese omelet. Oliver ordered the club sandwich.

"How long have you been flying?" she asked.

"Why?" Once again, he sounded suspicious. For heaven's sake, did the man have some big secret?

Emma sighed. "I don't know. It seemed like a good conversation starter, that's all."

"I'm not interested in being interviewed," he said curtly. "Besides, I have a couple of questions for you."

She smiled at the waitress who poured her coffee, then relaxed in the padded vinyl seat. "Wait a minute. You can ask me questions but I'm not allowed to know anything about you? Is that fair?"

"Fair doesn't matter. I'm your ride home—or I will be."

"So you think I owe you for that? Oh, never mind," she said, suddenly tiring of the argument. "Ask away."

"How long have you been with *The Examiner?*"

"About eight months—long enough to know I'm tired of writing obituaries."

Oliver frowned. "That's the only thing Walt lets you write?"

"For the most part. A month ago he let me cover the

school board meeting." Emma had written what she thought was a masterful commentary on the events. Walt hadn't agreed, to put it mildly, and had rejected her article in scathing terms. He said she was trying too hard. People were looking for a clear, concise summary, not a chapter from *War and Peace*. "What I want is a real story," she told Oliver in a fervent tone, "something I can really get my teeth into."

"Like fruitcake?" Oliver said, teasing her.

"It's a start."

"Yes." Once again, he was obviously trying to restrain a smile. "What are you going to write about Earleen Williams?"

Emma was mulling that over. "I don't know for sure. She's a complex woman. She's had a number of difficult relationships with men, and—"

"You don't date much, do you?" he broke in.

Emma stared at him. "Who says?"

"Phoebe."

"You know Phoebe?" Either her friend had been holding out on her, or Oliver was lying. If Phoebe knew him, Emma was positive she would've said so earlier.

"We've had a couple of conversations about you," Oliver admitted, nimbly twirling the fork between his fingers.

Emma found the action highly irritating. Stretching across the table, she grabbed his wrist. "Please don't do that."

He grinned; he seemed to do a lot of that around her. "You can't keep your hands off me, can you?"

She toyed briefly with the idea of getting up and walking out. She would have, too, but their food hadn't been delivered yet. Her stomach won out over her pride.

"How do you know Phoebe and when did you talk to her?"

"We met through…a friend of mine. Phoebe's a few years younger than me, but I've seen her around town. No big deal." He shrugged. "I stopped in at the office after your visit to the airfield and asked about you. Casually, you know. Phoebe sang like a canary."

Emma refused to believe it. Phoebe had never mentioned this supposed conversation.

"She said the two of you were hired at the same time and that you kept pretty much to yourself. So what gives?"

"What do you mean?"

"Where's the boyfriend?"

Emma's jaw sagged open. "You've got a lot of nerve!"

"Men are scum, remember?" His eyes twinkled. "So tell me, what's happening in the men department?"

"Nothing. I'm a serious writer—well, maybe not yet, but I intend to become one."

"Being a 'serious' writer means you don't have time for relationships?"

Emma didn't care for the direction this conversation was taking. "At present, no—not that it's any of your business."

"Why not?"

"Are you always so nosy, or is this expressly for my benefit?"

"Both." He picked up his fork and studied the tines with every appearance of interest.

To Emma's relief, their plates arrived just then. The waitress set the bill facedown in the middle of the table.

Emma spread the paper napkin across her lap, looked over her meal and lifted her fork. By the time she'd taken two bites, Oliver had wolfed down half his sandwich. She glared at him disapprovingly.

"What?" he asked, apparently perplexed.

"Nothing," she said, knowing it would do no good to explain.

He munched on a French fry, then glanced across the table at her. "If I asked you out on a date, would you go?"

"No," she said without hesitation. She didn't mean to be rude but she could read him like a book. He was her father all over again. Besides, she wasn't much good at relationships.

"Why not?" Oliver pressed.

Emma groaned. "Listen, I'm sure a lot of women would consider you charming—" she almost choked on the word "—and you're not unattractive..."

"In other words, you think I'm cute."

"No," she inserted quickly. "That isn't what I meant at all." The last thing she wanted was for Oliver to assume she was attracted to him. "I like that you're kind to animals."

"You want me."

Emma set her fork down, astonished at his audacity. "I most certainly do not!"

He cracked an even bigger smile. "Keep telling yourself that, but I know otherwise."

"This is exactly what bothers me," she said, sighing heavily. "Your arrogance is unbelievable. You assume that because you're reasonably good-looking, any woman would be grateful for the opportunity to date you. The fact is, it's simply not true."

"You're dying to find out everything you can about me."

This time Emma laughed outright. She couldn't help it. "*You're* the one asking all the questions—and making a lot of assumptions. *I* was making conversation. It seemed the polite thing to do, since we might end up spending the next few hours together."

Some women might find his smile sexy. Not Emma, of course, but others. She forced herself to look away, in case he misread her interest.

"All right then. What do you want to know about me?" he asked, leaning forward.

Emma considered his question. Anything she asked

him, Oliver was bound to interpret in such a way that it would seem she was falling head over heels in love with him. Really, his attitude bordered on the comical.

"How soon before we can fly out of here?"

He frowned. "I can't answer that until I get an updated weather report. Anything else you want to know?"

Plenty, but she planned on asking Phoebe first. "Not really."

She sliced into her omelet and saw that he'd already finished his sandwich. Only a handful of French fries remained.

"Are you going to eat your toast?" he asked.

She shook her head and slid the plate across the table.

Oliver took it, slipped out of the booth and headed outside to where Oscar waited. As soon as he left the café, Emma plucked her cell phone from her bag and pushed the button that speed-dialed the newspaper office. A moment later, she connected with Phoebe.

"This is Phoebe," her friend answered in her usual cheerful fashion.

"When did Oliver Hamilton ask you about me?" Emma demanded.

"Emma?"

"You know exactly who this is."

"I take it the muscle relaxant has worn off?"

So it was true. "Why didn't you say something?"

"Because," Phoebe murmured, "it was a short conversation. Two minutes, if that."

"You knew he was coming in to talk to Walt."

"Yes," Phoebe admitted. "All right, I'll tell you. I was afraid that if I mentioned I'd talked to Oliver, you'd have all these questions about how I knew and I didn't want to get into that."

"How *did* you know?" Emma asked. It could only be one thing—Phoebe was seeing Walt. Why she wanted to keep that a secret, Emma wasn't sure.

When Phoebe answered, it was in a whisper. "Walt and I are dating."

"You *are?*" Even though she'd already guessed, Emma was shocked. "Why didn't you tell me?" As soon as she asked the question, she knew. "Walt doesn't want anyone at the office to find out." It explained a lot.

"He doesn't think it's good policy. I hated not telling anyone, especially you, but I...couldn't."

"How long has this been going on?"

"Three months."

Emma was stunned into silence. She couldn't believe that her best friend had managed to keep this from her for *three months*. Obviously, Phoebe wasn't as timid around Walt as she'd seemed.

"You can't let him know that you know," Phoebe said anxiously.

"Fine." Emma blew out her breath. "But when I get back, I want you to tell me everything, understand?"

Phoebe laughed softly. "I'll make a full confession."

"Good. Now, what do you know about Oliver Hamilton?"

"Just that...he likes you. He specifically asked for an opportunity so the two of you could fly together."

"What?"

"You heard me."

Oliver had done that because he knew she was frightened to death to get into his little plane. The man was a sadist, and between them, her employer and her best friend had willingly handed her over.

"He told Walt you'd done a wonderful job of selling him on advertising and he wanted to give the newspaper his business because of you."

"Did you tell Walt that if I didn't get an assignment soon, I'd quit?"

"I couldn't let my best friend quit," Phoebe said—although Emma noted that she hadn't really answered the question. "Not if I could prevent it. Then Oliver showed up and, well, it was meant to be."

The truth was out. She'd gotten this assignment thanks to her friend. Walt hadn't thought she was ready; he was just trying to keep Phoebe happy.

"I can't understand why you don't like Oliver," Phoebe said.

Emma pinched her lips tightly together. "Oliver Hamilton is accustomed to women swooning over him."

"He's not like that," Phoebe protested.

Emma knew otherwise.

"You're not upset with me, are you?"

Emma considered the question. "I guess not."

"If our situations were reversed, you'd have done the same thing for me," Phoebe said. "Now tell me what's going on in Yakima."

Emma looked out the window and noticed that Oliver had walked across the street, presumably to get an updated weather report. "At the moment we're stuck."

"Together?" Phoebe asked with an inappropriate amount of amusement.

It figured she'd see this unfortunate situation in a humorous light. "For now, and trust me, I'm not happy about it."

"You should be. Oliver and Walt get along really well. He's a cool guy."

The problem was he knew it. Emma didn't bother to comment. She chatted with Phoebe a few minutes longer before ending the phone call.

The waitress refreshed Emma's coffee and took the money she'd left on the table. While she waited for her change, she read over her notes from the interview with Earleen Williams. But it wasn't the older woman who dominated her thoughts, it was her own mother.

Pamela Collins had wanted the very best for her, Emma knew. What she could never understand was why her mother had stayed in the marriage as long as she had. From as early as Emma could remember, she'd known her father was having affairs, betraying his wife and family. To this day, her father didn't get it. Her mother had been so forgiving; Emma wasn't. And she was too smart to be taken in by a man who had all her father's worst traits—and all his appeal.

She couldn't imagine what her mother would think of Oliver. No, she could imagine exactly. Her mother would think he was wonderful and treat him like a king, the same way she'd done with Emma's father whenever he'd seen fit to bless them with his presence.

The café door opened and Oliver returned, his leather jacket splotched with damp. He walked across the room, sliding into the booth. He handed her a sheet of paper.

"What's this?" she asked.

"The weather report. You aren't going to like it."

Emma's heart sank. "How long are we trapped here?"

He hesitated as if weighing how much of the truth he should tell her. "Overnight."

The word echoed in her brain. "No!"

"Have you looked outside lately?"

Emma hadn't. She stared out the window now. Thick flakes of snow drifted down; already the sidewalks were covered and the sky had grown darker. No wonder his coat was wet. She closed her eyes. "What are we going to do?" she whispered.

Oliver shrugged. "It happens, especially this time of

year. I don't like it any better than you do, but I try to make the best of it."

"How?"

"I don't know what you're planning, but I've already got a line on a poker game. I don't suppose you'd care to join us?"

Chapter Five

The snow fell fast and furious as the afternoon wore on. Although Emma strongly suspected Walt wouldn't be willing to reimburse her, she broke down and rented a motel room near the airfield, using her credit card since she was almost out of cash. Her knight in tarnished armor had disappeared inside one of the hangars with three other pilots for a poker game, and she hadn't seen him since.

The motel room was about what you'd expect for $39.95. The mattress and pillows were thin and no matter what she did, Emma couldn't get comfortable on the bed until she marched down to the office for extra pillows, which she propped up to support her back while she used her laptop on the bed. Her fingers flew across the keys.

Lessons from Fruitcake: Earleen Williams
by Emma Collins
For *The Examiner*

Earleen Williams of Yakima bakes masterful fruit-cakes but she's the true masterpiece.

It's no surprise to anyone who has tasted one of her fruitcakes that Earleen and her recipe have achieved national acclaim. With a shy smile, she'll laughingly say that her secret ingredient is stored in her liquor cabinet. But there's more to it than that.

Now Earleen's recipe has been chosen as one of the twelve nationwide finalists in *Good Home-making*'s fruitcake contest. The winner will be announced December 20th on the magazine's website. The January issue will feature a profile of the winner. That winner might be Earleen Williams.

Earleen admits her life hasn't been easy, not that she's complaining. She was married to her first husband, Larry, for sixteen years, but as she says, he was more trouble than she could handle. They parted, and in her pain and loss she returned to the days of her childhood and the happiness she'd known, surrounded by family and love.

Earleen's parents had little money for frivolous things, but there was an abundance of love in the home. And somehow, through good times and bad, there was always fruitcake at Christmas. It was this spirit of love, laughter and joy that Earleen sought to recapture in making her own fruitcake. Adding local apples, cooked down into a sauce, and using only ingredients of the highest quality, she began with her mother's recipe and expanded on it. When asked, Earleen was happy to share her secrets—liquor and apples. In the years since her divorce, her fruitcake has become a holiday staple for family and friends.

The former bartender continued baking through two subsequent marriages. Discussing her three husbands, Earleen commented that none of them appreciated her. Each pursued other women—or sought escape in a bottle. Over time, Earleen says, she gained perspective on her life and learned to recognize that her husbands' infidelity wasn't due to any lack in her.

Earleen Williams creates a moist, succulent fruitcake—a baking masterpiece. But she, too, is a masterpiece, just the way she is.

This was a draft, but Emma felt it was a good start. The more she read over her notes, the more she realized that the interview hadn't been about fruitcake as much as about Earleen. Briefly she wondered if all the interviews would be the same. Lessons about life, wrapped up in a fruitcake recipe. She hoped so.

By now it was past four o'clock; dusk had begun to fall in earnest. The room had grown chilly and Emma was ready to stop work for a while. The heater below the window belched and coughed before it sent out a blast of hot air. When she turned on the television, all she got was a blank screen and some strange noise. Bored and restless, she threw on her coat and wandered out to the office to complain.

The middle-aged woman at the desk looked up when she appeared. "The television doesn't seem to be working," Emma told her in a friendly tone.

"We've been having problems with the cable," the clerk said.

"I'd really like to watch the news." Listening to the weather report was vital at this point. She wanted out of Yakima, and the sooner the better.

"I'll send Juan over to see what he can do," the clerk promised. "He's our handyman. He knows what he's doing, but his English isn't very good. I'll do my best to explain it to him."

"Thanks. I'd appreciate that," Emma told her.

Since Oliver didn't know where she was, Emma decided she'd better inform him. If there was a break in the storm, he wouldn't appreciate having to search for her.

Unsure where to find Oliver, she stepped out of the motel office and turned toward the hangar where she'd last seen him. Pulling her wool coat more tightly around her, she trudged across the snowy street. Fortunately, Oscar trotted over to her, happily wagging his stub of a tail.

"Where's Oliver?" she asked the terrier, then followed the dog as he led her to a hangar not far from Oliver's Cessna.

When she walked inside, shaking the snow from her coat, Emma found Oliver sitting at a table with his poker-playing friends. Two were dressed in beige overalls, and Emma assumed they must be mechanics. Oliver sat across from a third man who wore a leather jacket similar to his. Probably another pilot.

Oliver pulled his gaze away from his cards, glanced up and frowned, almost as though he couldn't remember who she was.

"I wondered where you'd wandered off," he mumbled, returning his attention to his hand.

"I got a motel room."

At the mention of the room, his three friends stared at her. From her, they turned as one to Oliver. All speaking at the same time, the men made suggestive comments.

"Way to go, Oliver."

"Atta boy."

"Oo-la-la."

To her dismay, Oliver played along, grinning from ear to ear as if it was understood they'd be making wild, passionate love as soon as he'd finished his poker game.

Emma wasn't letting him get away with that. If he wasn't going to explain, then she had no qualms about doing so. "The motel room isn't for him," she said coldly. "There's absolutely *nothing* between Oliver and me."

One of the mechanics laughed. "That's what all the girls say."

"I'll be back shortly." Oliver set his cards down on the table and stood, his movements casual.

"Take your time, ol' buddy."

"Don't hurry on our account."

Emma glared at the men as Oliver took her by the elbow and steered her out of the hangar. She peered over her shoulder on her way out the door, strongly tempted to put them all in their place. That would be a waste of time, she realized. Besides, any argument was only going to encourage them.

"You got a motel room?" he asked.

"That's what I said, isn't it?" she muttered irritably. Then, repenting her sharp tone—at least a little—she added in a more conciliatory voice, "You said it would be morning before we'd get out of here." She hadn't wanted to spend money on the motel, but there was only so long she could sit in Minnie's Place, otherwise known as MICE.

"That was probably a good idea." Oliver looked both ways before jogging across the street, Oscar at his heels.

"I wanted to see the weather report. Unfortunately,

the television in my room seems to be on the fritz. The manager sent a repairman."

"I wouldn't mind getting a current weather update, either."

"The only reason I came to find you was so you'd know where I was." She wanted to make it clear that she hadn't gone searching for him because she wanted his company. She was being considerate, nothing more.

He nodded. "I'll see about getting a room for the night myself."

While Oliver filled out the paperwork, Emma went back to her room. She opened the door to find Juan, the repairman, sitting on the end of her bed, gazing intently at the television.

Emma took one look at the images flashing across the screen and gasped. He was watching the pornography channel. Obviously, a lack of familiarity with English was no impediment to following this kind of movie—not that there was much dialogue to worry about.

He grinned at her as if he'd managed some spectacular feat. "I fix," he said, beaming. He flipped off the television and handed her the remote on his way out. Emma stared at him openmouthed as he disappeared into the snowstorm.

Emma didn't know how long she stood in the doorway, still holding the remote, but it must have been more than a minute.

"Problems?" Oliver asked as he strolled toward her.

"The repairman was in my room watching porn." She was shocked by the other man's audacity.

Oliver followed her into the room. "Let me see the remote," he said, and took it from her. He pushed the power button; instantly the television returned to the scene she'd witnessed when she walked into the room.

"Change the channel," she insisted, whirling around so she wouldn't have to look at the entwined figures. This was so embarrassing. All she could hear were moans and groans.

Oliver made several attempts but the pornography channel was the only one that seemed to be working. Every other channel remained a snowy blur.

"Ah," Oliver said after a moment. "I get it."

"You get what?"

"You asked to watch the news, right?"

"Right," she concurred.

"Juan thought you wanted to watch the *nudes*."

"Oh, for heaven's sake." Half-laughing, Emma felt the heat radiate from her cheeks.

"I'm two doors down if you need anything." He tossed the remote onto the rumpled bed, where she'd been working earlier.

"I won't," Emma rushed to assure him. But when she closed the door she remembered that she still couldn't watch television.

Sighing, she sat cross-legged on the bed. Might as

well work, she decided. Emma reached for a pad of paper and a pen, one of a dozen she kept in a special compartment in her briefcase.

She wrote down the date, then chewed on the end of her pen while she mentally reviewed the conversation with Earleen. She needed an introduction to her first article.

Life is a journey, she began, *and as with any journey, a traveler will come upon unexpected twists and turns. Sometimes a person will follow the same path for so long that change seems imperceptible. Conversely, another will travel the shortest of distances and discover a completely new landscape. In a single lifetime, it is possible to live both experiences, as Earleen Williams discovered.*

When Emma finally glanced up, she was surprised to see that it was pitch-black outside, the darkness punctuated by the lights in the motel parking lot. There was a knock on her door.

"Who is it?" she asked.

"Who do you think?" Oliver called from the other side.

Emma opened the door.

"My television works if you want to trade rooms."

The idea was tempting.

"I'm going back to my poker game."

"All right," Emma said gratefully. "Thanks."

"Can Oscar stay with you?"

"Sure."

"Good." They exchanged room keys and he turned away. Then, as if he'd just thought of something, he turned back.

"What?" Emma asked.

"Nothing," he said. Without another word he kissed her.

At first Emma felt too stunned to react, but once she'd collected her wits, she was furious. He was trying to shock her, and she refused to give him a reaction. "What was that for?" she asked.

Oliver stopped, shrugged, smiled. "Can't say. All of a sudden, I had this urge to kiss you."

"Next time curb it."

He shrugged again. "Don't know if I can."

"Try."

Just the way the edges of his mouth turned up annoyed her. "Come on, admit it," he said. "You liked it."

Emma examined her feelings. If he wanted honesty, then she'd give it to him. "As kisses go, I guess I'd call it fair."

His grin slowly faded. "I don't think so."

Before she could take a single step back, he pulled her into his arms again and brought his mouth to hers.

Ample opportunity came and went for Emma to object. Her mind shouted at her to put an end to it right that minute but…she simply couldn't.

His mouth moved over hers with practiced ease.

Emma parted her lips and moaned involuntarily. On second thought, maybe it was Oliver who moaned.

They were still fully caught up in the kiss when Emma heard someone clear his throat. Even then, she didn't make an effort to break away.

"Oliver," a man's voice said.

"Yeah, Oliver. We playin' cards or not?"

Oliver lifted his mouth from hers and slowly opened his eyes, as if she were the one providing the answers.

"He's playing cards," Emma answered for him. She barely recognized her own voice. It didn't matter. Oliver got the message.

Chapter Six

"Emma! Open up." The words were accompanied by a loud knock on the motel room door.

The harsh sound of Oliver's voice woke her abruptly, and she bolted upright. Taking a moment to orient herself she realized Oliver had awakened her in the middle of a dream about *him*. She blamed Oscar for this. The terrier slept at the foot of her bed, a constant reminder of his master. Her face instantly went red as she tossed aside her covers and hurried to the door.

"What do you want?" she demanded without unlatching the chain. She'd slept in her shirt and her legs were bare.

"The weather's clear. We're leaving in fifteen minutes."

"Fifteen *minutes?* I don't know if I can—"

"Hurry up. I'll be waiting at the plane."

"Okay, okay. I'll be as fast as I can." Already she was fumbling about, looking for what she needed.

As soon as she heard him leave, she tore around the room, dressing as quickly as she could. Twenty-five minutes later she was strapped in the plane's passenger seat with headphones on. They sat at the end of the runway, awaiting clearance. Oscar was asleep in his dog bed in the cargo hold, oblivious to the tension up front.

Oliver ignored her and spoke to the tower, again rattling off a list of letters and numbers.

That was when it hit her. In her rush Emma had forgotten to take her pill. The muscle relaxant was wrapped in a small plastic bag at the bottom of her purse.

Her first instinct was to interrupt Oliver and insist he taxi the plane back to the hangar. She needed to swallow the pill and then wait thirty to sixty minutes for it to take effect. One glance at the intense expression on his face and she could see that wasn't the best plan. Just then, he pulled back on the throttle and the plane roared down the runway, gaining speed. Leaning against the seat, she closed her eyes and gritted her teeth. A few minutes later, the wheels left the runway and they were airborne. Okay, she'd survived.

Emma held her breath. Keeping her eyes closed, she tried to think happy thoughts. Unfortunately, her mind had other interests, drifting back to the scene in the doorway last night. In an effort to dispel the memory of their kiss, she opened her eyes. That, she immediately decided, wasn't a good idea. All she could see in the darkness was a blur of lights far below. Far, *far* below. Dwelling on exactly how far was not conducive to her peace of mind.

About twenty minutes into the flight, the Cessna hit an air pocket and bounced. She gasped and bit down on her lip. She'd grabbed a cup of coffee in the motel office; it was boiling hot, but after adding cold water, she'd managed to drink it. Now, with the slight turbulence, her stomach revolted. Feeling light-headed, she closed her eyes once more and pressed her cheek against the passenger window. It felt nice and cool against her skin.

As if he sensed her discomfort, Oliver glanced in her direction and asked how she was doing.

"I...is there any way it would be possible to land?"

"Land?" he repeated into his mouthpiece. "We can't land here."

Emma refused to look at him. "I think I might be sick."

Oliver chuckled. "Quit telling yourself that. You're going to be fine."

"Quit telling me how I feel. I've got nausea."

"Take deep breaths."

"I'm trying." He made it sound as though she had a choice in the matter.

Oliver took one hand off the controls and stretched his arm behind her seat. He appeared to be searching for something. Sure enough, a couple of seconds later, he triumphantly gave her a plastic bag.

"What's this?"

"A container for you to puke in," he said without the slightest hesitation.

Emma supposed she should be grateful, but she wasn't. "Thank you so much," she muttered sarcastically.

His scowl told her he didn't appreciate her sarcasm.

Her stomach settled down a few minutes later, and she slowly exhaled. "I think I'm going to be all right."

He nodded. "I thought you would be."

They exchanged no further conversation for the rest of the flight home.

Once they'd landed, Emma was out of the aircraft in record time, eager to be on her way. Unfortunately, her car was parked back at her apartment. Oliver offered to drop her off, and she accepted, but he certainly wasn't in any hurry. She chafed with impatience as he tended lovingly to his plane, exchanged protracted greetings with various other men, then retrieved his truck. Finally they arrived at her apartment. As she politely thanked him for the ride, Oscar took her place in the passenger seat—well, *his* place, she assumed.

Emma watched them drive away, more determined than ever not to get inside a plane with him again.

Somehow, she'd persuade Walt to listen to reason. With her mind made up, she headed into her apartment. After showering, washing her hair and changing clothes, Emma drove to the office.

It seemed that every eye in the newsroom was on her when she walked through the door. Judging by the looks cast in her direction, she could easily have been the page one story.

"How'd it go?" Phoebe asked the minute Emma entered The Dungeon. She hadn't even sat down at her desk before Phoebe rolled her chair across the aisle. "I think it's wildly romantic that you and Oliver Hamilton were stranded together like that."

"It wasn't." Emma refused to elaborate. Bad enough that he'd kissed her without permission. "I didn't even have a toothbrush with me. It wasn't an experience I care to repeat."

"But you were with Oliver."

Emma sent her friend a glower that said she wasn't impressed with the pilot.

"In case you haven't noticed, Oliver's pretty hot."

"There's more to a man than his looks." Her father was an attractive man, too, but his character wasn't any deeper than the average mud puddle. Emma suspected Oliver was like that. His glibness infuriated her. He took delight in making her uncomfortable, which she considered a juvenile trait—and one that seemed particularly typical of men.

Phoebe wouldn't be thwarted. "I'll bet he kissed you."

Emma ignored the comment. She set her briefcase on her desk and removed her laptop. As soon as she could, she'd review what she'd written and go over her interview notes one final time.

Phoebe grinned knowingly. "He did, didn't he?"

Her friend wasn't going to stop tormenting her. Emma sighed. "Not that it's any of your business, but yes."

"I *knew* it." Phoebe's eyes flashed with victory, as if she were personally responsible for that kiss. "And?" She waited for Emma to elaborate.

"And nothing," Emma returned. "It was okay as kisses go, but I didn't feel the earth move or anything."

"You didn't?" This seemed shocking to Phoebe. "But everyone says—"

Emma had no interest in hearing the details of Flyboy's amorous exploits, even if it was only by repute.

"The truth is," she broke in, "that ninety percent of the time we were stranded, Oliver was busy playing poker with his cronies."

Phoebe's expression suggested that she was terribly disappointed in both of them. The only way to end this inquisition, Emma decided, was to ask a few questions of her own. "While I have your attention, I want you to tell me what's going on between you and Walt," she said. "You promised."

Phoebe glanced over her shoulder and lowered her

voice. "I've probably said more than I should have already." She rolled her chair back across the aisle.

Emma followed her, and leaned against the cubicle wall with her arms folded. "I'm not sure whether I should thank you or yell at you for getting me this assignment."

"I did not," Phoebe insisted righteously. "I just felt Walt should know that if he didn't do something quick, he was going to lose you, so I...I told him what you said about quitting."

"That's practically blackmail!" Emma said in a horrified voice. "What if he'd fired me because *you* told him I threatened to quit?"

"Don't worry about that. I wouldn't have let it happen," Phoebe said calmly. "But you deserve a shot at something other than obituaries. I knew Walt couldn't afford to let you go—and he knows it, too."

"Okay, at least you used your power for good," Emma murmured. She was thankful that Phoebe had spoken to Walt on her behalf; still, she'd rather stand on her own merit. "Oliver said that when he asked about me, you sang like a canary. And that's a quote."

Phoebe laughed out loud. "Yeah, right, and if you believe *that,* then you don't know me at all."

"I thought he was exaggerating." Just then the phone on her desk rang. Reaching across the aisle, Emma picked up the receiver. It was Walt, wanting to see her. Now.

Phoebe's eyes widened in speculation when Emma hung up the phone.

"Wish me luck," she mouthed to her friend. Grabbing a pad and pen, she walked up the stairs. When she got to his office, her boss was on the phone, but he motioned her inside. He grinned in her direction, which boded well. She had no idea who he was talking to or about what—although the word "no" featured prominently—but after another moment he ended the conversation.

Emma sat in the chair on the other side of his desk.

"So. You're back."

She nodded, but resisted mentioning the motel bill.

"I understand you and Oliver Hamilton had a bit of an adventure."

She couldn't help wondering how much Walt knew about what had happened in Yakima. "You could say that." She mulled over how to tell him she refused to fly with Oliver again.

"The interview with Earleen Williams went well?"

She nodded. "Earleen was wonderful. She was flattered by the attention and excited about the article. Her recipe's terrific—I had a taste and, believe it or not, I loved it. By the way, she's already signed the legal documentation so we can print her recipe in *The Examiner*." If nothing else, Walt should be pleased by that.

He inclined his head slightly in apparent approval.

"I'd like the article about Earleen on my desk this afternoon."

Emma's mouth fell open. "This afternoon? As in today?"

Walt raised his eyebrows as if she'd contravened some kind of reporters' code by daring to ask such a question.

Swallowing hard, she offered him an apologetic smile. "It'll be there."

"Good." His eyebrows started to return to their usual position. "And be ready to leave for Colville first thing tomorrow."

So soon? She wanted to tell him she needed time to regroup after the flight from Yakima. Yes, it had gone fairly well. Other than the fact that she'd nearly vomited. The best part was that she'd survived without drugs. Her employer simply had no idea what she'd gone through just to get to the other town and home again in one piece. Then there was the problem of no transportation when they'd landed in Yakima. Not only had she risked her life for this interview, but she'd encountered germs besides.

Now all she had to do was find a way to tell Walt that she preferred to drive to her next interview. "If you have a moment, I'd like to talk to you about Sophie McKay."

Walt gave her a questioning look.

"As you know, I ended up spending the night in Yakima. In a motel room. A cheap one."

He sat back in his chair. "Hamilton said that was unavoidable."

So Walt had already spoken to Oliver. "There's no guarantee it won't happen again—being delayed due to weather, I mean."

He pinched his lips together. "True. Not to worry, the newspaper will reimburse you for the room."

Emma couldn't prevent a look of surprise at his easy capitulation on the matter of her expenses. Still, that wasn't her main concern at the moment.

"I appreciate it, but I was thinking, you know, that it'd probably be better if I drove to Colville this time, rather than fly. I realize it's a full day's drive, but—"

Walt raised his hand and stopped her. "Out of the question. I already have an agreement with Hamilton. He's got a run into Spokane tomorrow morning. He'll drop you off at Colville, fly into Spokane and then come back for you later in the afternoon."

Emma's heart shot to her throat. "You actually want me to do this again...tomorrow?"

Walt nodded. "Meet Oliver at the airfield same time as before."

"Oh." She stood, but her feet felt weighted down. In less than twenty-four hours, she was going back up into the wide blue yonder with Oliver Hamilton.

"Have a good day," Walt said, turning to his computer and dismissing her. "Remember, I want that first article before you leave this afternoon. We're already in the second week of December, and there's a time fac-tor here." He gestured at some limp Christmas garland draped on his window.

"It'll be on your desk," she promised, relieved that she had the rough draft on her laptop computer.

More by instinct than knowledge, she stumbled back down to her cubicle in The Dungeon, preoccupied by the fact that she'd be flying again so soon. She'd learned that—especially with the help of drugs—she *could* handle being in a small plane. She didn't like it, never would, but in all honesty, the flight hadn't been as bad as she'd feared.

Examining her reluctance to repeat the experience, she was forced to admit something she'd rather ignore. More than the flying itself, it was Oliver Hamilton she wanted to avoid.

Chapter Seven

A fruitcake is to a chef what love is to a gigolo—
an item we both desperately try to avoid.

—Michael Psilakis, executive chef
and owner of Onera, New York City

Oliver wasn't in the best of moods. He'd made a recent and rather disturbing discovery: Emma Collins wasn't good for his ego. Until he met her, he'd been doing just fine when it came to attracting the opposite sex. Better than fine.

His late-afternoon conversation with Walt had further eroded his ego. Apparently, upon their return from Yakima, Emma had attempted to get out of flying with him a second time. Fortunately, Walt had said no; a deal was a deal and Oliver didn't plan to let her kill his chances of advertising his air-freight business in the local paper.

Okay, he'd admit it'd been a mistake to kiss her, a mistake he didn't intend to repeat. If this was how Emma felt, then he could ignore her, too.

A glance at his watch told him she had five minutes to show up. If she wasn't at the airport by seven, he was leaving without her. He would've kept *his* end of the bargain, and she'd just have to explain to her boss that she'd been late. He'd only signed this new contract a few weeks ago, flying Alaska salmon packed in dry ice to restaurants in Spokane and Portland. It was a regular job and he couldn't afford to mess up the opportunity.

Just as he was about to board the plane, Emma hurried onto the tarmac, clutching her briefcase and a large takeout coffee.

"You're late," he snapped.

"I most certainly am not." Then, perhaps to reassure herself, she stopped and checked her watch. "I've got five minutes to spare," she announced with more than an edge of righteousness. "At least by my watch."

"Well, not by mine."

This time she wasn't having trouble remaining upright because—or so he assumed—of some stupid pill.

Regardless, he was going to stick to his policy of ignoring her; he'd simply fly his plane.

He felt her scrutiny. "Someone got up on the wrong side of the bed this morning," she said in a singsong voice.

He pretended not to hear. Oscar was already in the plane, ready and waiting to take off. The terrier poked his head out the passenger door as if to ask what was taking so long.

"Listen," Emma said, "why don't we start over, all right?"

"Fine, whatever."

She rolled her eyes and climbed into the plane with absolutely no complaints. He didn't know what had happened to get her to relax. She'd probably switched drugs and had swallowed some heavy-duty, industrial-strength mood enhancer. Nothing else could explain this cheerful state of mind.

Suddenly he wondered if she'd been drinking, although she'd denied it yesterday. He studied her and sniffed on the off-chance he could smell alcohol.

She glared at him. "Why are you looking at me like that? What's wrong with you, anyway?"

"Nothing," he muttered, returning to the task at hand. He walked beneath the wing, stepping in front of the engine to examine the blades.

Emma's headphones were in place, with the small microphone positioned by her mouth, before he'd finished his preflight check.

His faithful—or should that be faithless?—companion had obviously accepted her, barely raising his head when Oliver climbed into the plane. Oscar had settled onto his dog bed in the cargo hold.

"You didn't wear perfume this time, did you?" he asked.

"No, because I didn't want to get sneezed on again."

"Well, good for you."

Her eyes narrowed. "I don't know why you're in such a bad mood, but I wish you'd snap out of it."

As if to apologize for Oliver, his terrier stood up and poked his head between the two seats. When Emma bent toward him, he licked her ear. Smiling, she stroked his face. Traitor that he was, Oscar seemed to relish her attention. Not until the engine started did the dog go back to his bed.

"Finish your coffee," he said. "We'll be leaving in a couple of minutes."

"It's not coffee. It's latte. Eggnog-flavored." She had to argue about everything. But she obediently drained the large cup.

Oliver taxied to the end of the runway and waited for approval to take off. It wasn't long in coming. He was in the air before he realized that Emma's eyes were squeezed shut. Like yesterday, she held on to the bar above the door with what could only be described as a death grip. But at least she wasn't confessing at the top of her lungs that she'd lied about her weight. The memory produced a grin and for a moment he forgot that he was annoyed with her.

They hardly spoke the entire flight. Every now and then he felt her glance in his direction, as if to gauge his mood. An hour outside of Colville, he saw that she was squirming in her seat.

"What's the problem now?" he asked.

Emma shifted from one side to the other. "If you *must* know, I have to use the, uh, facilities."

"You should've gone before we left."

"I did," she said, not bothering to hide her indignation.

"There isn't a toilet on the plane."

She turned and scowled at him. "I noticed. Do you have any other suggestions?"

"You can do what I do," he told her. Reaching behind him, he grabbed a wide-mouth red plastic container.

She looked at it as if he'd just handed her a dead rat. "You aren't serious, are you?"

"You said you had to go."

"You don't honestly expect me to...go," she said, apparently not finding a more suitable verb, "in that."

"I use it."

"It's different for a man. There's a bit more effort involved for a woman."

"We're a little less than an hour from Colville."

She crossed her legs. "I guess I can wait."

"I thought you'd say that."

By the time he approached the Colville runway, Oliver's sympathies were with Emma. She was clearly uncomfortable, if the number of times she'd crossed and uncrossed her legs was any indication. He didn't have the heart to tell her there wasn't a terminal in Colville. The runway was next to a cow pasture, and while there was an office, that didn't necessarily mean anyone would be there to let her in. It'd been a while since his last visit and he didn't recall if there was a restroom of any kind in the hangar. For her sake, he hoped there was.

Emma bit her lower lip when the wheels touched down. Oliver taxied and parked the plane and leaped out. Just as he'd suspected, no one emerged from the office.

"There's a toilet in there," he said, helping her down. "But I'm not sure it's open...."

She had a desperate look.

Emma hurried toward the office, but no one answered her frantic knock. When she glanced over her shoulder, he shrugged, pointing at the hangar.

With that, she bolted for the large metal shed. She must have found what she needed because she didn't immediately reappear. While he waited, Oliver got on his cell and phoned the Spokane restaurant with his ETA. Someone would meet him at the airfield to pick up the salmon delivery.

When she returned from the hangar she was frowning. "The conditions in there were deplorable. Downright primitive."

"Hey," he said, holding up both hands in a gesture of surrender. "It wasn't me who gulped down that eggnog latte."

She threw him an irate look. "The least you could've done was warn me how long the flight was going to take."

"You're a reporter. You could've done the research." He was about to say something else when he saw the small black dog.

Emma had noticed the mutt, too, a curly-haired mixed breed, probably part poodle. From the matted hair and the lost expression in her brown eyes, Oliver could tell the dog was a stray.

"Where did you come from?" Emma asked, gently petting her. The dog stared longingly up at her and started to shake. "She's cold," Emma said.

Oliver felt bad, but there was little he could do. As it was, Oscar had seen her, jumped down, barking loudly, and then promptly did what dogs always do when they meet another of their kind. He sniffed her butt.

"I had no idea this town was so small," Emma commented. She looked over the cow pasture and wrapped her coat more securely around her. "Do you have anything to eat?"

"You're hungry?"

"No, but the dog is. I don't usually carry food with me." She checked the inside of her purse; the best she had to offer was a half-used package of antacid mints. Unfortunately, Oliver wasn't much help, either.

A lone car drove past the road next to the airfield. "Do you have my cell phone number?" he asked, following the vehicle with his eyes.

"You gave it to me in Yakima."

"Right." He remembered that now. "Call me when you're finished, all right?" As soon as she was picked up, he'd fly into Spokane.

"When will you be back?" she asked.

So she was going to miss him, he thought, warmed by the question. She wouldn't admit it, of course, but she *was* attracted to him. He decided it was better not to react.

"You're sure you have a ride," he confirmed.

"Sophie McKay said she'd come and get me."

She pulled out her cell and punched in a number from her little daybook. After a short conversation, she nodded in his direction, letting him know her ride was on the way.

Oliver hesitated. He didn't feel entirely comfortable about leaving her here alone, in what was virtually a deserted field.

"You can go," she said, her shoulders hunched against the wind. "Ms. McKay will be here any minute."

"How long will the interview be?"

"I'm not sure. I imagine an hour, two at the most."

Oliver estimated that he wouldn't be away more than a couple of hours himself, but it wasn't a problem if Emma required more time. The Indian casino was a few miles down the road, and if she was occupied, the gaming tables offered him ample entertainment. Emma might not want to ride his folding bicycle, but he didn't mind using it. He welcomed the excuse to try his hand at blackjack. The slot machines were pretty much a bust, but he did fairly well with a deck of cards.

"Take all the time you need."

She smiled and frankly he wished she hadn't. When she acted this pleasant, it was hard to remember what a pain she really was.

Emma wrapped the plaid wool scarf around her face to ward off the chill wind, then buried her hands in her pockets. At the moment, she looked about as pitiful as the stray dog huddled next to her feet.

"Just call my cell and I'll be back as soon as I can."

"I will," she assured him, her words muffled. "You'd better go or you'll be late."

"I know."

He hesitated a moment longer, then returned to the plane and opened the cargo hatch. To his surprise, Emma followed him.

"You're upset because you found out I didn't want to fly with you again," she said. Her hands remained in her pockets.

He shrugged as if it didn't matter either way.

"If not that, then is it because..." She stopped, her expression mildly embarrassed.

"What?" he demanded.

"Never mind."

"No," he said. "I want to know."

She looked at him hard. "Is it because I...I didn't react the way you wanted when you kissed me?"

He didn't want to answer that and climbed aboard the plane.

"I didn't see any fireworks when we kissed. Did you?" she asked, sticking her head in the cargo hold.

He snorted.

"Then it isn't any big deal, right?"

"Right."

"Friends?" she asked.

Without meaning to be rude, Oliver paused. "I guess. Why do you care?"

His question appeared to catch her off guard. "I don't know, but I do. If we're going to be spending time together for the next week or so, then I think it's preferable to get along."

"Of course. You have nothing to worry about."

She glanced nervously away. "My mother told me that when a man uses that line, I *should* start to worry."

He chuckled. "No, you don't. You're perfectly safe with me."

As if in disagreement, the little black dog at her feet snarled up at him.

Chapter Eight

Fruitcake is one of those foods that evoke lots of different feelings in people. For me it marks the holiday season that is accompanied by traditions and family. Sharing foods that you eat during certain times of the year is something that I look forward to. A warmed thin slice of fruitcake with freshly made ice cream is the way to go.

—Craig Strong, chef de cuisine, The Dining Room,
The Ritz-Carlton in Pasadena, California

Sophie McKay arrived at the airfield five minutes after Oliver left. Although Emma would never admit it, she found his reluctance to leave her somewhat comforting. She just might have to change her opinion of Oliver Hamilton.

Emma spent those five minutes alone paying attention to the small stray, whom she called Boots because she had two white paws and otherwise black fur. The poor thing shivered in the cold.

When a compact car turned off the road and onto the airfield, Emma straightened. The vehicle came to a stop not far from her, and the driver rolled down her window.

She was an elegant eighty or so, with thick white hair, fashionably styled. Her face glowed with pleasure. "Are you the reporter from *The Examiner*?"

Emma nodded. "And you must be Sophie McKay."

"I am. You seem half-frozen. Come on, I'll drive you to my house. It's warm and cozy, and I'll put on a pot of tea."

Emma looked down at the little dog. Crouching, she petted Boots.

"I see you have a friend," Sophie commented.

"Does she have an owner?" Emma asked hopefully, but considering the dog's appearance, she agreed with Oliver that Boots was most likely a stray.

"Not that I know of. The poor dog's been hanging around the area for a while. I put food out for her a few times, and I know other people have, too, but she's skittish. I think someone must've mistreated her because she doesn't let anyone get too close. Except for you, apparently."

Boots had taken to Emma right away, and she hated to leave the dog behind. "Would you mind if I brought her with me?" What she'd do with Boots after that was a quandary, but Emma didn't feel she could just walk away.

"That might be a problem because of my cats."

Emma gazed down at the dog, unsure what to do.

"Could you find somewhere warm for her to stay until later?" Sophie suggested. "Maybe in the hangar? I'll give you some food to bring back for her."

"Good idea." Emma hadn't thought of that. Boots followed her inside while Sophie dug up an old blanket from the trunk of her car. Emma folded it and placed it on the bathroom floor. Boots didn't object when Emma shut her inside the small room. At least the dog was out of the cold and out of danger. Squatting down, Emma stroked her thin sides and spoke in low, soothing tones, assuring her she'd be back soon.

A few minutes later, she left the hangar and walked over to Sophie's Taurus. A welcome blast of hot air warmed her the instant she slid into the passenger seat.

"I have to tell you," Sophie said as she slipped the stick shift into reverse and revved the engine. "You coming for this interview has really stirred up interest in town. We don't get much notice this side of the mountains. Of course, there's not much that's newsworthy coming out of Colville, so the western half of the state doesn't pay us much mind."

"Your fruitcake recipe is a finalist in a national contest," Emma reminded her.

"Yes," she agreed readily enough, "that was exciting news around here. It made the front page of our weekly paper. Still, none of us figured anyone in the Seattle area would care about my recipe."

"Why do you think yours was chosen?" Emma asked. She might as well get started with the interview now. She opened her purse and brought out her notebook and one of her pens.

"That's easy. It's different. How many recipes have you heard of for chocolate fruitcake?"

"Chocolate?"

"That's right. I created it for my husband years ago and he loved it. Christmas just isn't Christmas without it anymore. I've been baking my chocolate fruitcake every year for longer than I can remember."

"I imagine your husband appreciates that."

Sophie took her eyes off the road for an instant. "Harry's been gone twenty years."

"I'm sorry," Emma murmured awkwardly. "Um, when exactly did you create this fruitcake?"

"It all began shortly after Harry and I were married. Within a year he was off to fight in World War Two," Sophie told her. "I mailed the chocolate fruitcake to him and he got a real kick out of that because, you see, we'd had our first real fight over fruitcake. I'll explain all that once we get back to the house. He wrote to let me know how much he enjoyed it, and I've been baking it every year since. I still have all his letters. Now that he's gone, I read them every once in a while for the memories."

"You never remarried?"

"No, I never did. I found the love of my life. There wasn't another man like Harry and I knew it." Sophie shook her head as she drove down Main Street and the large clock that stood in the center of town. From there, she turned up a steep hill and past the city park.

Although Harry McKay was very different from her own father, Sophie's devotion reminded her of her mother's. Pamela had been like that, loving one man her entire life, despite his weaknesses and flaws. Bret Collins wasn't worthy of such adoration, such heartfelt affection. And Emma wasn't willing to be the daughter he seemed to want now that he was aging.

"Did you have any children?" she asked, unwilling to waste another moment thinking about her father.

"Two sons. Both live in other parts of the country. Harry was very proud of his sons. I am, too. They're good boys—handsome like Harry and smart like me." She laughed a little as she pulled into a long driveway that led to an older home with a large front porch. Sophie parked in the back and turned off the engine.

"The boys want to buy me a new car this Christmas," she said with a thoughtful look. "Lonnie wants to get me one of those old-style cars you see around. I forget what they're called—Cruisers, I think. Unfortunately, they don't come with a stick shift."

"You don't like automatics?" Emma asked.

"Never learned how to drive them and at my age, I'm comfortable with what I know."

That made sense to Emma.

Sophie ushered her onto the back porch. She stepped around pie tins filled with cat food, both kibble and canned.

"Sorry for the mess and the smell," Sophie apologized. "I feed the strays. Some of them have bad teeth, hence the soft food. God only knows how many cats I've got living under this old porch. I do what I can for them—take the sick ones to the vet and give them a bit of attention." She paused and smiled. "It makes me feel good, even when they don't appreciate it."

Emma looked out over the large well-maintained lawn and flower beds. "Your yard is lovely."

A fir wreath with pinecones and red bows hung in the kitchen window. "You should see my irises in the spring. I have them planted everywhere and the yard is full of color. Flowers, cats and chocolate fruitcakes are my passion. Harry and the boys, too, of course, but my husband is gone and my boys are living their own lives now. They don't need me the way they once did." She unlocked the back door and brought Emma into the oversize family kitchen. Three cats meowed as they entered. "These are Huey, Duey and Louey. They're the house cats. They're spoiled, ill-mannered and don't take kindly to strangers or dogs, so you'll have to forgive them."

Emma petted one, who instantly scooted into another room.

"This is the problem with living alone," Sophie said as she filled the kettle and placed it on the stove. "It's just me and the cats and we have certain ways of doing things."

"That's understandable."

Sophie walked into the dining room and returned with a large teapot. "I reserve this one for special company," she said as she measured out tea leaves. Motioning toward the table, she added, "Make yourself comfortable. Just pull out the chair if there's a cat in it and he'll move."

"All right." Sure enough, a large tabby was nestled on the seat cushion. As soon as Emma drew out the chair, the cat stretched and yawned and grudgingly vacated the seat.

"Here, let me brush away the cat hairs." Sophie brought over a whisk broom and swept off the cushion.

"Thank you." Emma sat down at the table, which was cluttered with magazines, newspapers, mail and sales flyers.

Sophie glanced at the wall-mounted clock. "Do you mind if I turn on the radio for a few minutes? It's bingo."

"Ah…sure." Bingo over the radio? Emma had never heard of such a thing.

The radio was on the table, too, next to an aged photograph of a young man in uniform. Harry, Emma guessed. His widow was right; he'd been a handsome man. Other pictures caught her attention—framed photographs of two families. Emma assumed they were Sophie's two sons and their wives and kids.

Her hostess turned on the radio, sat down and lined up her bingo cards in neat rows. Her timing was perfect. She reached for a round blotter pen and waited for the numbers to be called. Her eyes darted back and forth over the cards after each number was announced. Radio bingo was followed by the farm report, which Sophie immediately switched off.

"Sorry about that, but I'm on a winning streak. I've won two weeks in a row," she told her proudly as the kettle on the stove started to whistle. "My friends say I'm lucky, and it's true."

"I've never heard of radio bingo."

"You haven't?" Sophie shook her head as if this was a real shame. "The local merchants sponsor it. When you bingo, you call it in to the station and then take your card to the participating merchant for your prize."

"What did you win?" Emma asked, curious now.

"Five dollars off my next haircut at Venus de Milo Beauty Salon, and the week before, it was buy one, get one free at the A & W Drive-In. If you were going to be in town longer and it wasn't so cold, I'd take you down for one of their root beer floats."

Emma smiled appreciatively as Sophie poured the tea and brought out a dark wrapped loaf from the refrigerator.

"I thought you might want to try my chocolate fruit-cake."

"Uh, sure…"

"You'll be surprised—pleasantly so," Sophie told her. Within minutes, she brought two cups of tea and a plate of the most unusual-looking fruitcake Emma had ever seen.

"Taste it," the woman urged.

Emma helped herself to a slice, unsure what to expect. The flavors came alive in her mouth and she widened her eyes. Sophie hadn't exaggerated. This was incredibly good. "Is that pineapple I taste?"

"Yup, and coconut, too."

"Oh, this is *wonderful*." Emma took another bite and licked her fingers when she'd finished. For the second time, her preconceptions and prejudices about something—fruitcake—had been tested.

"I use lots of nuts. Harry was wild about pecans. My own favorite is walnuts. Do you realize how good nuts are for you?" she asked conversationally. "Just think about it. Inside each nut is the potential for an entire tree. They're packed full of nutrition. A lot of people are concerned about the fat content, but nuts have good fat, not bad fat."

Emma smiled. Being with Sophie was such a delight that she was having a hard time remembering to take notes. "How did you come up with the recipe?"

"That's the most interesting part," she said, joining her at the table once more. "The first year Harry and I were married, I wanted to make fruitcake at Christmas. My mother always had, and I wanted to be a good wife and homemaker, just like her. Harry told me he hated fruitcake and furthermore he didn't want me wasting money on ingredients for a cake he wouldn't even eat. This was toward the end of the Depression, when money was still scarce. I told him he was being selfish and mean, and I burst into tears." She paused and sipped her tea.

"You see, to me, Christmas *was* fruitcake. It felt as if Harry had asked me to give up my favorite holiday. That was our first big fight. Telling me I couldn't bake that fruitcake was like telling me we couldn't afford Christmas."

As far as this Christmas thing went, Emma's sympathies were with Harry.

"The next morning," Sophie continued, "Harry said if it meant that much to me, I should go ahead and do whatever I wanted. So I baked fruitcake, but I used the ingredients I knew Harry liked best. When I told him what I'd done, he put his arms around me and said it wasn't any wonder he loved me as much as he did. Harry had a real sweet tooth, especially for good chocolate."

"You used the ingredients he liked?" Emma thought that was a clever compromise.

"I admit chocolate fruitcake isn't run-of-the-mill fruitcake, but that's what got me into the finals, don't you think? I can only imagine how many recipes they received. Mine was different, and I have my Harry to thank for that."

Emma made another note on her tablet. Sophie was about to say something else when someone knocked on the back door.

"That'll be Barbara, my sister-in-law. I told her she could stop by and meet you. I didn't think you'd mind."

"Sure, that's fine."

Barbara came into the kitchen, wearing a heavy winter coat and a long hand-knit scarf with matching gloves. "Hello," she said, beaming Emma a warm smile. She removed her gloves, tucked them in her pockets, then extended her right hand. "It's a pleasure to meet you. We're all so proud of Sophie, and it's nice that the Seattle newspaper's doing this."

Emma didn't have the heart to tell her that *The Examiner* was a regional paper with a limited circulation. Of course, Puyallup was considerably bigger than Colville with its population of less than seven thousand, and compared to Colville's weekly, *The Examiner* was practically the *New York Times*.

"How was your flight?" Barbara shooed a cat out of a chair and joined them.

"Uneventful—just the way I like them." The discomfort of a full bladder was not a topic she wished to pursue.

Barbara wasn't the only visitor Sophie had. By the end of the interview, Emma had been introduced to Dixie, Sophie's next-door neighbor; Florence, her best friend; and Cathy, who cleaned her house once a week. They all gathered around the table with tea and chocolate fruitcake and told story after story. Their laughter echoed through the house. It was a party unlike any Emma had ever gone to; none of these women were close to her age but she felt like one of them.

By the time Sophie dropped her off at the airfield, it was almost two in the afternoon. The Cessna was parked at the end of the strip near the hangar, and Emma assumed Oliver was inside.

"I'll wait just to be sure," Sophie insisted.

Emma didn't want to hold up the other woman, but reluctantly agreed. She hurried over to the plane, seeking Oliver, disappointed not to find him immediately. She felt excited—no, elated—after the interview and wanted to talk about the experience. Share some of the wisdom she'd gained from Sophie and her friends.

In discussing the interview with Oliver, she might get a slant for her story. She had a thousand ideas and impressions chasing around in her head and needed to sort through them. It was important to her that she do Sophie and her friends justice.

"Oliver!" she called out. He might have curled up inside the hangar for a nap. "Oscar?"

No response.

Emma let Boots out of the restroom and bent down to feed her the can of cat food Sophie had given her. The dog would be too hungry to be finicky, Emma guessed, and she was right. Boots gobbled up the small can's contents and looked for more.

Emma found her cell phone and walked outside to make sure she'd get a good connection. She waved at Sophie, then punched in the number for his cell. The phone rang three times before Oliver responded.

"Hamilton."

"Where are you?" she asked.

"You're finished?"

"Where are you?" she repeated. She couldn't place the background noise, which sounded like some sort of circus.

"The casino. It's a couple of miles out of town."

After the poker experience, she should've known he'd be gambling. "Will you be much longer?"

"I'm in, I'm in," he shouted, obviously not to her. "Listen, I'm in the middle of a game and I can't quit. Find a way out here, will you?"

"You want me to come to the *casino*?" She couldn't believe the nerve of this man.

He didn't answer and the line was disconnected. She called again, but this time there was no answer, even after a dozen rings. Like it or not—and she didn't—Emma was going to the casino.

Chapter Nine

On the short drive to the casino, Emma brooded about the unreliability of Oliver Hamilton. She hoped Sophie didn't notice how upset she was with her so-called pilot. In case he'd forgotten, she needed to get back to the newspaper office sometime before the end of the Christmas season.

"Colville's a pleasant little town," Sophie was telling her. "I wish you had more time to look around. There's a lumber mill on the other side of town, which helps keep the local economy afloat."

Emma smiled politely, finding it difficult to concentrate. Boots was curled up next to her feet and had gone to sleep. She still didn't know what she was going to do with the stray. Maybe she could persuade Phoebe to take her until Emma moved into a new apartment that allowed pets.

When Sophie pulled up in front of the casino, Emma had to look twice. The place resembled nothing so much as an overgrown tavern. Other than a sign on the roadway, there wasn't a single indication that this was a casino. Emma had expected flashing neon lights, a fancy restaurant offering steak and lobster dinners at cut-rate prices, uniformed valets. Instead, Sophie parked on a gravel lot.

"I can't thank you enough," Emma told the other woman as she climbed out of the vehicle. Boots hopped out with her as Emma reached for her purse and brief-case.

"It was lovely to meet you," Sophie said, leaning across the front seat. "I hope you win today. I'll be out here on Sunday after church—for bingo. I won eight hundred dollars a year ago." She grinned. "Like I said, I'm just plain lucky."

The door to the casino opened and out sauntered the largest lumberjack Emma had ever seen. Not that she'd seen many lumberjacks. This man had to be close to seven feet tall and wore a red plaid shirt, dirt-smudged jeans with suspenders and a red wool cap. She glanced around, just to make sure Babe, the blue ox, wasn't fol-lowing behind.

He took one look at Emma and pointed a beefy fin-ger in her direction. "You. Be my woman."

Emma gasped.

Shaking her head, Sophie got out of the driver's seat. "Grizzly, you leave this young lady alone."

Grizzly looked crestfallen and rubbed the side of his face. "I shaved before I came into town."

"It takes more than a shave to attract a woman. Now apologize."

Grizzly shuffled from one foot to the other. "I didn't mean no offense."

"None taken." After a final wave for Sophie, Emma grabbed Boots and tucked the dog under her arm as she scurried into the casino. When she found Oliver, she intended to let him know *exactly* what she thought.

Oscar was patiently waiting for Oliver just inside the door. As soon as he saw Emma and Boots, he barked twice. This appeared to be the cue Oliver was waiting for, because he turned abruptly and faced the door.

He was at a table near the entrance playing some card game. Blackjack? It was hard to tell in the smoky haze. The entire place was shrouded in cigarette smoke, and she gave an involuntary cough. Oscar sneezed, but she managed to jump back in time.

"Won't be long," Oliver called out. "Make yourself comfortable."

"In here?" The smoke was likely to kill her first.

With a disgusted grimace, he left the table and walked toward her. "I'll be ten minutes or so."

At her horrified expression, he looked over his shoulder at the blackjack table. "You want something to eat?" he asked quickly.

"No, I want to go home. How are we supposed to get back to the airfield? And why did you make me come out here, anyway?"

He gazed at her a moment, pure innocence in his eyes. "Why, Ms. Collins, I thought you'd enjoy being introduced to another fascinating aspect of Washington state culture. Maybe you could write a travel piece. And like I said, you can get a meal here. Or try one of the slot machines. Don't worry about getting back, either. A friend of a friend said he'd give us a ride to the airfield. You'll like Grizzly. And don't be put off by his name. He's as gentle as a lamb."

"Grizzly?" That completely distracted her from the sarcastic remark she'd been about to make.

"Now, don't judge a man by his name. He's a sweetheart."

"Big guy in a red plaid shirt?"

Oliver nodded. "You know him?"

"He just asked me to be his woman," she said from between clenched teeth.

Oliver blinked. "I'm sure he didn't mean it."

Emma's eyes opened wide. "What is *that* supposed to mean?"

"He doesn't come into town often. Don't worry, you're safe."

If that was supposed to reassure her, it didn't. From

the sound of it, the big guy hardly ever saw a woman. And since she was going to be stuck in some vehicle with him, he might well think he'd hit the jackpot.

"I'm in the middle of a lucky streak." For the first time Oliver seemed to notice that Boots was with her. "What do you intend to do with the dog?"

"I...I haven't figured that out yet."

Someone impatiently shouted Oliver's name.

"Be right with you," he yelled over his shoulder. "Can't you entertain yourself for a few minutes?"

He spoke as if she were ten years old.

"Don't be concerned about me," she said. Next time she was going to insist on driving, and she wouldn't take no for an answer.

"Hamilton, you in or not?"

"In," he shouted back.

Emma watched him sprint over to the table. This was great; it was either breathe in smoke or risk facing Paul Bunyan in the parking lot. Emma decided her chances were better in the casino. But she didn't like it there. Boots didn't, either. The dog trembled in her arms, alarmed by all the lights and noise. Oscar, however, despite an occasional sneeze, relaxed in his corner by the door. He appeared to be an old hand at this, which no doubt he was.

After a few minutes, Emma couldn't tolerate the smoke anymore. She needed fresh air. She stepped outside and wasn't completely pleased when Oliver's terrier followed her into the pale wintry sunlight. She didn't like the way Oscar was eyeing Boots. Her hold on Boots tightened. No way was she letting Oscar have his way with this sweet dog.

"If you're thinking what I think you're thinking," she told the other dog, "forget it. Boots is off-limits. Understand?" Once she got home, there'd be a veterinary appointment for Boots—checkup, shots and spaying. She planned to be a responsible pet-owner, and that included thwarting Oscar's evil-minded intentions.

It was cold outside, and her fashionable leather boots weren't enough to keep her feet warm. Her toes lost feeling; reluctantly she retreated inside once again, determined to drag Oliver away from the gaming table if necessary.

Fortunately, he was finished with his game. Counting his money as he walked toward her, he looked up as if nothing were amiss and smiled. "I won three hundred dollars."

She ignored that. "Can we leave for the airfield now?" she asked, keeping her voice as level and even as she could manage.

"Sure thing. And considering your worries about Grizzly, I got us another ride."

"Good."

"You don't have any objection to riding in the back of a pickup, do you? It's only a couple of miles."

"What?"

"Just kidding."

"Ha, ha." She wasn't amused.

"Come on, Emma, loosen up. Where's your Christmas spirit?"

She didn't answer. The less said regarding her feelings about Christmas, the better. Instead she asked, "Three of us are supposed to cram into a truck cab?"

"You have a problem with that?"

"As a matter of fact, I do. I'll find my own way back to the airfield." Oliver was really starting to get on her nerves. "Why did you have me come out here, anyway?" she demanded. "Seriously. Don't give me any nonsense about culture or travel, either."

He sighed. "I was on a winning streak. I didn't know how long it was going to last. But sending for you was the stupidest thing I could've done. The minute you showed up, I started losing."

"You're blaming *me?*" Emma had to get away from this Neanderthal. "Go ahead without me," she told him. "I'll phone for a taxi."

Oliver nearly doubled over as he burst into laughter. "La-di-da. Her highness requires a private conveyance. Do you actually believe a town the size of Colville has a taxi service?"

"Oh." Emma had assumed there was one.

"Don't worry. I'm the forgiving sort. I'll still let you ride with me and if you're real nice I won't make you sit in the back of the truck."

By this time Emma was so angry with Oliver, she wanted to smack him upside the head. "Have you been drinking?" she snapped.

"Absolutely not." His smile faded. "FAA regulations don't permit it. I worked too hard for this license to mess it up over a beer."

She had half a mind to lean over and smell his breath. She didn't, for fear he'd try to kiss her again. And yet... the thought was strangely appealing.

She and Oliver clambered into a rickety old truck driven by a bearded taciturn man named Michael Michaels—known as Mike-Mike. He had remarkably little to say, which was fine with Emma. Preferable to Grizzly's idea of conversation, anyway.

On the ride back to Colville Emma reminded herself that she wasn't attracted to Oliver Hamilton. Still, if he wanted to kiss her—not now, of course, but later—she was afraid she might let him. Perhaps she was experiencing altitude sickness. There was definitely something in the air, but it wasn't Christmas and it sure wasn't love.

Emma sat between the two men with Boots, plus her purse and briefcase, on her lap and Oscar down by Oliver's feet. When they arrived at the field, Emma climbed out of the truck once Oliver had leaped to the ground. She thanked Mike-Mike politely for the ride.

Oliver handed his new friend a few dollars. With

the two dogs trotting behind them, Emma and Oliver headed toward the Cessna.

"How'd the interview go?" Oliver asked as they approached the plane.

The tension left her shoulders. "I think Sophie is one of the most interesting women I've ever met."

"Really." Oliver walked around the Cessna, giving it the usual inspection.

"She's loved one man her entire life."

He nodded, although she doubted he was listening.

"Harry died twenty years ago, and she's loved him and only him all these years. I find that so romantic."

"Romantic," he repeated absently.

"Did you hear me?" she asked.

Oliver glanced back at her. "I heard you. So what's the big deal? Men and women stay in love all the time."

"They don't," Emma said. "Do you know what the divorce rate is in this country? One out of every two marriages fails. That's a fifty-percent failure rate. Men and women *don't* stay in love, and do you know why?"

He yawned.

"It's because there aren't any genuinely romantic men left in this world. Where's Cary Grant when we need him? What about Humphrey Bogart? Rock Hudson? No, wait. Not him. Although he was very romantic in all those Doris Day movies."

"Donald Duck. Daisy thought *he* was pretty romantic."

This time she couldn't resist and slapped his shoulder. "It's all one big joke to you, isn't it?" Without giving him a chance to respond, she said, "I'm serious."

"There are romantic men in this world, Emma. Lots of them, and they don't look anything like a bunch of old movie stars, either. Real romance isn't about candlelit dinners or diamonds or champagne. As for couples staying in love, my parents have been married for thirty-six years."

Suddenly Oliver Hamilton was the expert. "You know all about this subject, do you?" She let him hear the sarcasm in her voice.

"You'd probably consider my brother a romantic. At least he tried to be. Unfortunately, the whole thing backfired on him."

Emma knew he wanted her to ask what happened and she refused to. She needn't have worried because Oliver was intent on telling her, whether she wanted to be told or not.

"Jack took his girlfriend to a fancy restaurant in order to propose. He wanted to do it up big, you know. So he had the chef bake the engagement ring into a piece of chocolate cake." He was smiling as he described the details of his brother's attempt at romance. "The problem is that when Ginny ate the cake, she swallowed the diamond ring." He slapped his knee now, overcome by mirth.

"Oh, let's just get in the plane."

But Oliver seemed determined to finish his story. "I told him he was lucky Ginny didn't choke to death on that diamond. They've been married for six years now and have two little rug rats, both as cute as can be."

Emma was about to comment when a white van drove into the airfield. Boots started barking frantically. Emma bent over and picked up the dog in order to calm her. She'd welcome the opportunity to clean her up. Maybe she could sneak her into the apartment and do that later today.

The van pulled up next to the plane. Emma read the lettering on the side of the vehicle and groaned. Animal Control.

"It's the dogcatcher," Oliver said out of the side of his mouth, in case she wasn't smart enough to read it for herself.

"I can see that."

"Afternoon, folks," the tall thin man said as he climbed down from the van.

Boots growled and Oscar joined him in perfect harmony.

"Good afternoon, Officer Wilson," Emma said formally, reading the nametag on his jacket.

"Do you know that dog?"

"Ah…we only just met."

"Before you ask," Oliver said, distracting Officer Wilson. "Oscar's license is paid in full. He's not a local but he's legal." He grinned, apparently at his own cleverness.

"I'm more concerned with the stray your lady friend's holding."

"I named her Boots."

The dogcatcher nodded in a friendly fashion; he seemed to approve of her choice of names. "Do you plan to adopt Boots officially?"

"Ah..." Emma didn't know how to respond. She needed time to work something out. If Mr. Scott discovered she had a dog, he'd evict her from the apartment so fast her head would spin. She'd probably end up living at the office.

"It seems she's taken a liking to you." His expression grew somber. "You know, for some reason she's been hanging around the airfield lately. That's dangerous, for her and for the pilots."

Boots growled again and squirmed as if begging for the opportunity to nip at the dogcatcher's heels.

"This dog doesn't have an owner," Officer Wilson informed her, "and we've had complaints. That's not good."

Emma gathered Boots closer to her side.

"If I take her to Animal Control, I'm afraid she'll be euthanized."

"No!" Emma's protest was immediate. She looked to Oliver for help, although she didn't know what he could do.

"Emma wants to adopt Boots," Oliver said. "It's obvious those two have bonded. What are the fees?" Oliver pulled a wad of cash from his pocket.

Officer Wilson frowned. "Adoption isn't my department. But…" He gave Emma an assessing glance. "I'll turn the other way if you want to take her with you."

"Thanks," Oliver said, steering Emma toward the plane.

"Yes, I'll take her," Emma cried. She couldn't bear the thought of Boots going to the shelter. She didn't know how long the poor thing had fended for herself, but that was about to end. Somehow or other, she'd figure out a way to keep the dog hidden until she found an apartment that accepted pets.

The dogcatcher pulled two dog biscuits from his pocket and offered one to Oscar and the second to Boots. "No hard feelings, girl, I was only doing my job." He gently petted the small dog's head. "Glad it worked out for you."

As if accepting Officer Wilson's apology, Boots licked the man's hand.

"You'll see to buying Boots a license when you get home?" he reminded them.

"We will," Oliver promised.

Mr. Wilson seemed pleased and drove off with a "Merry Christmas" and a jolly wave.

Sophie McKay's
Chocolate Fruitcake

Make 3-4 weeks in advance. Store in refrigerator.

Place into large bowl:

2 cups maraschino cherries, sliced in half
2 cups chopped dates
2 cups pineapple tidbits, well drained
1 cup coconut
2 cups walnuts
2 cups pecan halves
2 12 oz. packages semisweet chocolate chips

Beat the following ingredients on low for thirty seconds, then on high for three minutes:

3 cups flour
1 ½ cups sugar
1 tbsp. baking powder
½ tsp. salt
¾ cup shortening
¾ cup butter
⅔ cup crème de cacao
½ cup cocoa powder
9 eggs

Pour batter over fruit and nut mixture. Pour into two well-greased loaf pans. Bake at 275 degrees for 2 ½ to 3 hours. After two hours, check with a toothpick every fifteen minutes.

When cool, set each loaf on a large piece of plastic wrap and pour a jigger of crème de cacao over them. Wrap tightly and place inside a Ziploc bag and keep refrigerated for 3–4 weeks.

Chapter Ten

It was dark by the time Oliver and Emma landed back at the airstrip in Puyallup. They hadn't talked much during the flight, which was unexpectedly turbulent. Emma had white-knuckled it, choosing to close her eyes and pray. She hadn't prayed this much since grade school.

As soon as they taxied to the end of the runway, Oliver parked the plane. Emma climbed out and reached for Boots, who came willingly into her arms. The poor dog trembled, and Emma realized it hadn't been an easy flight for her, either.

"I'll be in touch," Oliver said after Emma had collected her things.

Her legs felt shaky and her stomach queasy, so she merely nodded, eager to get home. It was too late to return to the office; besides, she had more pressing concerns that had nothing to do with her job. Somehow, she had to find a way to smuggle Boots into her apartment. Even more of a challenge would be keeping the dog hidden until she located someplace else to live. Maybe Phoebe could help. Money was tight already, this close to payday, and she needed to make a veterinary appointment, plus obtain a license for Boots and buy a collar and leash. Groceries weren't necessary, Emma decided; besides, she needed to lose a few pounds. Somehow she'd make it to the end of the month, despite the unexpected drain on her cash reserves. There were real advantages to avoiding Christmas, and this proved it.

On the drive back to her apartment, Emma explained the tricky situation to Boots. She took her eyes from the road for just a second to smile at the little black dog. Boots gazed at her adoringly, but it would be ridiculous to assume the dog understood her dilemma and would voluntarily remain out of sight. And what about walks? She'd have to sneak Boots in and out for her walks.

Fortunately, when she arrived Mr. Scott was nowhere to be seen. Clutching Boots with one arm, Emma wrapped her coat around the dog. Anyone who noticed her bulging side would guess she was making a poor attempt at hiding something. That being the case, she could only hope no one suspected it was a dog.

Her mind was whirring from her afternoon with Sophie McKay and the woman's community of family and friends. Sophie's chocolate fruitcake recipe was unusual, and it didn't surprise Emma that it was a finalist. As soon as possible, she wanted to sit down with her laptop and begin drafting the article. First, however, she had to give Boots a bath.

The moment Emma entered her small one-bedroom apartment, she closed the drapes. She didn't want Mr. Scott walking past and peering through her window. Her neighbors on both sides had decorated Christmas trees on display in theirs. Not Emma.

After checking the refrigerator and discovering an open box of baking soda, two small containers of yogurt and a shriveled-up orange, she realized she'd need to go out later for dog food.

Because she was hungry, she ate the yogurt as she ran warm water into her bathtub. Boots sauntered from room to room, sniffing and exploring her new home. The dog didn't object when Emma placed her in the water and gave her a bath. Using her own shampoo, she worked up a good lather, then rinsed Boots off and repeated the process, finishing with a cream rinse that left the black fur glossy and soft. The muck on Boots's coat had deposited a dirty residue on the bottom of the tub. The dog had been completely filthy. She licked Emma's hand as if to thank her.

"You're a darling." Emma laughed as she dried Boots off with a thick towel, and then cleaned the tub.

The doorbell chimed and Emma froze. She'd barely been home an hour. It didn't seem possible that someone had already gone to Bud Scott and reported that she was in violation of the *No Pets* clause.

Perhaps it was Phoebe, who sometimes stopped by in the evening. Cautious, she locked Boots in the bathroom and checked her peephole.

"Oliver?" she said aloud, surprised to see him. She unlatched the lock and opened the door.

He stood on the other side of the threshold with a pizza box in one hand, a bag of dog food in the other.

"You said there weren't any romantic heroes left in this world," he said, balancing the pizza box on the tips of his fingers. "I'm here to prove you wrong."

Impressed by his thoughtfulness, Emma stared at him, hardly knowing what to think.

"Can I come in?" Oliver asked.

"Oh, yes…sorry." It didn't even occur to her to refuse him. She stepped aside and as he passed, the scent of warm pizza made her stomach growl. The yogurt hadn't taken her far.

With flair, Oliver set the pizza down on the kitchen table. "Deluxe, with extra cheese," he announced. "Plus two cans of Coke."

"Where's Oscar?" Emma asked as she took a couple of plates from the cupboard.

"In the truck. Where's Boots?"

"In the bathroom. I'll let her out in a minute," she said, thinking it was probably for the best that Oscar had stayed in Oliver's truck. No need to raise Mr. Scott's suspicions by letting another dog inside her apartment.

"Boots has a thing for him, you know." Oliver pulled out a chair, sat down and served her a slice of pizza.

"Don't be ridiculous." She would've argued further but she was too hungry for a full-blown argument. "You're making that up."

Oliver's mouth twisted into a lazy smile and he wiped his fingers on a paper towel.

Boots scratched at the bathroom door. When Emma opened it for her, she hurried into the kitchen. Sitting on her haunches, she stared longingly at the steaming pizza. "Look what Oliver brought us," Emma told her dog. She got a cereal bowl from the cupboard and filled it with dog food. Setting it on the floor, she watched as Boots gobbled up the entire amount and then begged for more.

She was about to refill the dish when Oliver stopped her. "Don't overfeed her," he said. "Especially now. She's been semistarved for some time. You don't want her getting sick."

Emma nodded, rinsed out the bowl and ran clean water into it.

While she did that, Oliver glanced around the apartment. "Do you have something against Christmas?" he asked.

"Not really." She didn't feel like launching into a long explanation.

"The least you could do is put up a sprig of mistletoe."

"Very funny." She rolled her eyes.

"I mean it." He gestured around him. "You have a deficit of Christmas cheer. When are you planning to put up your tree?"

"I'm not." Leave it to Oliver to press the issue. "I don't really like Christmas."

"Why not?"

"It's personal."

"You *have* to have a Christmas tree," he said. When she shook her head, he murmured, "Come on. Why don't you enjoy Christmas, Ms. Scrooge?"

She frowned at him, struggling to maintain her composure. "Not everyone lives and breathes Christmas, you know."

"Most people do. Take my mom. She's really big on Christmas, with family dinners and parties—the whole nine yards. I thought all women were."

"I'm not." He was really irritating her now. "But you, of course, know women so well."

"Hey." He shrugged. "It was just a question."

Emma realized she was overreacting. Oliver had been very kind to her this evening and didn't deserve to be snapped at. "My mother was a big fan of Christmas," she said quietly, paying a lot of attention to her pizza slice. "She used to bake cookies and decorate the house and make a big fuss over the holidays."

"So you spend the day with her," Oliver said, smoothly accepting her explanation. "That makes sense."

Emma turned away. A part of her wanted to let him assume that was true. But she couldn't, although she wasn't sure why. "My mother died several years ago."

Her announcement was followed by an awkward silence. "I'm sorry."

Emma raised one shoulder in a half shrug. "I've gotten over it."

"Do people really get over losing their mothers?" he asked softly.

She looked at Oliver then. Really looked at him. A small shiver of awareness went through her. It occurred to Emma that he was working hard to prove he could be a romantic hero, *her* romantic hero. Emma wasn't sure she was ready for anything like that, with anyone.

"What?" he demanded after a lengthy pause.

Emma blinked, embarrassed that she'd been staring at him. "Nothing."

"No," he said. "You were thinking about something and I want to know what."

"Ah…"

"I'll bet it was me." He raised his eyebrows. "You want me, right?"

"Would you stop?"

"No." Oliver smiled. "A little pizza, a bag of dog food, and you're ready to fall at my feet. Who would've thought it'd be this easy." He'd abandoned all seriousness and seemed absolutely delighted with himself. Grinning widely, he took a giant bite of pizza.

Emma could see it was going to be impossible to have a real conversation with this man.

"Come on, admit it," he urged.

She pretended to be absorbed in her dinner. "The dog food was a nice touch," she finally said.

He nodded. "Actually, it was Oscar who thought of that."

"You carry on conversations with your dog?" She didn't mention the little heart-to-heart she'd had with Boots on the drive home.

"All the time." Oliver motioned toward the apartment door. "Now that Boots has eaten, would it be okay if I brought Oscar inside? He hates being left in the truck for very long."

"He doesn't mind the plane."

"No, but he knows Boots is here."

Emma thought about warning Oliver not to let anyone see his dog, and decided against it. "Boots would enjoy the company." If they were caught, it would be easy enough to explain that the terrier was only visiting. Surely Mr. Scott couldn't object to that.

Oliver stood and headed for the door and then, as if he'd forgotten something, he turned back.

Emma glanced up, wondering what he was doing, when he leaned over and kissed her. This wasn't any peck on the cheek, either. His mouth was warm, insistent, and Emma felt overwhelmed by sensation. By excitement. His hands found their way into her hair and she instinctively opened to him. Thankfully, she was sitting, otherwise she feared her knees would have given out. Oliver was gentle, coaxing, as the tip of his tongue outlined the shape of her lips. When he pulled away, he reached for the back of the chair as if he, too, needed something to ground him.

"Nice," he whispered, not sounding anything like his normal self.

Wanting to make light of it, Emma tossed her head. "It was all right, I guess."

Oliver grinned, and she could see he wasn't fooled. "You could really damage a man's ego."

But not his, she suspected.

"I'll be right back." He started for the door again.

Emma remained where she was in order to gather her scattered wits. This man's kisses were a lot more potent than she'd been willing to acknowledge. Earlier, the first time he'd kissed her, she'd deluded herself into thinking it'd been rather pleasant but nothing earth-shattering. Wrong. *This* time, she'd experienced a response of seismic proportions.

Oliver was back and let himself in the apartment door. Oscar barreled inside and the instant Boots saw the other dog, she barked joyfully. Oh, dear, was it possible Oliver was right about that, too? But Oscar played it cool, his head at a cocky tilt. It was true, Emma thought, unable to hold back a smile. After a while, dogs and their masters began to look alike.

Emma bent down and stroked Oscar, then poured him a bowl of dog food, too.

"Was that a dog I saw just now?"

At the sound of Bud Scott's brusque voice, Emma nearly fainted. He'd opened her—regrettably un-locked—door and was peering into the apartment.

"Yes," Oliver answered gruffly. He'd clearly taken exception to Mr. Scott's offensive tone.

Emma hurried to stand next to Oliver, hoping to block the landlord's view of the two dogs. "Oscar belongs to my friend," she explained, trying to sound innocent and accommodating.

Mr. Scott's eyes narrowed. "I thought I saw *two* dogs in here."

"You did," Oliver confirmed.

Emma elbowed him hard in the ribs.

"Ouch." Oliver glared at her and rubbed his side.

"There's only Oscar," she said sweetly. Unfortunately, Boots chose that moment to bark excitedly. Oscar joined in, and Emma sagged against the doorjamb.

"You know this is a pet-free zone." Bud Scott scowled.

"Yes, but…"

"We have a no-tolerance policy in regard to pets, especially cats and dogs."

"Friendly place you chose to live," Oliver muttered.

"You aren't helping," she said furiously. It would've been a whole lot better if he'd just gone home, taking his leftover pizza with him.

He made a resigned gesture and stepped back.

Emma folded her hands. "Please, Mr. Scott," she implored. "I…only got Boots this afternoon. She was a stray—"

"You brought a *stray* into this complex?" He looked at her as if she were insane. "Do you have any idea what you've exposed your neighbors to?" He retreated a step as if he feared an infestation of some kind at any moment.

"But—"

"One week," Mr. Scott intoned. "One week and you're out."

"One week," she echoed, aghast.

"I want you and that…that mutt out of here one week from today."

Both dogs growled when she closed the door.

"Now what am I going to do?" she asked Oliver. Money was already tight, and she couldn't possibly come up with first and last month's rent in that short a time.

Chapter Eleven

I've had the honor to cook for seven presidents
of the United States here at the Waldorf–Astoria.
Unless President Bush asks me to make it, fruitcake isn't on the menu.

—John Doherty, executive chef,
The Waldorf–Astoria

"I have to move," Emma moaned to Phoebe when she
arrived at The Dungeon the next morning.

"What happened?" Good friend that she was, Phoebe
immediately rolled her chair across the aisle.

"It's a long story." Emma didn't want to explain just
now; it would take half the morning and she had an
article to write. What bothered her most wasn't the
problem of having to be out of her apartment in seven
days. That was bad enough, but it wasn't what had

kept her up half the night. Instead, all she could think about was Oliver's kiss. By morning, with her eyes burning from lack of sleep, she hoped she'd never see him again. It wasn't true, though, Emma admitted reluctantly. She very much wanted to be with him, and that frightened her. Maybe she wasn't so different from her mother, after all.

"I have news," Phoebe whispered.

Emma glanced up expectantly.

"Walt and I are having some…serious conversations."

"That's great." The look in Phoebe's eyes was rapturous, suggesting that the couple was on the brink of announcing their engagement.

"Unfortunately Walt's having a problem telling anyone at the office that we're seeing each other."

Even Emma hadn't known until just recently. She was astonished that they'd managed to keep their romance such a well-guarded secret.

"He wants to wait awhile," Phoebe said. She lowered her voice again as someone came down the stairs and passed their cubicles. "I don't know why, but Walt seems to think we should wait until after the holidays."

"Why?"

"I don't know."

"And you agreed?" Emma asked. Like Phoebe, she didn't understand Walt's hesitation. She doubted anyone at the office would object to his relationship with Phoebe. There might be a few raised eyebrows, but so what?

"I think Walt's concerned about setting a good example. You know—doing things the way his father would. I mentioned that, but he denies it."

"I guess this means I won't be able to move in with you if I don't have a new apartment by next week?" Emma muttered. "It would only be for a few days—until I can find a place."

Phoebe frowned. "In case you've forgotten, I only have a one-bedroom apartment and my sofa's pretty ratty. What's going on, anyway? I was so absorbed in my own news that I'd completely ignored yours."

"I have a dog now."

"A dog?" Phoebe's eyes rounded with surprise.

"Like I said, it's a long story."

"That no doubt involves Oliver Hamilton."

"How'd you guess?" Emma sighed. "Although I'd like to blame Oliver, the dog sort of chose me. Now I have to move because the landlord is dead set against animals."

"In other words, you're desperate?"

Emma sighed again; she still had six days. "Close, but not panicking yet."

"I'm sorry, but I can't have a dog, either," Phoebe said. "I'll check and see if a visiting dog is allowed, okay?"

Emma was grateful; this was a lot to ask, but she might not have any other choice. She wouldn't need to move in until next week—if at all. She'd certainly do her best to find something else before that.

"How did the interview go? The one in Colville?" Phoebe asked.

"Really well." Emma glanced longingly toward her blank computer screen. "I have all my notes, but do me a favor, would you? Don't let Walt know I'm here just yet. He's going to want this article and I haven't even started writing it. I intended to, but then... Well, it's complicated."

"Oliver Hamilton is somehow involved, right?" This was becoming a refrain.

"Isn't he always involved?" Emma said, reaching in her briefcase for her notes on Sophie McKay.

As she'd told Phoebe, she wanted to blame Oliver for her current troubles, but that would be decidedly unfair. In bringing Boots home with her, Emma had taken a calculated risk. Now she had to write this article and quickly, because she needed to spend her lunch hour making phone calls. At least she had access to the very latest rental listings, she told herself. If only she could find a decent place that allowed pets and required a minimum cash outlay...

Without wasting another moment, she began drafting her article.

Lessons from Fruitcake: Sophie McKay

Sophie McKay, the second of the Washington State finalists in the *Good Homemaking* fruitcake contest, resides in Colville, the seat of Stevens County in the northeast part of our diverse state.

Sophie believes her entry, Chocolate Fruitcake, caught the judges' interest because it was different. She first created this fruitcake with its unusual mixture of ingredients during the Depression. Her husband, Harry, claimed to hate fruitcake, but it was an important aspect of Christmas for Sophie. Her compromise was to use his favorite foods and flavors—including chocolate.

Although Harry's been dead for twenty years, Sophie continues to bake the fruitcake in his honor. And while the ingredients are indeed unusual, what makes Sophie's fruitcake special are the memories she bakes into each one.

In life, as in fruitcake, this mother of two adult sons reminds us all to use the ingredients we love. For her that includes cultivating a beautiful garden, rereading her beloved husband's wartime letters, feeding and caring for any cat that comes her way. And, of course, enjoying her family and friends.

Sophie says we shouldn't skimp on the "ingredients" that matter to us, at Christmas or any other time. Like her, we should surround ourselves with family members and friends and share stories and laughter with them. We should cherish our memories and treat all creatures with kindness. We—

Hearing someone approach, Emma looked up to discover Oliver Hamilton leaning against the partition in the narrow aisle that separated her cubicle from Phoebe's. At first, she was too shocked to respond.

"Hi," she managed, before her throat went completely dry.

"Hi, yourself. I don't suppose you've had a chance to check out new apartments yet?"

"Ah—no, not yet." As it was, Emma had barely made it to work on time. After she'd dropped Boots off at a veterinarian Oliver had recommended, she'd been hard pressed to get to the office by nine.

"Well…" Oliver wore a cocky grin. "I have good news. There's a vacant apartment on Cherry Street. The tenant got married and he's already moved out. It'll be available right away."

This was a lovely area of Puyallup and within walking distance of the office. The cherry trees that lined the boulevard gave the street its name; they bloomed each spring in a profusion of pink blossoms. Apartments there were coveted and hard to come by. "Cherry Street?"

He nodded. "If you want, I can pick you up at lunchtime and you can take a look."

"How much?" Not only were those apartments at a premium, but more than likely they'd be way out of her price range.

"Same as you're paying now," Oliver said, seeming pleased with himself.

This sounded too good to be true, and things that sounded too good to be true generally were. But just maybe... "What about the first and last month's rent?"

Oliver shrugged as if this were a minor consideration. "A friend of mine owns the complex, and he said if your credit rating's okay, he'd be willing to waive that."

"Wow." This came from Phoebe.

"Boots won't be a problem?"

"Not at all. But Jason will want a $150 deposit in case of damage."

Only a hundred and fifty dollars—this was unbelievable. She'd expected it to be much more than that. She'd heard of apartments that asked for five-hundred-dollar deposits when the tenant owned a pet. Emma wondered for a moment whether Oliver had gotten his facts straight. No, wait. There had to be *something* he wasn't telling her. "No strings attached?" she asked with a skeptical look.

Oliver raised both hands. "None."

Emma felt as if she'd won the lottery. "How come?" She didn't want to examine this gift too closely, but she was still terrified there might be a catch.

Oliver ignored her question.

"Oliver?" she persisted.

"Oh, all right. Jason owes me a favor. I flew him

and his wife to San Francisco—and I promised I'd do it again."

"Oh…"

"I put a hold on it for you, but Jason said he can't keep the apartment off the market any longer than one o'clock this afternoon."

"I'll take it." Emma didn't want to risk losing this opportunity. She smiled at Oliver.

"Sight unseen?" he asked.

"Maybe you'd better go see the place," Phoebe cautioned. "In fact, you should go now."

Emma nodded; her friend was right. Still, she hesitated. Walt would be looking for that article and all she had was an unfinished rough draft. She was going to need several hours to work on it and to shape it into the piece she wanted it to be.

"We'll take thirty, forty minutes, tops," Oliver said. "We can run over, do a quick tour and you can make up your mind then."

"I'll cover for you," Phoebe promised.

"But Walt—"

"Don't worry. If Walt asks where you are, I'll explain the situation to him. He'll understand."

"Won't he be upset if he finds me skipping out in the middle of the morning?"

Phoebe's eyes brightened and she shook her head. "Let me take care of that."

"Okay, I will." Emma reached for her coat and purse.

Although she'd never admit it—at least not to Oliver—
she was delighted to see him again. She wasn't quite sure
why he was being so helpful, but then she remembered
his comments about ordinary men and real romance as
opposed to romantic gestures. A real hero brought you
and your dog a meal; he didn't worry about providing
the perfect setting. He made you laugh instead of pre-
senting you with poetic words. He found you an apartment when you needed one....

When they approached his truck, he opened the
passenger door for her. Oscar barked a welcome and
seemed to be looking for Boots.

Emma raised her eyebrows. "You're really taking
this romantic-hero stuff to heart."

"Absolutely," he said, grinning. "If a pizza and a bag
of dog food results in a kiss, I can only dream about
what finding you an apartment will do."

"Don't get your hopes up." It figured—he wanted
something. What all men wanted, apparently. And after
she'd had all these lovely thoughts about him, too.

He chuckled. "Want to go flying with me later?"

She stared at him. "No way!"

"You're getting to be a pro at this. There was hardly
a peep out of you the entire flight home."

"I was busy praying."

Oliver shook his head. "Come on. We'll have a good
time."

Oliver Hamilton was *not* getting her back in the

air, especially for the so-called fun of it. To her, fly-ing simply wasn't entertainment. "No. N-O," she said, spelling it out.

"That's a pity."

Not to her. It was life preservation.

The apartment, a ground-level corner unit, was small but well-designed. The single-story complex was fairly new but beautifully maintained, and each unit had its own front door. The surrounding doors were all dec-orated with wreaths and pine swags and lights. Inside, Emma was thrilled to see brand-new appliances, in-cluding a dishwasher. Sliding glass doors off the kitchen led to a fenced area in the back that would be perfect for Boots. There was even space for a container gar-den, which pleased Emma. Her mother had always had a garden. Emma had hated weeding and watering it as a girl. She'd never believed she'd miss it, but she did.

Oscar walked around, cocking his head as if con-fused. He looked up at Oliver, who ignored his ca-nine friend.

"Well, what do you think?" Oliver asked, leaning against the kitchen counter in a nonchalant pose.

"It's wonderful!"

He grinned knowingly. "I thought you'd like it."

"I do. Thank you, Oliver, thank you so much." Im-pulsively she kissed his cheek.

Not one to let an opportunity slip away, Oliver

grabbed her around the waist and brought her into his arms. "You can thank me properly, you know."

She was tempted to do just that when there was a sudden knock at the open door and Oliver's friend Jason let himself in. Emma had met Jason when Oliver took her to the owner's unit to collect the key.

"Have you made a decision?" he asked.

Embarrassed, Emma quickly disentangled herself from Oliver's embrace. "I'll take it. Just show me where to sign."

Jason had the paperwork with him, and after reading the lease agreement, she quickly signed her name at the bottom and wrote him a check.

Jason handed her the keys, assured her she could move in anytime, and left.

"You *are* my hero," Emma said once the other man had gone.

"I know," Oliver murmured in modest tones.

She was half-tempted to kiss him again, but changed her mind. "I suppose I should get back to the office," Emma said reluctantly.

"Okay, but I need to stop at my place first."

She couldn't quibble, since he'd driven her here and, more, had arranged for her new home.

He walked out, turned right and went down two doors.

Emma followed. She didn't understand, until he inserted the key into the lock, that this was his place—two doors down from hers.

"You live here?" she asked. *"Here?"*

He nodded, opening the front door. It had the biggest Christmas wreath of all, and the front window sparkled with tiny white lights.

"It didn't occur to you to maybe mention this before now?" She'd asked him earlier if there were any strings attached and he'd promised her there weren't. She should've known.

Her tone must have conveyed the fact that she wasn't happy with this unexpected turn of events. She remained standing in the doorway, resisting the impulse to look inside, although she did catch sight of a gaily decorated Christmas tree.

"What's the matter? Don't you want me for a neighbor?"

She found it hard enough to keep him out of her thoughts as it was. Living two doors down from him would make it impossible. "As a matter of fact, no. Why didn't you tell me?"

"Didn't enter my mind. You should be grateful I found you an apartment."

"Which I wouldn't have needed if you hadn't opened your big mouth," she said, even though that was only partially true.

"So it's *my* fault?" he cried out at the unfairness of her accusation.

"Yes, yours."

Oliver glared at her. "Fine."

She crossed her arms and glared right back at him.

Jason stepped up to his vehicle on the other side of the street and raised his hand. "Merry Christmas," he shouted.

"Right," Oliver muttered back. "And goodwill to all mankind."

Chapter Twelve

Late that afternoon, Oliver joined Walt Berwald at the tavern down the street from the newspaper office. Walt sat at the bar with his shoulders hunched forward, looking as if he'd just received some piece of devastating news. His demeanor was at odds with the cheerful rendition of "Deck the Halls" playing on the tavern's crackling sound system.

Oliver shared Walt's sentiment. He had no idea what he'd done that was so terrible. There was no mistaking Emma's irritation with him, although he'd expected her to be overjoyed that he'd found her an apartment. Oh, no, that would've been far too rational. He should've remembered that there was nothing rational about most women. His mother and one of his three sisters were the exception that proved the rule.

What *really* got to him was that he hadn't purposely hidden the fact that he lived in the same complex. It just hadn't seemed important, and he didn't understand why it mattered. The ride back to the newspaper office had been silent and uncomfortable. Emma hadn't been able to get out of the truck fast enough.

Walt slid his gaze to Oliver when he claimed the stool next to him, nodding morosely. The bartender looked over and Oliver motioned toward the beer in Walt's hand. "I'll take one of those. And get another for my friend."

"Thanks," Walt said.

"My pleasure."

Neither spoke again until the beers arrived.

"What's got you so down in the dumps?" Walt asked.

"I don't want to talk about it. What about you?"

Walt shrugged. "Same."

Women were beyond Oliver's comprehension. He had sisters and knew from experience that Emma was probably talking to Phoebe right now, describing every aspect of his many faults. Things had begun to look promising, too. He'd been attracted to Emma from the start and he'd been certain she felt the same way. After this morning, he was no longer sure.

"How's it going with that reporter of mine?" Walt asked, reaching for his cold beer.

"Not bad." Oliver didn't elaborate.

"Emma's got real potential as a journalist, you know."

Oliver believed that, even if he hadn't read anything she'd written. This was her big shot and despite their differences, he wished her well. "She's got a few hang-ups." He didn't mean to say that aloud and was surprised to hear his own voice.

"All women do," Walt said, as if he were an authority on the subject.

"You know this from your vast research, do you?"

Walt laughed and shook his head. "Hey, when it comes to women and relationships, I'm a disaster waiting to happen."

Oliver gave him a second look. Walt had always seemed secure and confident. He knew his stuff, as befitted a man who was the third generation of his family in the newspaper business. Now, however, Walt seemed to feel downright miserable.

Oliver did, too. And it was all because of Emma. It was times like these when he felt like sitting in the dark, listening to Harry Connick Jr., bourbon in hand. Either that, or go and visit his mother. Knowing her, she'd pry out of him what was wrong, give him some common-sense advice and then feed him a huge dinner, as if her cabbage rolls would solve all his problems.

Oliver loved her and her stuffed cabbage, but even his mother wouldn't be able to help him understand Emma Collins.

After a second beer, Oliver slid off the stool and

placed a twenty-dollar bill on the bar. "See you around," he mumbled at Walt.

Neither one of them had been very talkative.

"Yeah, sure," Walt responded in the same weary tone. "Thanks for the beer. I'll buy next time."

Oliver nodded, and got up to head back to his truck, where Oscar was waiting impatiently inside the cab.

"You got plans for the evening?" Walt asked unexpectedly.

"Not necessarily." It was either his mother's cabbage rolls or listening to Harry. "What have you got in mind?"

"You are a friend indeed," Emma said as she came out of the bedroom dragging a cardboard box filled with books. She and Phoebe had left work early, once Emma had finished the article, skipping lunch to do it. They'd collected boxes on the way to Emma's place and spent the past two hours packing. Fortunately, Boots was still at the vet's and therefore not underfoot.

Phoebe didn't seem to be listening. "You'd help me move, too, if our circumstances were reversed."

"Something on your mind?" Emma asked. Phoebe hadn't been her usual self since she'd returned from lunch.

Sighing, her friend straightened. "I met Walt for lunch. We left separately and went five miles out of our way in order not to be seen. It's ridiculous! I love Walt, but I told him I was through sneaking around."

Emma didn't blame her.

"I won't do it again." Phoebe sounded firm about her decision. "If he wants to wait until after Christmas, then fine, we'll wait. But I won't see Walt again until he's willing to be open and honest about our relationship."

"You're right." Emma admired her friend's courage and conviction. "What did Walt say?"

Phoebe's shoulders slumped. "He thinks I'm overreacting."

"You aren't!"

"I know. I've been feeling dreadful all afternoon, and when I left, I didn't let him know I was going to help you move. Instead, I let him assume—" a slow smile formed "—that I had...other plans."

"Other plans? Like being with another man?"

Phoebe gave a careless shrug. "Never mind. It'll do him good to wonder where I am."

"I really do appreciate the help," Emma said earnestly as they both walked out to the parking lot with loaded boxes.

"I know. You'd do the same for me," Phoebe said again. "When's the next fruitcake interview?" she asked, although Emma wasn't sure why she'd changed the subject.

"Next week—Tuesday, I think."

Emma didn't welcome the reminder that Oliver was scheduled to fly her into Friday Harbor. She didn't want to think about him—or the fact that she'd soon be in the air again.

"Are you ready to take these over to the new place?" Emma asked in an effort to derail her thoughts. She was eager to show off her apartment. An apartment she wouldn't have if it wasn't for Oliver, her conscience pointed out.

"Sure," Phoebe said. "Let's go." But her enthusiasm seemed forced.

Emma hesitated. "Do you want to talk some more?" This disagreement with Walt had really depressed her friend.

"Not especially," Phoebe murmured, revealing a little more life. "Let's go," she said again.

It was nearly seven and completely dark out. The first thing Emma noticed when she pulled up in front of the complex on Cherry Street was that Oliver's apartment lights were off; only his Christmas lights flashed a festive message. He was probably out on some hot date, she thought glumly. Despite her best efforts, her spirits sank. It shouldn't matter where he was or with whom—and yet, it did.

She stood by her car, fumbling for the door key, as Phoebe's SUV drove up behind her. Carrying a couple of plants she'd transported on the front seat, she joined Emma. "What's wrong, Em?"

Emma looked at her blankly.

"You just growled."

"I did? I was thinking what a bother moving is," she said, inventing an explanation that was also the truth.

"I'll work as long as you want tonight."

Emma nodded her thanks. She wanted out of the old place as quickly as possible. Because she didn't own much, it hadn't taken long to pack. Books, bedding and towels, clothes, kitchen stuff. Her TV and CD player. Odds and ends. Only a few pieces of furniture remained.

They made two trips, with both her car and Phoebe's loaded, rooftop and all. Back at the old apartment, they surveyed the things that still had to be moved.

"We should take the bed over tonight," Phoebe suggested, hands on her hips as she stood in the almost-empty bedroom. "That way you'll be able to sleep at the new place."

The idea appealed to Emma. "Are you sure you're up to this?"

Phoebe nodded.

Oliver's lights were on when they arrived with the bed and nightstand. So he was home. Not that she cared.

The mattress was the most difficult to handle. With Phoebe on one end and Emma on the other, they wrestled it out of the SUV.

"I'm starved," Emma said as she paused to take a

breath. She hadn't eaten lunch; her only sustenance had come from a vending-machine pack of peanuts. "When we finish, I'm treating you to dinner. What time is it, anyway?"

Phoebe didn't answer. When Emma looked around the protruding mattress, she saw why.

Oliver's apartment door was open, and Walt Berwald and Oliver stood just outside the doorway, watching them struggle.

Phoebe dropped her end of the mattress. "Walt," she said in a choked voice.

"Oh, could you use some help?" Oliver asked coolly as he stepped forward.

"Phoebe?" Walt sounded nervous.

Even in the dark, Emma swore her friend's cheeks blossomed brighter than the cherry trees across the street ever would. She looked directly at Walt and then—reluctantly—at Oliver. She realized she owed him an apology. Her ungracious and ungrateful behavior toward him had worried her all day, and she needed to make it right.

"I'll take that," he said, hurrying toward her end of the mattress.

"Thank you," she whispered, and moved aside so he could grab the mattress. "For everything."

Oliver nearly stumbled. He dropped his corner of the mattress. "What did you just say?"

"I, ah, was attempting to apologize."

"That's what I thought," he said. "It felt good to hear that. Would you mind saying it again?"

Emma considered refusing, since he just wanted to rub it in. Oh, well, she supposed he deserved to hear her apology twice. Not that she intended to use the word *sorry* even once. She cleared her throat. "I wanted to thank you for all your help," she said more loudly.

He seemed gratified. Nodding his head, he said, "You're welcome." He lifted his end of the mattress again and grappled with it for a moment until he noticed that Walt hadn't taken hold of the other side. He propped the mattress against the back of the vehicle.

Emma saw that Walt and Phoebe were staring at each other. He'd come to stand beside her, ignoring the mattress, Emma, everything.

"When you said you had 'other plans,' you let me think they were with someone else," Walt murmured, frowning.

"It was what you deserved to think."

"What's going on with those two?" Oliver whispered, moving closer to Emma.

"They had a disagreement."

"They're seeing each other?" This seemed news to him. "They're a couple?"

Emma nodded, watching her friend and their boss.

"I wasn't joking, Walt." Phoebe held her ground. She crossed her arms.

Walt exhaled and looked at Oliver. "Did I just hear you ask if Phoebe and I are a couple?"

"That's your business, man."

"No," Walt countered, "I want you to know. I love Phoebe and she loves me." He turned to face her. "There, does that satisfy you?"

Phoebe grinned. "It's a start."

With that, Walt opened his arms and Phoebe walked into his embrace. A second later, they had their arms around each other and were locked in a passionate kiss.

"Hey, about this mattress?" Oliver whispered to Emma.

"Shh," she whispered back. This was a scene normally reserved for the movies; all it lacked was a soundtrack. Emma didn't think she'd seen anything more romantic in her life. "Isn't this just so…so perfect?"

"What?" Oliver demanded, leaning against the mattress.

She scowled up at him, then understood that he really didn't get it.

"Hey, anyone interested in Chinese?" Oliver asked.

Chapter Thirteen

Fruitcake—love it or hate it—is about the ritual of a family recipe. The longer the ritual is repeated, the more it becomes part of what is "done" at the holidays. With that in mind, there are only two fruitcakes that matter to me, and I eat them over the Christmas holidays every year. One is the recipe of my Grandma Prendergast, which my dad now makes at Christmas. It never turns out exactly the same as Grandma's did, but it tastes good because it reminds me of her at the best time of year—when I'm with family. I eat it spread with butter, just the way Grandma served it. The other belongs to my mother-in-law, who labors over her versions for weeks on end. In addition to the obvious fact that everyone should eat what their mother-in-law serves, hers are actually moist.

—Kevin Prendergast, executive chef,
New York Marriott Marquis

Bright and early the next Tuesday morning, Oliver pounded on Emma's apartment door. When she didn't immediately answer, he peered inside her front window. He saw her run into the living room and stare back. Smiling, he raised a small white bag and a large cup of coffee.

If she needed any inducement to unlock her door, that was it. She was dying for a latte.

"You sweetheart," she said, letting him into her apartment. Boots was at her feet, the ready protector. She'd been pronounced healthy and was scheduled to be spayed right after Christmas.

Oliver smiled and handed her the take-out latte. "I have another surprise for you."

"Another surprise?"

"More of a Christmas surprise."

"All right." Emma didn't trust that gleam in his eyes, and adding Christmas wasn't a bonus. "Tell me."

"I got us a float plane for the trip to Friday Harbor." He smiled again, as if this was something that should excite her.

"A float plane," she repeated slowly. It'd been difficult enough to deal with an aircraft that landed on the ground. "As in a plane that lands on *water?*"

"Yup." He positively glowed with the news. "You'll love it."

The one small sip of latte she'd taken curdled in her stomach. "I don't think so."

"Sure you do. We're flying out of Lake Union. A friend of mine is letting me use his plane and—"

She felt the sudden urge to sit down, but didn't.

"Now, listen," Oliver said, steering her into the kitchen and placing the white sack on the counter. It contained a large cranberry muffin, but Emma couldn't eat, nauseated as she was by the thought of flying— and worse, landing—in a float plane. "Everything'll be fine," he said soothingly. "Just one thing."

"What?"

"You should wear sensible shoes because those docks can get slippery."

"In other words, there's a chance I could fall in the water?"

"It's not likely, but it's been known to happen, so be extra-cautious when you're climbing into the plane, okay?"

"Is this a trick?"

"Of course not." He marched out of the kitchen, and Emma followed. Boots hung behind, gazing eagerly at the white sack.

"You can bring Boots," Oliver said before she could even ask.

Emma threw on her coat, scooped up Boots and

grabbed her briefcase for this last interview, which would be in the San Juan Islands. Emma had spoken to Peggy Lucas by phone, and she sounded like a woman in her thirties, much younger than the other finalists. Emma was looking forward to chatting with her about her No-Bake Fruitcake recipe.

Oliver opened the truck door for her and Boots, and Emma thanked him politely.

"It's all part of being a romantic hero," he reminded her with what she thought was a smirk.

Both dogs were in the truck, and the cab was crowded. "If I slip off the dock, I'm going to blame you," she said as she fastened the seat belt around her and Boots. Before they left, Emma had changed her shoes twice. In the end, she'd decided on tennis shoes with rubber soles, although they didn't do much for her dark-gray pantsuit.

"Why would you blame me?" Oliver asked as they merged into the traffic on Interstate 5.

She tapped her finger against her temple. "You're the one who put the idea in my head." He'd added a brand-new element to her fears, as if she needed more to worry about.

"You can swim, right?"

"Yes." Actually, Emma was a capable swimmer. "Why do you ask?"

"Well, it's only fair to let you know that if you go in the water you're on your own."

She rolled her eyes. "My hero."

"My hero, nothing. The water this time of year is damn cold."

Emma performed some contortions to look at the soles of her shoes once more, checking the treads.

"Don't worry, you'll be fine." His eyes sparkled with delight; Oliver Hamilton was enjoying himself far too much.

Lake Union was situated between Puget Sound and Lake Washington, with canals that connected both. One of Emma's favorite movies was *Sleepless in Seattle,* and she remembered that the houseboat the Tom Hanks character and his son had lived in was situated on Lake Union. She knew these houseboats were *very* expensive, and as Oliver drove closer, Emma saw a number of them in the distance. Cheerful, flashing Christmas lights strung around the decks were reflected on the still surface of the lake. One houseboat had Santa poised on the roof with a sleigh and eight reindeer. Everyone who lived on the lake was apparently serious about observing the holiday spirit. Just like all her new neighbors....

As they continued on the road around the lake, the float planes came into view, and Emma immediately tensed. From her long-ago yoga classes, she knew the best cure for that was to draw in deep, even breaths. In to the count of eight, out to the—

"What's with you?" Oliver asked.

"I'm practicing my breathing exercises."

"I thought that was for when you're in labor."

"You've spent time in labor rooms, have you?"

"No, but my sister has, and she told me all about that breathing thing."

"I'm just trying to remain calm."

"Driving frightens you, too?"

Emma looked out the window. "Never mind."

Once they arrived at the dock where the float planes were tied up, it was immediately apparent that Oliver was well-known and well-liked. He introduced her to his friends and then led her out to the dock. Emma tested her footing with each step.

"You aren't going to fall from the middle of the dock," Oliver said scathingly. Boots and Oscar ran circles around them both, barking and playing.

"Can't be too careful."

He said something under his breath that she couldn't understand, but considering the irritation lining his mouth and eyes, that was probably for the best. Taking slow, careful steps, it took her five minutes to get to the end of the dock. Oliver got there maybe three minutes earlier, and he didn't conceal his impatience for one second of that time.

Stepping onto the pontoon, he opened the door to the cockpit. Then he lifted Oscar and placed the terrier in the back. Next he swooped Boots into his arms and set her inside, as well. Emma stood there frozen, afraid to inch forward.

"Will you put my briefcase and purse in, too?" she asked, pushing them toward Oliver.

Oliver did as she requested and then extended his arm, urging her forward. "You ready?" he asked. He was balancing one foot on the dock and the other on the pontoon.

She nodded anxiously. Her heart was beating so fast she could hear the echo in her ears. Putting all her faith in Oliver, she stretched her arm toward his and stepped off the deck. She made the transition from dock to plane easily and was astonished that she'd allowed his warnings to fill her with dread.

"I did it!" she said, feeling triumphant.

"Yes, you did." Oliver smiled. "I'm proud of you."

Emma crawled into the passenger seat, pulled the seat belt toward her and locked it into place. Both Oscar and Boots were in the back, next to her purse and briefcase.

A boat went past and the wake rocked the plane. Standing on the dock, Oliver untied the craft and pushed off. Not a second later, Emma heard a tremendous splash. She didn't immediately understand what had happened. Then it hit her.

Oliver had slipped and fallen into the lake.

Caught in the boat's wake, the plane drifted toward the middle of Lake Union.

Scrambling out of her seat belt, Emma was on her knees in the pilot's seat. "Oliver! Oliver! What should I do?"

In response, he started swimming out after her. She covered her mouth. With part of her she wanted to laugh, and with the other she was holding back tears.

Oliver reached the plane a moment later. He levered himself up onto the pontoon and glared at her. "Don't you *dare* say a word," he managed from between clenched teeth.

"But Oliver..."

He stood on the pontoon, water streaming off him, and grabbed the plane's wheel, steering the aircraft back toward the dock. A couple of pilots were waiting for him. Oliver tossed them the rope and they efficiently tied down the plane. One handed him a towel as he climbed onto the dock. There was a lot of good-natured teasing, but she noticed that Oliver didn't have a whole lot to say.

"It happens to all of us at one time or another," his friend consoled him.

Oliver threw the towel over his shoulders, shivering visibly.

His lips were blue.

Emma felt terrible.

"I've got an extra set of clothes," she heard one of the other pilots tell him as they led him away.

She stayed where she was, unwilling to risk climbing onto the dock again. Twenty minutes passed before Oliver reappeared. His mood didn't seem to have improved.

"You okay?" she asked tentatively.

"I feel like a damn fool."

"Oh, Oliver, you were wonderful."

Her comment didn't amuse him. "So you enjoyed that spectacle, did you?"

"Well, no, not really, but you swam after me. That was the most romantic thing you've done."

"It was?" He sounded a bit puzzled.

She nodded. "You truly are my hero."

"I knew *that*," he said confidently.

"Oh, for goodness' sake."

They taxied farther onto Lake Union with only a minimum of fuss and took off.

Unexpectedly, Emma enjoyed the flight. She wasn't nearly as afraid as she'd been in the Cessna Caravan. Thinking about it, she realized it was because of the pontoons—if the plane went down, they'd float. That might be false security, of course; if they did crash on the water the plane would probably disintegrate on impact, but she didn't let that destroy her illusions of safety.

While flying, Oliver acted as a tour guide, showing her various points of interest. The San Juan Islands, she learned, were a cluster of 743 rocky islands of different sizes, situated in the Strait of Juan de Fuca and Puget Sound. Only about sixty of the islands were populated, according to Oliver, who seemed to know the area quite well.

The largest of the islands, San Juan Island, was

home to the bustling town of Friday Harbor. Emma remembered reading about the annual jazz festival in late summer. The island was also a popular site for whale watching. Emma hoped to join one of the expeditions next summer, since she'd never seen a whale in the wild. She didn't think she could count visiting Sea World.

"I have a confession," Oliver said, frowning. "I'm not as much of a hero as you seem to think."

"You are. You swam out and saved me."

"I hate to disillusion you, Emma, but I wasn't swimming after you. I was going for the plane. Do you know how much one of these is worth?"

"In other words, if I'd been in a canoe you would've let me drift off into the sunset?"

"Well…"

"Come on," she said, "be honest."

"I would've taken a hot shower and changed clothes and then gone looking for you in a speedboat."

Okay, so maybe he was right. He wasn't as much of a hero as she'd assumed.

He sneezed violently.

"You're catching a cold. You should take care of yourself."

He dismissed her concern. "I'll live."

"You need hot soup and extra vitamin C and—"

He placed his hand on her arm. "And a whole lot of lovin'."

Boy, had she asked for that.

"I'm fine," he said with a smirk. "Go do your interview. I'll be waiting here when you're finished."

Emma had been looking forward to this interview ever since she'd spoken to Peggy on Monday afternoon. Her sudden reluctance to leave Oliver was hard to explain.

He climbed out, tied up the float plane and then helped her out. Clasping his hand, Emma leaped from the plane onto the dock, which rocked gently when she landed.

Oliver retrieved her purse and briefcase and handed them to her.

One of Peggy's neighbors was waiting to drive her to the Lucas home.

"I won't be gone long," she promised.

"The dogs and I will be fine. Now go." For the first time since he'd crashed into the water, Oliver grinned.

Emma couldn't stop herself. Still holding tightly to her purse and briefcase, she kissed Oliver. He slid his arms around her and kissed her back. Soon they were so involved in each other, it was a wonder they both didn't slip off the dock.

That was when Emma knew she'd fallen in love with Oliver Hamilton.

Chapter Fourteen

Those who don't like fruitcake have never had a white fruitcake.

—Nathalie Dupree,
cookbook author and television personality

Peggy Lucas's matter-of-fact humor had Emma laughing even before she was in the front door of the fifties-style tract home in Friday Harbor. The neighbor, Sally, had dropped her off with a cheerful goodbye, after telling her repeatedly how proud everyone was of Peggy, how delicious her fruitcake was, how they were all convinced she'd win.

Peggy and her husband, Larry, had four small children. Children's toys littered the lawn surrounding a bigger-than-life blow-up snowman that was anchored to the ground.

The oldest child, Rosalie, was in first grade and the second daughter, Abby, was a year younger. Two little boys, Trevor and Dylan, rushed onto the small front porch to greet her, hiding behind their mother's legs. Emma guessed the boys' ages to be around four and two. The two younger ones seemed to be best buddies, although they were constantly bickering.

"Please excuse the mess," Peggy said as she ushered Emma into the living room. A small Christmas tree stood in the corner, decorated with what appeared to be hand-crafted ornaments. It reminded Emma of the tree in the "Peanuts" cartoons, the Charlie Brown tree— a little skimpy and with a definite homemade quality. The children had made a chain of colored paper loops and strung popcorn and cranberries. A small array of badly wrapped gifts circled the base.

Peggy hurriedly removed clean laundry from the recliner and motioned for Emma to take what was clearly the best seat in the house.

Emma appeared to be the main attraction. All four children gathered around their mother and stared at the stranger in their living room. Rosalie was still dressed in her pajamas.

"She's home from school today because of a cold," Peggy explained. "Abby, too. This is cold and flu season. It's the last week of classes, and I hate to have them miss out, but I can't expose the entire class to their germs."

Emma nodded, sympathizing with the young mother.

"Go and play," Peggy instructed the kids, but they refused to budge. Emma wondered if they feared that the minute they left the room, she'd abscond with the Christmas presents.

Peggy sat down on the ottoman with her children gathered around her like a small herd of lambs.

"Tell me about your fruitcake recipe," Emma said when she'd retrieved pen and pad from her briefcase.

"There's not much to tell. I concocted it myself a little while ago, using several fruitcake recipes I found in one of my mother's old cookbooks. I also found a newspaper clipping that dated back to the 1960s, which must've been mailed to my mom by my grandmother. Everyone in the family loves fruitcake."

"So you grew up with fruitcake?"

Peggy smiled. "Mom bakes it every Christmas. It's a family tradition."

"So you do, too?"

Peggy smiled again. "With some significant differences. My recipe isn't a typical one, although I use all the same ingredients most everyone uses in fruitcake."

"I like Mama's fruitcake," Rosalie whispered, her face averted so she wouldn't have to look at Emma.

"Is it good?"

"*Real* good," Abby added without a hint of shyness. "It's the best, and my mama's going to win. That's what our daddy says."

"What made you submit the recipe to *Good Home-making* magazine?" This wasn't a question she'd asked the other Washington State finalists, but Emma found she was curious about Peggy's reasons. Both Earleen Williams and Sophie McKay had perfected their recipes through the years. That didn't seem to be the case with Peggy.

The young mother blushed. "My husband encouraged me to enter, so I did. No one was more surprised than me when I found out I was a finalist." She lifted Dylan onto her lap and the little boy leaned his head against her shoulder and promptly placed his thumb in his mouth.

"Exactly how long have you been using this recipe?"

"How long?" Peggy repeated, and the question seemed to fluster her. Her hand went to her hair, as if she was afraid it needed attention. "Actually, the first one I baked was last December—a year ago."

"Wow. It must be good." If this relatively untried recipe was a finalist, it had to be impressive.

"Would you care to taste a slice?" Peggy asked. Setting Dylan aside despite his mumbled protests, she stood.

Emma imagined this young mother wasn't accustomed to sitting down for any length of time. A buzzer went off in the distance, signaling that the dryer had finished its cycle.

"Rosalie, take the sheets out of the dryer, would you?"

The oldest girl left the room, and the three remaining children all stared at Emma, the youngest with his thumb still firmly planted in his mouth.

Rosalie returned a minute later, her arms wrapped around a huge load of fresh laundry. "Where should I put them? The reporter lady is sitting in the chair." Apparently the recliner was the spot for sorting clean laundry.

"I can move," Emma volunteered, although she didn't know where. The one other piece of furniture was a sofa, and that appeared to be functioning as a sickbed for the two girls.

"Go and put them on my bed," Peggy shouted from the kitchen.

"Okay."

"Mama," Abby cried in sudden alarm. "Dylan has to go potty."

Emma hadn't noticed but, sure enough, the youngest boy was holding himself and crossing and uncrossing his legs.

"Where's his blankie?" Peggy asked calmly, coming in from the kitchen.

Peggy and the three children sprang into action, launching what was obviously a familiar and well-rehearsed routine. The two girls hurried out of the room and Trevor scrambled under the coffee table, crawling on all fours. Emma stood, fearing she was in the way.

Peggy grabbed Dylan and, holding the two-year-old at arm's length, carried him from the room. She disappeared into the hallway.

Never having witnessed anything like this, Emma followed and watched with interest as Peggy got her youngest son on the kiddie toilet. Dylan madly waved his arms, resembling a young bird about to take flight. Rosalie leaped into the room with a tattered yellow blanket.

"The duck?" Peggy asked. "Has anyone found the duck?"

Trevor was the hero of the hour. He slid into the tiny bathroom on his stocking feet, then thrust the plush duck at his brother.

As soon as Dylan had both his yellow blanket and his duck, he let out a tremendous sigh. His shoulders relaxed and a slow smile came over his face. Apparently he could now relax enough to concentrate on the job.

"Good boy," Peggy cheered and started to clap.

So did Dylan's three siblings, and because it seemed the thing to do, Emma joined in.

She didn't want to get sidetracked from the interview, but she couldn't help being curious about the minor production she'd just witnessed.

"Dylan's afraid of the potty chair," Abby explained

after Emma asked. "The only way he can go is if he has his security blanket and his favorite duck."

"He has more than one?"

"He's got three—white and orange and yellow, but he only wants the yellow one." Again it was Abby who explained. "It *has* to be that one."

Dylan smiled and his thumb came out of his mouth when he'd finished his task. Peggy pulled up his pants and led the youngster to the sink. Dylan pushed the step stool over, then by himself turned on the water and washed his hands. When he'd finished, he looked to his mother and siblings for another round of applause.

"Sorry for the interruption," Peggy said, lifting the little boy into her arms. The six of them returned to the living room, a ragtag parade.

"Let me get you that fruitcake," Peggy said. "I left it in the kitchen." Still holding Dylan, she retreated to the kitchen and came back with a small plate.

To Emma's surprise the fruitcake was a light brown. The candied fruits liberally spread throughout the slice made her think of a stained glass window. "It's different, all right," she told Peggy. "Very pretty."

"The recipe is no-bake."

Emma nodded. "I know, but what exactly does that mean? The ingredients aren't raw, are they?"

"Oh, no," Peggy said with a laugh. "I use graham cracker crumbs. Not surprisingly, graham crackers are

a staple around here. That's the base that holds everything together."

"Oh." She took a small bite. This cake really was unusual, filled with nuts and the brilliantly colored candied fruit and something else—something she couldn't
quite identify. Could it be marshmallows? Peggy had
kindly agreed to share the recipe.

"I'm not the first person who's come up with this
no-bake concept. It's surprising how well it works."

Emma's second bite confirmed her initial opinion.
The flavors melded together in a delectable sweet taste.
Sweet but not too sweet, Emma decided. At the start
of this assignment, she hadn't liked fruitcake, and now
she was a connoisseur. Every recipe she'd sampled was
unique, although each was based on traditional ingredients. If the three finalists' recipes from Washington
State were this innovative, she could only speculate
what the other nine recipes must be like.

"With my family, a cake doesn't last more than a
day or two," Peggy said, describing what had inspired
the revised recipe. "My children don't understand the
concept of leaving a cake for several weeks in order to
refine the flavors. They want to eat it *now*. The traditional fruitcake my mother makes is excellent. Every
year she starts baking right after Thanksgiving. She'll
bathe the cake in rum for weeks and then on Christmas Eve we have this ceremony and Dad slices it for
the first time. In theory that's great, but it doesn't work

around here." She grinned. "And the quantity of booze isn't appropriate for kids, either."

"Trevor ate Mom's cake," Abby said, pointing to her little brother. "Last year. At Grandma's."

"Did not."

"Did, too. And then he fell asleep."

"Enough." Peggy raised her hand and the squabbling ceased. "That convinced me to try something different. So I came up with this idea."

"She doesn't always make it the same, either," Rosalie said proudly. "Sometimes Mom adds different stuff."

"Like what?"

"She put caramels in one time," Trevor said.

Rosalie made a face. "I didn't like that."

"I won't do it again, although I like the version with melted marshmallows."

That sounded interesting, too. "Will you tell me about yourself?" Emma asked, turning to Peggy.

"Me?" Peggy said, sounding surprised. "There's not much to say."

"You married young." That much was obvious.

Peggy nodded. "I met Larry shortly after I graduated from high school. I wasn't sure what I wanted to do with my life and was working at a Starbucks and taking a few college classes. Larry was working for a plumber and had just become certified by the Department of Labor and Industries. He's almost five years older than me, and we both wanted children. We'd been dating for a while and decided to marry." She smiled and looked slightly embarrassed. "We didn't start out wanting four children, but now that we've got them..." Peggy wrapped her arms around her brood. "We wouldn't change a thing."

"What will you do with the prize money if you win?" Emma asked. This was a new question.

"That's easy," Peggy said. "We'd use it as a down payment on a small farm. Larry has always been an animal person and we were hoping to buy an alpaca or two. Eventually I'd like to weave my own yarn. It's something I've always dreamed of doing."

"I hope you do win," Emma said, and meant it. She wished that for all three of the Washington State finalists.

"Would you like another piece?" Peggy asked.

"I would," Trevor volunteered.

"It's almost lunchtime," his mother told him.

The little boy's eyes brightened. "I can have fruit-cake for lunch?"

"We'll see."

"I want it *now*," Trevor said.

That comment could serve as part of the opening paragraph. Emma stayed long enough to have a cup of tea and another slice of fruitcake with Peggy Lucas. While Peggy worked in the kitchen, preparing peanut-butter-and-jelly sandwiches for her children and heating up soup, Emma sat at the kitchen table and they talked.

Eventually the children lost interest in her and wandered back to their bedroom to play. All four, Emma noted, slept in the same room. It made for tight quarters but no one seemed to mind.

By the time Sally, Peggy's neighbor, returned her to the waterfront, ideas for the article were tumbling over each other in Emma's mind.

Oliver stood on the dock next to the plane, waiting. Whatever business had brought him to Friday Harbor seemed to have been completed. Oscar and Boots wandered up and down the pier, sniffing around curiously, but as soon as they saw Emma, both dogs leaped up repeatedly and barked for joy.

"How'd it go?" Oliver asked, walking toward her in his borrowed leather jacket. It was a little too small and his wrists stuck out, looking oddly vulnerable.

Her heart jumped when she saw him, leaping about in a way that reminded her of the dogs' exuberant display.

"Good," she said and then amended, "Very good."

"You liked the fruitcake?"

"Loved it." She opened her purse and brought out a small slice wrapped in plastic. "Peggy insisted I bring this for you."

A cocky grin slid effortlessly into place. "So you mentioned me?"

Emma had, in an offhand manner, during their conversation in the kitchen. Something in her tone must have indicated that Oliver was more to her than a means of transportation, because Peggy picked up on it right away. Despite Emma's protests that it wasn't necessary, Peggy had given her a slice of fruitcake for Oliver, too.

When she didn't immediately respond, he added, "I'll bet you told her you're crazy about me."

Emma had no intention of pandering to his ego. "I didn't say anything of the kind," she told him briskly. "Are you ready to leave?"

Oliver laughed. "You're that eager to fly again?"

"Not really. I just want to get it over with." That was true enough. More importantly, she wanted to sit at her computer and organize her thoughts while they were fresh in her mind.

"One of these days you'll admit you can't live without me." He stepped onto the pontoon and opened the plane's door.

"I just might," she agreed.

Her words appeared to shock him because Oliver nearly slipped. He grabbed hold of the door; otherwise he would've fallen into the icy water a second time.

"*What* did you just say?" he demanded gruffly.

"Never mind," she said, highly amused. "It was a joke."

"Very funny."

As a matter of fact, Emma thought so, too. Even if there was more truth in that remark than she wanted him to know.

Peggy Lucas's No–Bake Fruitcake with Marshmallows

1 cup raisins (dark or golden)
2 cups dates
2 cups mixed candied fruit
4 cups chopped nuts (you can reduce this to 3 cups if desired)
¾ cup evaporated milk
2 cups marshmallows
2 cups very finely crushed graham crackers

Mix raisins, dates, candied fruit and chopped nuts in a large bowl. In a saucepan (or in a bowl in the microwave) bring evaporated milk to a boil, add marshmallows and stir until thoroughly combined and marshmallows are melted. Grind the graham crackers in the food processor (one package at a time) until they are very finely ground (like flour). You can also use packaged graham cracker crumbs. Stir the graham crackers into the fruit-and-nut mixture. Add the marshmallow mixture. With wet hands, mix all ingredients. Rinse hands, wet them again and press the mixture into a 9 inch x 5 inch loaf pan lined with wax paper. Press it down well and refrigerate for 2 days until set.

Note: If you use ½ cup candied fruit, ½ cup

flaked coconut and 1 cup candied pineapple instead of 2 cups candied fruit, the cake has a tropical taste. If mixture seems too dry, add a little orange juice or strawberry jam. Don't worry if it seems too wet, because as it sets the graham cracker crumbs will absorb the liquid.

Chapter Fifteen

The first time I had fruitcake was as an adult at a coffee shop in Paris. The amount of sherry is simply overwhelming and the cake is too heavy and sweet for my taste. And with so many fruits, there is no specific taste. For my family, the apple-cranberry tart is our traditional holiday cake.

—Jasmine Bojic, executive pastry chef,
Tavern on the Green, New York City

Emma sat at her computer, which she'd set up on the kitchen table, trying to work on her article. When Oliver had finally landed at Lake Union again and they'd started back to Puyallup, it was rush hour. The Seattle traffic inched along Interstate 5; what normally would have been an easy half-hour drive took almost ninety minutes. Emma's nerves were frayed and she didn't even attempt to go to the office.

Oliver had dropped her and Boots off at the apartment. "Would you like to come in and have a hot drink?" she'd asked. It was the first time she'd made such an offer and she'd expected him to accept her invitation instantly.

Oliver hesitated. "Some other time."

His rejection took her by surprise. Not knowing how to respond, she mumbled her thanks for the ride and climbed out of the truck, retrieving Boots and her briefcase. She stood on the sidewalk and watched him drive away. He obviously wasn't going home.

Oliver was out of sight within seconds. Emma had wanted to demand that he tell her where he was going, but she couldn't. It was none of her business. Besides, she reminded herself, she had a dozen things to do, all of which were more important than frittering away time with an unresponsive and ungrateful man. "I have an article to write," she mumbled to no one in particular.

But even now, an hour after he'd left, Emma's mind continually wandered back to Oliver. Boots seemed unsettled, too. Her dog ran back and forth from the kitchen to the front window, hopping onto the chair and peering out at the street. Boots obviously missed her two companions.

Emma shared the feeling. She didn't *want* to care

about Oliver, but she did. This was too similar to the way her mother had behaved toward her husband, which Emma had hated. Bret had acted as if Pamela should be grateful for whatever crumbs of his life he offered them.

Emma forced herself to think about the interview with Peggy Lucas. She'd enjoyed meeting Peggy and her children, and…

Oliver was up to something. Emma knew it—there, she'd done it again. No matter how hard she tried, her mind was filled with thoughts of Oliver.

She got up and walked over to the window, petting Boots, who'd jumped into the chair to stand guard. This late in the afternoon, there was little activity outside. The streetlights had come on, casting a warm glow that illuminated the Christmas bells that hung from each lamp post.

Emma drew her sweater more tightly around her. She refused to think about Oliver anymore. No—not for another second. She sat down at the kitchen table again with a cup of tea and read over the opening paragraph she'd drafted. With her interview notes propped next to the monitor, she resumed writing.

Lessons From Fruitcake: Peggy Lucas

Peggy Lucas is the third Washington State resident to place in *Good Homemaking* magazine's national fruitcake contest. Her motto—inspired by her children—is EAT IT NOW. The young wife and mother, who lives in Friday Harbor, married her plumber husband as a teenager, and they have four children ranging in age from two to six.

It was for her children that Peggy created the recipe for this no-bake Christmas fruitcake. Like all kids, her children lacked the patience to wait months for a traditional fruitcake. As four-year-old Trevor said, "I want it now."

His three siblings agreed with him, and Peggy devised this unusual recipe.

As with the two previous finalists, there are lessons to be learned from Peggy's fruitcake. Earleen Williams was determined to bake the perfect fruitcake, a masterpiece, and while it took her many years and three marriages, she discovered that *she* was the masterpiece.

Sophie McKay bakes her fruitcake using unexpected ingredients, including maraschino cherries and semisweet chocolate chips, because those were the ingredients her late husband enjoyed. She blends pineapple and coconut with chocolate liqueur, and her recipe is a compromise between the traditional way of doing something and individual preferences. Her lesson: Use the ingredients you like. Do what you love.

Last, there is Peggy Lucas with her four young children, eager to partake of anything Christmas.

She couldn't bear to make them wait even a day for their special cake. Her fruitcake is meant to be enjoyed right away. According to Peggy, life's like that. Enjoy it now.

Three finalists, three valuable lessons that—

Emma sighed and saved her draft, then shut down her computer. She couldn't concentrate on fruitcake anymore, or metaphors for life. Her mind wasn't on Peggy but on Oliver.

In order to distract herself from memories of the man, she phoned Phoebe.

"Hello, Emma," Phoebe said, picking up after five rings, just before the answering machine came on.

"What took you so long to get to the phone?" Emma wanted to know.

"Ah…"

Emma could almost hear her friend blush and suddenly understood. "You're not alone, are you?"

Again the hesitation. "Not at the moment."

"Is it, by chance, anyone I know?"

"Could be."

Her friend's face would be beet-red by now. "Is it… drumroll, please…Walt?"

"Ah…"

"Say no more," Emma murmured. "Call me when you're free."

"Okay. Bye."

"Bye." Emma replaced the telephone receiver, more depressed than before. Everyone she met was in love. Okay, maybe not everyone; it just felt that way. Ever since the night Phoebe had helped Emma move, she and Walt were practically never apart. They hadn't made a big announcement, but everyone at the office knew. Emma didn't understand why Walt had been so concerned. Their romance had barely been a blip on the office gossip monitor. They seemed to suit each other; Phoebe's sense of adventure balanced Walt's caution. Their relationship struck her as natural and healthy, now that it was out in the open.

Emma gave another deep sigh. What did *she* know about healthy relationships, anyway? With her parents as an example, she was destined to mess up. Falling for Oliver Hamilton was a prime example of that.

Emma covered her face with her hands, hating this sense of despair.

The doorbell chimed and her heart kicked into overdrive. It had to be Oliver! She hoped it was him. No, she didn't. Yes, she *did*.

If ever Emma understood her mother's feelings about her father, it was now. She wanted to slam the door in Oliver's face and yet, at the same time, she wanted to hug and kiss him.

The doorbell chimed again.

"Who is it?" she asked, stalling for time.

"Look through your peephole."

It was Oliver's voice. "Uh, is there something you want?" she asked. Should she let him in or not?

"You didn't check the peephole, did you?"

She did, then gasped at what she saw. Oliver stood there with the largest, most beautiful Christmas tree she'd ever seen. It was the kind of tree the White House put up every year. Or Rockefeller Center. Definitely not as big, but about as perfect as a tree could get.

"Are you going to let me in?"

She unlatched the lock and swung open the door.

Boots and Oscar raced toward each other as if it'd been years since their last meeting. Emma had wondered if they'd ever get beyond the stage of sniffing each other's butts. Although she supposed that was like saying "Hello" or "What's new?" in the dog world.

"Well," Oliver said proudly, clutching the tree by its trunk. "What do you think?"

Emma stared. "It's gorgeous. Absolutely gorgeous." She tried to figure out where he planned to put it. In his dining room, perhaps? She recalled catching a glimpse of one in his living room last week, glittering with decorations.

He smiled as he thrust the tree at her. "Merry Christmas."

She backed away a step. "Merry Christmas to you, too."

He cocked his head to one side. "Where do you want it?"

Emma leaned closer in order to hear him better. "*Want* it? This tree is for *me?*"

He nodded. "Yes. Isn't it obvious?"

Emma took another step backward.

He blinked, as if he'd been expecting her to throw her arms around him in gratitude. "You don't like it?"

"Of course I like it. That's the most beautiful Christmas tree I've ever seen."

"It's yours."

Emma froze. He'd been serious about giving her the tree. Her—a woman who didn't have a stand or ornaments or anything else one needed for a Christmas tree.

"It's kind of…big, don't you think?" she asked.

"I might need to take a bit more off the bottom, but no, it's not too big. I thought you could do with a bit of Christmas cheer, and I decided to make a contribution."

"But…"

"You'll thank me later."

Emma wasn't sure about that. Not sure at all.

Chapter Sixteen

"I've never seen anything so big in my life," Emma complained to Phoebe. "He didn't even *ask* me if I wanted a Christmas tree." Thanks to her unenthusiastic response, Oliver hadn't spoken to her in two days. Now Emma was miserable and needed to talk with her friend.

Phoebe frowned. "But don't you think bringing you a Christmas tree was very romantic of Oliver?"

Emma stopped her pacing, deep in The Dungeon, as she considered this. "Oh, my goodness." That hadn't even occurred to her. She pressed her hand to her forehead, then flopped down in her chair. "That's it." She should've realized earlier what had prompted him to buy her a tree. "Oliver thought he was being romantic." They'd had this ongoing conversation about romantic heroes and she'd failed to recognize what he was doing. The tree was his way of being romantic according to his theory of "show, not tell" romance. Action rather than words.

"Yes! Oliver was being romantic," Phoebe insisted. "You've really fallen for him, haven't you?" She smiled—a smile that could only be described as smug.

"I think he's arrogant and dogmatic, opinionated and—"

"Yeah, yeah." Phoebe's smile grew even wider. "I thought so." She returned to work as if there was nothing left to argue about.

Emma felt she couldn't leave her friend with that impression. Phoebe might say something to Walt, and Oliver and Walt were pals. She wasn't ready to acknowledge her feelings for Oliver, wasn't even sure those feelings would last long enough to be worth acknowledging.

"I think Oliver's a good pilot," she said, carefully weighing her words. "We've each made an effort to make the best of an uncomfortable situation."

Phoebe ignored her.

"You're right…." Emma admitted reluctantly, walking over to her friend's desk. She folded her arms and spoke casually. "There *was* a slight attraction in the beginning. We even joked about it." Well…Oliver had joked.

Phoebe turned and looked up at Emma. "Did he or did he not kiss you?"

"He...ah, okay, yes, there were a couple of times when I...that happened. So technically, yes, he did kiss me." This was all she was willing to say on the subject.

"So there was *more* than the one time?" Phoebe probed.

"There might have been." Emma wanted her friend to stop studying her with that appraising light in her eyes. "It wasn't a big deal."

"But you said Oliver's your romantic hero."

"No. I said it looked like Oliver was just proving a point." She wished he wouldn't try so hard, but she didn't know how to make him stop. The entire conversation about romantic heroes had come about by chance. But now he seemed to be going out of his way to prove that he was every bit as romantic as Humphrey Bogart or Cary Grant.

Emma sat at her desk, hardly able to concentrate. She'd be leaving the office in a few minutes to drum up advertisements for the newspaper. During the fruit-cake interviews, Walt had excused her from that responsibility. Apparently his arrangement with Oliver had sparked an idea, and Walt was now willing to trade newspaper space for goods and services. Rumor had it that the Subway Express down the street would be catering the company Christmas lunch. Talk around the water cooler was that Walt had worked out some sort of deal with the owner—three weekly ads in exchange for thirty turkey sandwiches, pickles and coleslaw on the side. Thankfully, he hadn't been negotiating with the Mexican restaurant/sushi bar. Cross-cultural restaurants weren't so rare in small towns, but this was a combination Emma found a little bizarre.

"How are things going with you and Walt?" Emma asked, deciding it was her turn to ask personal questions.

Phoebe glowed. "Fabulous."

"Define fabulous."

"He asked me to have Christmas dinner with his family."

This was big, and Emma released a low whistle.

"We're having two dinners that day," Phoebe went on to explain. "First with my mom and dad, and then later with his."

"I hope you like turkey."

"I do," Phoebe assured her. "But my mom's serving prime rib and I don't know about his mother. What are you doing for Christmas?"

Christmas fell on a Sunday this year, and Emma wouldn't be doing anything special. She'd probably do what she had the year before—attend a movie and have buttered popcorn for dinner. It would be a day like any other.

"Emma?"

"I have plans." She hated to lie, so she remained

vague. If she mentioned going to a movie, Phoebe would feel sorry for her and then find a way to include her. Emma didn't want to intrude on Phoebe and her family, or on Walt and his.

"What sort of plans?" Phoebe pressed.

Emma didn't want to be rude or arouse her suspicions, so she played it coy. "Private plans," she said, dropping her voice until it was almost a purr.

This was a mistake because Phoebe's curiosity was certainly piqued now. "They involve Oliver, don't they?"

"They could." Emma reached for her coat and purse, anxious to leave.

"You'll tell me later?"

Emma sighed deeply. "Yes, but only if you torture it out of me."

"That could be arranged," a gruff male voice said from behind her.

Both Phoebe and Emma gasped as Walt stepped between their desks. "I should come downstairs more often to see how the two of you spend your time." He frowned at Emma and handed her a sheet of paper printed with a list of businesses. The highlighted ones were the companies he wanted her to approach. Oh joy, The Taco Stand and California Rock & Roll were on the list, the combination ethnic restaurant so recently in her thoughts.

Emma stared at the paper and squelched a groan. She did not consider ad sales her forte.

Half an hour later, Emma was sitting with Mr. Garcia of The Taco Stand and his wife, Suki, who operated the other half of the restaurant. There weren't any lunch customers yet, and they'd chosen a booth on the Mexican side of the building with its strings of red chili pepper lights proclaiming Christmas cheer. Emma carefully reviewed the newspaper's advertising rates. Suki, whose English was poor, looked to her Hispanic husband to explain what Emma had suggested. Emma glanced from one to the other and realized they had a language all their own.

"Is it for newspaper?" Suki wanted to know for the third time.

Emma smiled and nodded. "Yes," she said. She found herself speaking slowly and deliberately. "Advertise your good food to all the people in Puyallup so they will come in and place many orders." After five minutes of talking to the young Asian woman, Emma sounded as if she were the one struggling with English. It embarrassed her; she didn't want to offend the gentle young woman, but in her effort to make herself understood, she was overemphasizing each word.

Carlos, Suki's husband, nodded. "Very good for business."

Suki brightened. "We talk," she said and smiled softly at her husband.

A bell tinkled in the Japanese half of the restaurant, separated by a doorway. "Suki, where are you?"

Emma would recognize that voice anywhere.

Suki's eyes widened with pleasure. "Mr. Oliver," she said and immediately scooted out of the booth.

Carlos laughed. "She has a big crush on the pilot. It's a good thing she met me first."

Emma didn't doubt Oliver's appeal to the opposite sex for a moment. He had that effect on women; she knew from her own experience.

"Leave the information with me," Carlos said. "I'll call Mr. Walt later."

"So you think you'll buy an ad?" Emma asked hopefully.

Carlos hemmed and hawed. "Maybe. I'll talk it over with Suki."

It happened like this every time. She nearly had a commitment, and then the business owner would back off. She had no idea what she needed to do in order to get businesses to advertise in their local paper. Some of the businesspeople she talked to practically gave her the impression that they were afraid of attracting more customers. She didn't know how else to explain it. Fortunately, she'd had one success—Badda Bing, Badda Boom Pizza. They'd seen an increase in pizza sales and had happily signed a new contract.

She couldn't resist. After thanking Carlos, Emma walked over to the other half of the restaurant. Sure enough, Oliver sat on a stool with his back to her, while Suki worked behind the counter, assembling his order.

"I would never have taken you for someone who enjoys sushi," she said, and slid onto the stool beside him.

Oliver didn't look surprised to see her. "Really? I love it. My guess is you've never tried it."

He was beginning to know her. Then again, he seemed to have that ability from the moment they met. "You're right, I haven't."

"California rolls for the lady," Oliver told Suki.

"Oh, I'm not hungry," she said, which wasn't true.

Oliver didn't allow her to protest. "At least give it a try."

She'd been saying the same thing all afternoon. The least she could do was follow her own advice. "All right, I will."

Oliver gave her a warm smile, and she couldn't help basking in his approval. "See?" he said. "You didn't like fruitcake but you were willing to try it. And look how well that worked out." Emma could have stared into this man's eyes forever; instead, she quickly glanced away.

"I wondered where the name California Rock and Roll came from," she said casually. "Now I know."

Suki placed both orders on the counter and Emma examined hers. On a rectangular plate, Suki had arranged four California rolls. They seemed to be rolled logs of rice around a thin sheet of processed seaweed, with strips of avocado and various vegetables tucked in the center. On the same plate were two small bowls. One held soy sauce and the other was filled with a thin guacamole. Apparently Carlos and Suki had found a way to cross their foods culturally. Emma was intrigued. While Oliver reached for his chopsticks, she spread a liberal portion of the guacamole across the top of one California roll.

Oliver watched her with raised eyebrows.

Emma was about to take her first bite when he stopped her.

"You might want to scrape off some of the wasabi."

"The what?"

"Wasabi."

She must have looked confused, because he dipped the end of his chopstick in her guacamole and offered her a taste. The minute her lips touched it, her mouth was on fire. She grabbed her cup of tea and swallowed the entire contents. Waving her hand in front of her mouth, all she could do was feel grateful for Oliver's intervention.

"Oh, my goodness," she gasped.

"You thought that was guacamole?"

She nodded. "Thank you. Oh, thank you."

His eyes crinkled with a smile as he returned to his sushi.

Once Emma had tasted her first real bite, sans wasabi,

she was surprised by how delicious the California roll was. "Hey, this is good."

"Told you."

She merely smiled.

They sat in companionable silence, and Emma had to admit she was thrilled to see him. She wanted to explain why she'd reacted the way she had to his gift of a Christmas tree, but was afraid any attempt would destroy this fragile peace.

"You came here for an early lunch?" Oliver asked.

"No, I was on another of my advertising treks for Walt."

"How's it going?"

She hated to admit how unsuccessful she was at this selling business. It was so much harder than she would've expected. Oliver listened and nodded. Then he told her, "You're doing it all wrong."

"What do you mean, I'm doing it wrong?" *He* wasn't the one hoofing it from business to business, putting on a smile and talking his heart out, only to be shown the door.

"Emma, listen to me. You're an attractive, charming young woman and it should be difficult for people to tell you no."

She scoffed, although she took note of the "attractive" and "charming." "That hasn't been a problem today."

"You've gotten nothing but *no?*" He seemed astonished by that.

She wasn't proud of it, but that was exactly what had happened. If she didn't get a flat rejection, it was "we'll think it over" or "later, maybe."

"Like I said, you must be doing it wrong."

That annoyed her. "*You* turned me down," she reminded him, allowing her temper to flare just a bit.

"I most certainly did not. I couldn't afford you, but I wanted you."

"It was the advertising you wanted, not me," she told him, stiffening at the implication.

"Whatever. I got you in my plane, didn't I? *And* I got advertising in the paper."

"Okay, okay, I'll concede the point." She reached for the teapot and refilled her cup. "If you think it's so easy, you try."

"All right. I'll bet I can prove to you that people can be talked into anything. What do you want me to do?"

Another man had entered the restaurant and sat at a table by the window. Emma pointed at him. "Ask that man to pay for your meal and watch how fast he tells you no."

"Okay, you're on." Oliver slid off the stool and walked toward the gentleman dining alone. He looked like a midlevel bank employee. Possibly a loan officer, judging by the fact that he was smartly but conservatively dressed.

Oliver didn't hesitate. He strolled over to the other man and when he spoke, he made sure it was just loud enough for Emma to overhear the conversation.

"Excuse me," he said in a friendly way.

The other man glanced up from his menu. "Yes?"

"I just ordered lunch for my girlfriend and me, and I've discovered I left my wallet at home. Would you mind paying for our meal? I'll repay you, of course."

The other man didn't say anything for a long moment. "How much is it?"

Emma was shocked he hadn't immediately laughed in Oliver's face and told him to get lost.

In a display of false humility, Oliver shook his head. "I haven't got the bill yet, but I'd guess around ten dollars." He shrugged. "I just assumed I had my wallet."

"You didn't think of that before you ordered?" the man asked.

Oliver gave him a look that said he was absolutely right. "I know I should've but...I didn't."

"You seem like a decent sort," the other man said slowly.

Emma couldn't stand it. She climbed off the stool and hurried to Oliver's side. "You can tell him no," she said eagerly. She'd hate it if Oliver won this bet so easily. Besides, they hadn't decided what the winner would get.

"Now, Emma." Oliver frowned at her. "This is man to man. Don't you worry about it."

Emma wasn't going to let him win this bet without a struggle. "My friend is being irresponsible. It certainly isn't up to you to pay for his mistake. All you have to do is say no."

The gentleman nodded. "True, but it is the holiday season, and ten dollars won't break me."

Oliver grinned triumphantly. He stretched out his hand to the other man. "Thank you very much. I'm Oliver Hamilton, by the way."

"Gary Sullivan. Nice to meet you." Gary stood and reached for his wallet.

"No," Oliver said, refusing the money. "I was just proving a point to my girlfriend. This is Emma Collins, of *The Puyallup Examiner*."

"I'm not his girlfriend." Emma felt it was important to clarify that. "We're friends...." She let the rest fade, embarrassed to have said anything.

Gary looked confused.

"You could've just said no," Emma repeated, unable to understand why it had been so easy for Oliver and so difficult for her.

"I didn't mind. Like I said, this is Christmas, I could afford it and your boyfriend—Oliver—is very persuasive. The idea of paying for your meal actually made me feel good. Christmas spirit and all."

Emma gave up then and walked back to the counter.

"See," Oliver said as he returned to his stool. "People *want* to help and it's the same in sales. If you just remember that, and remember to show them what *they'll* get out of it, then you'll have a better chance of selling advertising for Walt."

She sighed loudly. "Okay, you win."

"I beg your pardon?"

"You win," she said a little louder this time, although she nearly choked on the words.

"Good. I'll be by for dinner around seven."

"Dinner?"

"Yes. Didn't I mention my prize?"

"I'm afraid you didn't."

"You're going to make me dinner." He grinned. "I hope it's all right if Oscar comes, too."

Chapter Seventeen

As children growing up in Ireland, we would watch our grandmother make fruitcake and she would always let us lick the bowl afterward. I liked fruitcake simply because of the association with Christmas and spending time in the kitchen with my grandmother. However, it always seemed that the cake lasted until the next century and there was always the possibility of broken bones if the cake accidentally fell on you!

—Frank McMahon, executive chef at Hank's Seafood in Charleston, South Carolina

Oliver was pleased with himself. His spur-of-the-moment experiment couldn't have gone any better. Later, as they left the restaurant, Emma seemed to think she'd been tricked. She claimed Oliver must have known Gary beforehand. He didn't, and she'd eventually believed him.

He hoped his little lesson in sales would help—and not just with her ad quota. The fact was, you had to persuade people that they were going to get something out of the deal. It was more of an emotional thing than it was a practical or financial one. Look at Gary for instance—he felt good about helping someone out. Oliver wanted to convince Emma that there'd be an emotional payoff for her, too, if she bought his sales pitch. Only what *he* was selling was himself.

She'd described them as friends, but he was interested in more than friendship, and if his intuition was right, so was Emma. The problem, and he considered it a minor one, was that she hadn't acknowledged it yet.

After his lunch, Oliver returned to the airfield, did some paperwork and then drove home. Emma had called to say dinner would be ready around seven-thirty and he took that to mean she had some grocery shopping to do before he came by. He was thinking a big, juicy T-bone steak would suit him just fine.

On his way home, Oliver bought a bottle of his favorite merlot. Humming a Christmas carol, he hopped back inside his pickup. Oscar, waiting for him in the passenger seat, yawned ostentatiously.

"So how's it going with you and Boots?" Oliver asked his terrier. "You looking forward to having dinner with her?"

Oscar cocked his head to one side.

His cell rang and when he checked caller ID, he saw that it was his mother. He picked up on the third ring, and they discussed Christmas Day and the dinner she had planned. "Hey, Mom," he said, glancing in his sideview mirror before he changed lanes. "Would it be all right if I brought a guest?"

"For Christmas?"

"Yeah. A...friend of mine." The word *friend* made him feel self-conscious. He hoped that by Christmas Day their relationship would have progressed to something a little more exciting.

His mother knew him far too well. "I'm assuming this guest you want to include is female?"

"Yes."

"Is she someone special?"

He was silent for a moment. "Yes," he finally admitted. "Yeah, she is."

"What's her name?"

"Emma Collins."

"Emma Collins?" his mother repeated. "That sounds familiar."

"No reason it should," Oliver said, changing lanes a second time. "She works for *The Examiner*. I met her earlier in the month when she came down to the airfield to—"

"She works for the newspaper?" his mother said excitedly, cutting him off. "She's that reporter!"

"What reporter?"

"The girl who wrote those articles about fruitcake," she told him, her tone suggesting he must be a simpleton.

"Well, yes, but I didn't know they'd been published." He'd been too busy to read the paper this last week and when he did, he rarely looked past the front page and the sports section.

"She interviewed the three Washington State fruitcake recipe finalists."

"I know." Oliver realized he probably sounded smug. "I was the one who flew her in for the interviews. Don't you remember I told you about that?"

"Yes, but you didn't tell me who you were flying or what for."

"She usually writes obituaries, Mom."

"You haven't read her articles, have you?"

"I've been busy."

"Everyone in town is talking about them," his mother informed him. "At my bridge club luncheon, we all said we were surprised someone that young could be so wise."

"How do you know her age?"

"The paper ran her photo at the bottom of the last article. She's an attractive woman."

Oliver agreed.

"My son is dating Emma Collins."

"She's making dinner for me tonight." He didn't

think now was the time to mention that Emma had agreed to this only because she'd lost a bet.

"I can't believe you haven't said anything!"

"Sorry."

"You should be. That girl is gifted. Those articles were *so* good."

"Save them for me, would you?" He'd look through the papers in his recycling bin, but just in case...

"I already used one of the recipes and I'm going to serve it on Christmas Day."

Oliver liked fruitcake, and there always seemed to be plenty of it around his parents' house. "So I can bring Emma?"

"Don't you *dare* show up without her."

"Wouldn't dream of it."

As soon as he arrived home, Oliver collected a week's worth of papers and sat down with them, searching until he located the first article—about the Yakima interview. He studied a picture of Earleen Williams displaying her fruitcake. Emma wasn't a bad photographer. He recalled that first flight and how nervous she'd been. Then he remembered her problem with the television in the motel room and her effort to hear the news that turned out to be nudes. At that he laughed outright.

His mother was right; the article was insightful and well-written. Within a few paragraphs, Oliver felt he knew Earleen. He'd certainly met women like her who didn't recognize their own worth or, as in Earleen's

case, recognized it later in life. Emma had character-
ized her with real sensitivity. Logically but subtly, she
led the reader to her own conclusion—that this was a
generous woman who'd spent her life loving men who
didn't deserve her devotion.

He found the article about Sophie McKay next. Sophie was a woman who enjoyed life. Neither she nor
her fruitcake recipe was in any way typical. She took
the ingredients she liked best and combined them into
a truly unique recipe, just as she'd done with her life.
Both she and her beloved husband, Harry, had been
willing to compromise on the fruitcake issue and, no
doubt, on the more important conflicts within their
marriage. After his death, she'd mourned him and continued to love him but also continued to live. Sophie
McKay, like her fruitcake, was one of a kind.

As Oliver rummaged through discarded papers for
the third and final article, he understood what had intrigued his mother and her friends about Emma. She
was special, and her understanding of these women's
lives was compassionate as well as incisive.

When he found the third article, he smiled at the
picture of Peggy Lucas surrounded by her children. He
almost wished Emma had been in the photograph. The
theme for that article was *eat it now* and the No-Bake
Fruitcake recipe followed. With Peggy, too, Emma had
found just the right tone.

In all three articles, she'd managed to write about

fruitcake—on the surface a rather limited subject—in ways that gave it a larger meaning. Fruitcake as a symbol for life. Hmm...

Emma might not be much good at garnering advertising dollars for Walt, but she shouldn't worry. What she lacked in sales ability she more than compensated for with her writing talent.

Oliver saw that it was almost seven. Rubbing his hand down his cheek, he decided to shave. He was in a good mood and knew he should credit Emma with that. She'd impressed him with her work and she made him laugh. There was a lot to be said for a woman who possessed a sense of humor. After throwing on his leather jacket, which had survived its icy bath in Puget Sound, he reached for the wine bottle, called Oscar and together, man and dog headed out the door.

Striking what he hoped was a sexy Cary Grant pose, Oliver rang the doorbell. He leaned his shoulder against the doorjamb and crossed his ankles, bottle tucked under one arm. It didn't take Emma long to answer. Unlatching the lock, she opened the door and immediately made a fuss over Oscar. She hardly seemed to notice Oliver was even there. Apparently she was immune to his many charms—or wanted him to think she was. Definitely hard on the ego.

"That's all the greeting I get?" he chided.

She wore a towel apron over jeans and looked lovely. He couldn't resist. Slipping his hand behind her neck,

Oliver bent forward and kissed her. She tasted wonderful—a little spicy, a little sweet.

She blinked several times when he released her. "Hi," she said in a husky voice, sounding flustered. When they'd first met, he'd enjoyed teasing her about how much she wanted him. Actually, the reverse was true. *He* wanted *her.* In an effort to derail the direction of his thoughts, he asked, "What's for dinner?"

"If I don't get back to the stove in a hurry, it'll be takeout." She dashed across the room and returned to her kitchen.

Oliver bent down and petted Boots. The two dogs resumed their ritual sniffing.

"Ever heard of puttanesca?" Emma asked, emptying a large can of crushed tomatoes into a pan.

"Putin what?" Oliver asked as he set the wine bottle down on the crowded countertop. "Is it some Russian dish?"

"Puttanesca," Emma repeated. "It's an Italian pasta sauce. My mother used to make it. I have to warn you it's kind of spicy."

The scents in the kitchen were delectable. He smelled garlic and tomatoes and something else he couldn't identify. He saw an empty anchovy can and wondered if that was it. Oliver enjoyed the little fish on his pizza. So far, that was the only time he'd ever eaten anchovies.

Emma stirred the simmering sauce, her back to him.

"Mom told me that women of the night would put a pan of this sauce in the window in order to entice men."

"Are you trying to entice *me,* Emma Collins?" Oliver asked softly.

As if she realized what she'd said, Emma whirled around, her eyes wide. "No...you misunderstood. This has nothing to do with you and me."

It was probably wrong of him to find amusement in her obvious discomfort, but he grinned and said, "Pity."

She held his gaze. "Could I?" she asked, her voice hesitant. "Entice you, I mean."

He shrugged carelessly. "You could always give it a try." He grinned again. "In fact, why don't you?"

She smiled in response and the tip of her tongue moistened her lower lip before she turned back to the pasta sauce.

Oliver was convinced she had no idea what an effective job she was doing of enticing him right then and there. He fought the impulse to kiss her again. "Is there anything you'd like me to do?"

She nodded. "You can roll the lemon."

Oliver was sure he'd misheard. "You want me to what?"

"Roll the lemon between your hands," she explained. "I'd normally roll it against the countertop, but as you can see, I don't have much space here."

He pressed the lemon between his hands, then crushed it with all his might. "This is for the pasta?"

"No," she said with a laugh. "The salad. I'm squeezing fresh lemon juice over the greens and then tossing them with a little extra-virgin olive oil."

Extra-virgin, was it? Oliver didn't even want to know what that meant. Then again, maybe he did.

"The bread's warming in the oven."

"Of course." The table was already set, and when he'd finished pulverizing the lemon, he opened the wine. After giving it a couple of minutes to breathe—he'd read about that once in an airline magazine—he poured them each a glass.

Emma certainly seemed to know what she was doing. He asked her about it over dinner as he swallowed every noodle and scraped up every last drop of the delicious sauce.

"My mom was the cook in the family. I miss her so much," she said quietly. "This is the first time I've made puttanesca since she died and I was a little concerned it wouldn't be the same."

"If it isn't, don't change anything. This was fabulous."

Emma smiled and picked up her glass of wine.

She rarely mentioned her mother. Oliver knew the subject was a painful one, but he sensed that she wanted to talk about her now.

"She taught you to cook, right?"

Emma nodded. "Mom insisted I should know my way around a kitchen. Isn't that something in these days of convenience food? I can't remember Mom *ever* resorting to processed food. I didn't taste macaroni and cheese from a box until I was almost an adult." She grimaced comically. "That's what comes of living on a student budget."

"Do you like cooking?" he asked.

She nodded again. "I don't do it often enough. If Mom were alive, I'm afraid I'd be a disappointment to her."

"I'm sure that's not true." He was sincere; her mother would be very proud of Emma and rightly so. "Speaking of mothers, I talked to mine this afternoon and she read your articles."

Emma's eyes brightened. "Did she enjoy them?"

"Mom was very impressed." Oliver was a little disgruntled that Emma hadn't let him know those fruitcake pieces had been published. He'd also been put out over her lack of appreciation for the Christmas tree. She had the tree up, but it didn't have a single strand of lights or even one decoration. It leaned rather forlornly against the corner of her living room. She hadn't bought a stand; she'd just stuck it in a large, dirt-filled flower pot.

"That's great." Emma seemed pleased by his mother's reaction.

"What did Walt say?"

Emma chuckled. "His only comment after he read the final drafts was that I gave him clean copy. Which is high praise from Walt."

Oliver helped himself to the last of the pasta sauce and sopped it up with his bread. "Getting back to my mother, she wants to meet you."

"She does?"

Oliver played this part cool. "Yeah. I told her I could arrange it."

"I'd be delighted to meet her."

"How about Christmas Day?" he asked, again casually.

Emma's smile faded. "Christmas Day," she said slowly.

"Is that a problem?" Oliver felt like smacking his forehead. He should've realized she'd have plans. Everyone did on Christmas.

"I'm sorry, it won't work." At least she had the good grace to look regretful.

"You've already got plans?"

"Sort of," she said after a brief hesitation.

Oliver straightened. "Either you have plans or you don't. Which is it?"

Emma set her napkin on the table, stood up and carried their plates to the sink. "I know you have a hard time understanding this, but I don't 'do' Christmas."

He looked over at the bare tree he'd gotten her. Point taken.

"It isn't anything religious," she explained. "Christmas just hasn't been the same since my mother died. I tried to continue all the traditions we'd done together. It was too sad. So I stopped."

She returned from the kitchen, carrying a pie and a couple of small glass plates. "My...father and I are estranged. He invites me out of obligation, but I can't go to him and his new wife. I just can't."

She sat down at the table again. "Friends invited me over a couple of years in a row, but it made me feel like a charity case." She lowered her head. "People tend to feel sorry for me and I don't want that. The last two years I've spent the day alone and, really, it isn't so bad. I've come to enjoy it."

Oliver shrugged off her rejection as if it didn't matter. His invitation had been issued in an offhand manner, which he now decided was a mistake. He should've made a big deal of it.

Because it *was* a big deal. Christmas was important to him and to his family, and he wanted Emma to be part of that. He wanted Emma with him.

Now all he had to do was figure out how to convince her.

Chapter Eighteen

Emma knew she'd disappointed Oliver and she felt bad about that. She was quite fond of him and— Okay, that was a mild assessment of her feelings. She was crazy about him.

"I think I blew it with Oliver," she told Phoebe on the phone later that evening.

"What happened?"

Emma sat down and put her feet up as she mentally reviewed their dinnertime conversation. "He invited me to meet his mother."

"That's terrific! Oh, Emma, Oliver's letting you know that you're more than just a friend. He's asking you to meet his family. That's a huge step in a relationship."

"It was all very casual," she murmured.

"Of course it was...." Phoebe paused. "You're not going to tell me you refused, are you?"

"He invited me to Christmas dinner."

The line went silent for a moment. "You mean to tell me that Oliver invited you to meet his parents on Christmas Day and you *turned him down?*"

"Yes." The word was barely audible, even to Emma.

"Don't you understand that's as good as it gets with a guy—his parents *and* Christmas?"

"But..."

"Tell me you're joking."

"Well, no."

Phoebe groaned. "I was afraid of that. I thought you liked Oliver."

"I do," she said in a small voice. Emma was afraid to admit how much. She knew now that he wasn't like her father. Oliver was caring, generous and had a great relationship with his family. He was kind to animals. He had a sense of humor. If she were to make a list of what she wanted in a man, those traits would be at the very top.

"How can you be so smart and so stupid at the same time?" Phoebe muttered.

"It's a gift," Emma said sarcastically.

"What did Oliver say after you told him no?"

Emma closed her eyes and pressed her palm against her forehead. "Hardly anything. I'd made dinner, he offered to help with the dishes, but there weren't that many and—"

"Stop right there," Phoebe commanded. "Oliver offered to help with the dishes and you refused that, too?"

"That was wrong?"

"Never, I repeat—never—turn down a man's offer to do the dishes. Men are like puppies that have to be trained. This training takes place during the courtship period. Men will take their cues from you and if you let them know you're fine with doing all the housework, they'll simply accept it. Who wouldn't? That, my friend, was mistake number two. Okay, now tell me what happened next."

"Nothing much. He said he had an errand to run and he left."

"Did he thank you for dinner?"

"Oh, yes. He really seemed to enjoy it." His enjoyment gratified her. This was a special recipe—a special meal. In her own way, she'd been letting him know he was important to her.

"But he left almost right afterward?"

"Yes." Emma was feeling worse by the minute.

Her friend exhaled slowly. "You're right, you blew it."

Emma swallowed around the lump forming in her throat. "Any suggestions on what I should do now?"

"Call and tell him you've had a change of heart and

would love to spend Christmas with him and his family." She gulped in an urgent breath. "And do it soon."

This wasn't what Emma wanted to hear. "But I *haven't* changed my mind."

"Do you love this guy or not?" Phoebe demanded.

Love? Love. Love! She didn't know. Okay, maybe she did. She loved him. And deep down she knew that if she didn't act quickly, she might lose him.

"But I don't do—"

"Don't say it," Phoebe interrupted. "Do you honestly think this is how your mother wants you to spend Christmas? You told me how much she liked the holidays and all the things you used to do together."

"I know. I'm not opposed to Christmas for other people," Emma said, defending herself. "But it's not for me. Christmas makes me sad and—"

"You didn't answer my question."

When had Phoebe become so dictatorial? "No…"

"No what?"

"Mom would want me to be with people at Christmas," she murmured.

"That's what I thought."

Emma knew Phoebe was right about this. Her mother had always said there was something special about Christmas. Oliver had tried to tell her there was something special about her, too, and she'd brushed him off.

"Okay, you've made your point." Now all she had to

do was explain to Oliver that she'd been wrong. That she'd mourned her mother in a negative way instead of a positive one. That she should have celebrated all the things they'd shared—like Christmas. Phoebe was right about something else. This dinner had been a turning point in Emma's relationship with Oliver. Unfortunately, she'd made the wrong choice once again.

"Call him."

"Okay."

"Tell him you've changed your mind and *mean* it," Phoebe said.

Emma nodded dutifully. "What do you think he'll say?"

Phoebe didn't answer for a long moment. "I don't know. Call me back after you talk to him, okay?"

"I will," Emma promised. This wasn't going to be easy. Before she lost her nerve she punched out his phone number. After three rings, voice mail came on and she left a message. "Hi," she said awkwardly. "This is Emma... Listen, about Christmas. I am so honored that you invited me. I'd love to meet your mother. I was thinking I might've offended you and I'd never want to do that and so—" BEEP.

Emma had been cut off. She dialed the number again, then replaced the receiver before the recorded message began. She wondered if Oliver was screening his calls and preferred not to talk to her. The last thing she wanted to be was a pest.

Sleeping was out of the question. The big office party was the following afternoon. The Subway Express lunch had fallen through—apparently the county Health Department had some concerns about them—and Walt had made another deal with a brand-new catering company. Emma had purchased the requisite gift and dutifully wrapped it for the Secret Santa exchange, but her heart wasn't in it.

The following morning when she showed up at the office, Phoebe met her with a cup of coffee. "Here, you look like you need this. Why didn't you call me back?"

"I didn't talk to Oliver."

"You tried?"

"Yes, twice." She hadn't left a message the second time. One message was enough, she reasoned.

Phoebe frowned. "It's still early."

Two days was all she had. The office closed for the holidays at the end of business hours today. Saturday was Christmas Eve and then Sunday was Christmas Day itself. She had to settle this with Oliver and soon.

Needless to say, Emma wasn't looking forward to the office party, but she was required to attend. No one said as much; it was simply understood. Staff and freelance writers mingled in the upstairs office, and the conference room table was covered with an elaborate culinary display.

Emma wasn't sure how much free advertising Walt had agreed to with the catering company. A lot, she assumed. The spread was gorgeous, with huge shrimp arranged around a bowl of cocktail sauce, smoked salmon and cream cheese on small rounds of rye bread, chicken teriyaki tidbits, veggie trays, cheese and crackers and enough desserts to send the entire staff racing to Weight Watchers on the second of January. To Emma's delight, among the desserts was a large platter of sliced fruitcake.

"You're Emma Collins?" the young female caterer asked when Emma paused to admire it.

"I am."

"I really enjoyed your articles," she said. "My name is Dixie Rogers."

They shook hands. "I enjoyed meeting the finalists— and trying their fruitcake," Emma told her.

"Has the winner been announced?"

Emma nodded. "It was a woman from South Carolina." She'd checked the web last night, just before she went to bed, and had seen the results.

"Oh. I hope the Washington State finalists aren't too disappointed."

Emma thought that Earleen, Sophie and Peggy were thrilled to have made the final cut. She'd heard from each one after the articles were published and they'd all been pleased.

"As you probably guessed, the no-bake fruitcake is Peggy Lucas's recipe." Dixie pointed to the tray Emma had recently admired. "I think everyone who normally dislikes fruitcake will be eager to give it a second try after reading your articles. I know I was."

The praise felt good. "Thank you again."

"Next year I'm determined to bake all three fruit-cakes. The chocolate one especially interests me."

"It's wonderful," Emma assured her. The three final-ists had made a believer out of her. Her intense dislike of fruitcake had come about more because of its asso-ciation with Christmas than any aversion to the cake itself. It was an unreasonable dislike, she recognized, since she'd only tasted it a couple of times. Next year, she'd bake one herself. Maybe even all three.

Emma filled her plate and joined Phoebe while Walt made the traditional Christmas champagne toast. The Secret Santa gift exchange turned out, surprisingly, to be a lot of fun, and Emma ended up the proud pos-sessor of a pair of Christmas tree earrings. Soon ev-eryone was getting ready to leave for the night. There were plenty of hugs and holiday greetings as the office staff began to drift away.

Bundled against the cold, Emma walked out of the office, Phoebe and Walt behind her. Being alone over the holidays had never troubled Emma this much in the past. It was the thought of not being with Oliver. She wanted to be in his life and she wanted him in hers.

Just before the office party, Walt had sought her out. He hadn't openly praised her work; that would've been asking too much. But he'd given her another assignment. Shortly after the first of the year, the big Bridal Fair would be held at the Tacoma Dome. Walt seemed to feel she'd find plenty of human interest stories at an event like that.

It wasn't a random choice, Emma realized. When Phoebe returned to work after Christmas, Emma expected to see her wearing an engagement ring. In fact, she was virtually certain that Phoebe had whispered the idea for her new assignment in Walt's ear.

The wind sent icy shivers down Emma's back as she headed toward the parking lot. A dog barked. Could it possibly be Oscar, which meant Oliver would be close by? She scanned the area but didn't see either Oliver or his terrier.

As she drove through town, Emma noticed—as if for the first time—all the street decorations. Wreaths, striped candy canes and snowmen were suspended from light posts, with evergreen boughs stretched from one side of the street to the other. These decorations were truly an expression of the community's spirit. Before, she'd barely glanced at them, viewing it all as evidence of the commercialization of Christmas. Now she looked at the scene in front of her with fresh eyes.

Snowflakes floated down. She caught her breath at the sheer wonder of it. Carolers stood in the center of a roundabout with their songbooks open. Even through the noise of the traffic, Emma could hear the harmonic blend of voices. It was lovely and peaceful and festive—

and so was Christmas.... Just like it'd been when she was a kid growing up.

Emma thought about the women she'd met and the articles she'd written. Earleen had taught her to look at her mother and herself in an entirely different way. Pamela Collins had made her own choice, and that choice had been to remain in a failed marriage. Even though she knew Oliver was nothing like her father, Emma had been afraid of repeating her mother's mistakes. But she was her own woman, a masterpiece in her own right. From Sophie she'd learned about the value of compromise and the importance of recognizing what you want and making it part of your life. And Peggy had shown her how to live in the moment.

Fortified with enthusiasm, Emma drove to the local Wal-Mart and, using her Christmas bonus, bought lights and decorations for her tree. While she was there, she loaded up on groceries. Then she went to a local strip mall and did her first real Christmas shopping in years.

Nothing had been resolved with Oliver; still, she felt wonderful. Christmas music played loudly from her car radio as she arrived home and carried all her bags into the apartment. Boots jumped up and down with happiness at her homecoming.

She didn't stop to see if the red light was blinking on her answering machine. It didn't matter if Oliver had tried to return her call or not. Riding on the crest of her newborn appreciation for Christmas—and for him—she went directly to his apartment with Boots in tow. She didn't hesitate before she rang his doorbell.

He looked surprised to see her. He waited for her to speak.

She smiled warmly. "Hi."

"Hi, yourself," he repeated without much animation.

Her smile grew wider. "Merry Christmas."

His eyes widened. "Merry Christmas? The original Ms. Scrooge is wishing me Merry Christmas?"

"Oh, yes." With that, she launched herself into his arms and spread eager kisses over his face. She started with his cheek, gradually working her way to his mouth.

Sliding his arms around her waist, Oliver lifted her from the ground. His mouth hungrily covered hers. Somehow he managed to bring her into his apartment—Boots scurrying past them—and kick the door shut. Emma wrapped her arms around his neck and hung on tight. This was exactly where she wanted to be. If the fervor with which he returned her kisses was any indication, Oliver shared her feeling.

"Did you get my message?" she asked when she could breathe again.

"Did you get mine?"

"No."

His lips went back to hers. "I decided to give you another chance."

"Good." She kissed his jaw, then cradled his face between her hands so she could gaze into his eyes. "Can I still join you and your family for Christmas?"

Oliver's expression grew solemn. "Sorry, I've already asked another girl."

His answer shocked her until she realized he was teasing. Playfully she punched him in the ribs. "That wasn't funny."

Oliver laughed. Emma had always loved his robust laughter and closed her eyes to hold on to the sound of it as long as possible.

"Do you want to help me decorate the tree?" she asked.

"What?" Oliver pretended to stagger back, hand to his heart. "This is indeed a complete transformation. Sure."

"Also," she said, slipping her arm around his waist. "If I'm going to be joining your family for Christmas dinner, it's only polite that I bring something."

Oliver disagreed. "Mom won't hear of it. You're our guest."

"No, I insist. Besides, I've already been to the grocery store."

"Okay, okay. Bring whatever you want."

She tilted back her head. "Don't you want to know what I intend to make for your family?"

"Okay, tell me."

So she did. "Fruitcake, of course."

Epilogue

I'm not a fruitcake fan generally speaking, but then there's my mother's. She makes a fabulous, upscale fruitcake using a high-quality sherry. She bakes the cakes in November, wraps them in cheesecloth and lets them marinate for a couple of weeks, routinely adding sherry to keep them moist. Each year she sends me a few of her superb fruitcakes and they always disappear surprisingly quickly—especially for fruitcake!
—Robert Carter, executive chef at Peninsula Grill in Charleston, South Carolina

A year later

Her mother had been right; Christmas was good for the human spirit.

"Emma, would you take this out to the table?" Oliver's mother asked, handing her a bowl piled high with fluffy mashed potatoes. She didn't wait for a response before she gave Oliver's sister, Laurel, a second bowl, and picked up a third, filled with Brussels sprouts, herself. Walking in single file, the Hamilton women brought the serving dishes to the huge dining room table for Christmas dinner.

A turkey, roasted to golden perfection, rested on a huge oval platter at the far end of the table for Oliver's father to carve. Nieces and nephews, plus dogs and cats, raced around the house with sounds of glee.

Oliver was talking to his father but glanced up when she entered the room. They exchanged a smile. For the second year in a row, she'd joined his family for the holiday festivities. Only this year, Emma was a member of the family. Oliver and Emma had been married in June, two months after Phoebe and Walt. Following the reception, they flew—yes, flew—to Hawaii for a two-week honeymoon. Thankfully, their flight was aboard a 747 and not Oliver's Cessna Caravan.

With Oliver's urging and support, Emma had called her father. That first conversation had been tense, and she'd realized Bret Collins wished their relationship was different. To her surprise, he showed up for the wedding. He attended the reception, too, and made a point of meeting Emma's in-laws. Though he'd left shortly afterward, they'd talked a number of times since. In fact, he'd called that very morning to wish her and Oliver a merry Christmas.

It was a start.

Emma's journalism career was progressing, and although she was still responsible for her share of obituaries, she routinely wrote feature articles for *The Examiner.* Walt sometimes offered suggestions, but lately he'd allowed her to write whatever she chose. Emma's work had even garnered attention from some of the larger newspapers in the area. For now, she was content to continue writing for *The Examiner.* She enjoyed living in Puyallup, home of the Western Washington Fairgrounds and the Victorian Christmas extravaganza. She'd covered both events for the paper this year.

Oliver's freight business was doing well, too. He'd managed to pick up another exclusive contract with an Alaska fishing company. Five days a week, he flew in fresh salmon and other seafood to restaurants in Washington and Oregon. Emma was proud of his company's success. In November Oliver had hired another pilot and leased a second plane in order to meet demand. He advertised regularly in *The Examiner,* and Emma wrote all his ads.

Oliver's mother stepped out of the kitchen and removed her apron, signaling the start of the Christmas meal. "Ollie, dinner's on the table," she called to her husband. The family migrated to the dining room.

Oliver and Emma stood in front of their chairs as his sisters and brother and their families found their way to the table. Emma smiled, admiring the meal. In addition to turkey and all the fixings, there were a number of salads and vegetable dishes, plus fresh-baked rolls still warm from the oven. Desserts lined the sideboard. For the second year in a row, Emma had brought fruit-cake—three varieties this year, all made from the recipes contributed by the three women she'd interviewed last Christmas.

When the family surrounded the table, they all joined hands and Oliver's father offered a simple grace. Emma closed her eyes; at the end of the prayer she whispered a heartfelt "Amen." She was in love, and she felt as though she'd reclaimed herself—and reclaimed the joy of Christmas.

With dinner came a lot of good-natured teasing between Oliver and his younger brother and three younger sisters. Although he was the oldest, he'd been the last to marry.

"I don't know how you put up with him," Laurel said, speaking to Emma.

"You wouldn't believe the stuff he pulled on us as kids," Carrie added.

"Do you remember the time Mom made you babysit, and Donny put a huge hole in the living room wall?" Jenny asked Oliver.

"Remember it?" he said with a groan. "I knew the minute Mom saw that hole, I'd be grounded my entire senior year."

Oliver's mother waved her fork at him and turned

to Emma. "Do you know what he did? My genius son rearranged the living room furniture so the wall was covered."

"I hid the hole," Oliver said in a stage whisper.

"Then he demanded extra pay because he claimed he did housework in addition to babysitting," his mother reminded them.

The whole family laughed.

Laurel spoke to Emma again. "Okay, you've been married to our big brother for six months now."

"Six months," Donny repeated. "Leslie was pregnant a month after our wedding. What's the problem?"

Oliver laughed. "Trust me, there's no problem."

This was her cue, Emma realized. "We're due in July."

Amid cheers and gasps, Oliver's parents rose to their feet and applauded. His siblings and their spouses joined in.

Oliver slipped his arm around her shoulders. "I told you they'd be happy," he murmured.

"You'd think this was their first grandchild," Emma said, overwhelmed by the family's reaction to their news. She'd never known families could be like this.

By the end of a memorable Christmas Day, Emma was tired and ready to go home. After a series of hugs and promises to meet again soon, Oliver steered her to the car parked out front, his arm protectively around her. The dogs followed obediently in their wake.

"It's a bit overpowering, isn't it?" he said.

"What?" she asked.

"My family, when we're all together."

"They're wonderful, each and every one." Oliver's sisters were among her closest friends. Her circle of family, friends and acquaintances had increased from the day she'd met him.

"They love you, too." He opened the car door for her and helped her inside. Oscar and Boots piled into the back.

As they neared their newly constructed home, Oliver glanced at her. Emma's eyes were closed, her head back against the leather seat. "You've really taken to Christmas," he said. "Hard to believe that just over a year ago you didn't want anything to do with it. Now look at you."

Emma opened her eyes and smiled. Their home was decorated with not one, but two, Christmas trees. The second, a smaller one, was for the dogs. She'd written a series of articles about Christmas customs around the world. And she'd started baking right after Thanksgiving. As Oliver had said last year, the transformation had been complete.

"I don't know what to tell you," she said with a laugh, "except to repeat what my mother told me."

"And what would that be?" he asked, a smile in his voice.

"There's something special about Christmas."

★ ★ ★ ★ ★

Still in the holiday spirit?
Keep reading for a sparkling bonus story from
Debbie Macomber — a special gift from us to you.
It is Christmas, after all!

Chapter One

Greg Bennett had always hated Christmas.

He'd never believed in "goodwill toward men" and all that other sentimental garbage. Christmas in the city—any city—was the epitome of commercialism, and San Francisco was no exception. Here it was, barely December, and department-store windows had been filled with automated elves and tinsel-hung Christmas trees since before Thanksgiving!

Most annoying, in Greg's opinion, was the hustle and bustle of holiday shoppers, all of whom seemed to be unnaturally cheerful. That only made his own mood worse.

He wouldn't be in the city at all if he wasn't desperately in need of a bank loan. Without it, he'd be forced to lay off what remained of his crew by the end of the

year. He'd have to close the winery's doors. His vines—
and literally decades of work—had been wiped out by
fan leaf disease, devastating the future of his vineyard
and crippling him financially.

He'd spent the morning visiting one financial insti-
tution after another. Like a number of other growers,
he'd applied at the small-town banks in the Napa Valley and been unsuccessful. His wasn't the only vineyard
destroyed by the disease—although, for reasons no one
really understood, certain vineyards had been spared
the blight. For a while there'd been talk of low-inter-
est loans from the federal government, but they hadn't
materialized. Apparently the ruin hadn't been thorough
enough to warrant financial assistance. For Greg that
news definitely fell into the category of cold comfort.

It left him in a dilemma. No loan—no replanted
vines. Without the vines there would be no grapes,
without the grapes, no wine, and without the winery,
no Gregory Bennett.

What he needed after a morning such as this, he
decided, was a good stiff drink and the company of a
charming female companion, someone who could help
him forget his current troubles. He walked into the
St. Francis, the elegant San Francisco hotel, and found
himself facing a twenty-foot Christmas tree decorated
with huge gold balls and plush red velvet bows. Disgusted, he looked away and hurried toward the bar.

The bartender seemed to sense his urgency. "What

can I get you?" he asked promptly. He wore a name tag that identified him as Don.

Greg sat down on a stool. "Get me a martini," he said. If it hadn't been so early in the day, he would have asked for a double, but it was barely noon and he still had to drive home. He didn't feel any compelling reason to return. The house, along with everything else in his life, was empty. Oh, the furniture was all there—Tess hadn't taken that—but he was alone, more alone than he could ever remember being.

Tess, his third and greediest wife, had left him six months earlier. The attorneys were fighting out the details of their divorce, and at three hundred dollars an hour, neither lawyer had much incentive to rush into court.

Nevertheless, Tess was gone. He silently toasted eliminating her from his life and vowed not to make the mistake of marrying again. Three wives was surely sufficient evidence that he wasn't the stay-married kind.

Yet he missed Tess, he mused with some regret—and surprise. Well, maybe not Tess exactly, but a warm body in his bed. By his side. Even at the time, he'd known it was foolish to marry her. He certainly *should* have known, after the messy end of his second marriage. His first had lasted ten years, and he'd split with Jacquie over… Hell if he could remember. Something stupid. It'd always been something stupid.

"You out shopping?" Don the bartender asked as he delivered a bowl of peanuts.

Greg snorted. "Not on your life."

The younger man smiled knowingly. "Ah, you're one of those."

"You mean someone who's got common sense. What is it with people and Christmas? Normal, sane human beings become sentimental idiots." A year ago, when he and Tess had been married less than eighteen months, she'd made it clear she expected diamonds for Christmas. Lots of them. She'd wanted him to make her the envy of her friends. That was what he got for marrying a woman nineteen years his junior. A pretty blonde with a figure that could stop traffic. Next time around he'd simply move the woman into his house and send her packing when he grew bored with her. No more marriages—not for him. He didn't need any more legal entanglements.

Just then a blond beauty entered the bar, and Greg did a double take. For half a heartbeat, he thought it was Tess. Thankfully he was wrong. Blond, beautiful and probably a bitch. The last part didn't bother him, though—especially now, when he could use a little distraction. He'd be sixty-one his next birthday, but he was trim and fit, and still had all his hair—gone mostly gray, what people called "distinguished." In fact, he could easily pass for ten years younger. His good looks had taken him a long way in this world, and he'd worked hard to maintain a youthful appearance.

"Welcome," he greeted her, swerving around on his stool to give her his full attention.

"Hello."

Her answering smile told him she wasn't averse to his company. Yes, she might well provide a distraction. If everything worked out, he might stay in town overnight. Considering the morning he'd had, he deserved a little comfort. He wasn't interested in anything serious—just a light flirtation to take his mind off his troubles, a dalliance to momentarily distract him.

"Are you meeting someone?" Greg asked.

"Not really," she said, her voice sultry and deep.

Greg noted the packages. "Been shopping, I see."

She nodded, and when the bartender walked over to her table, Greg said, "Put it on my tab."

"Thanks," she said in that same sultry voice. He was even more impressed when she asked for a glass of Bennett Wine. A pinot noir.

He slipped off the stool and approached her table. "I'm Greg."

"Cherry Adams."

He liked her name; it suited her. "Do you mind if I join you?"

"Go ahead. Why not?"

The day was already looking brighter. He pulled out a chair and sat down. They made small talk for a few minutes, exchanged pleasantries. He didn't mention his last name because he didn't want her to make the connection and have their conversation weighed down by the problems at Bennett Wines. However, it soon became clear that she was knowledgeable about wine—and very flattering about his 1996 pinot noir. Tess had been an idiot on the subject, despite being married to the owner of a winery. She didn't know the difference between chablis and chardonnay. And she never did understand why he couldn't call his own sparkling wine champagne, no matter how many times he told her the name could only be used for sparkling wines from the Champagne region of France.

After another glass of wine for her and a second martini for him, Greg suggested lunch. Cherry hesitated and gazed down at her hands. "Sorry, but I've got a nail appointment."

"You could cancel it," Greg suggested, trying to hint that they could find more entertaining ways to occupy themselves. He didn't want her to think he was being pushy. Later, after lunch, he'd surprise her and announce who he really was. He was pleased—no, delighted—by her interest in him, particularly because she didn't know he was the man responsible for the wine she'd described as "exquisite." He grinned; wait till he told her. Cherry's interest proved what he'd been telling himself ever since Tess had walked out on him. He was still young, still vital, still sexy.

That was when it happened.

The look that crossed Cherry's face conveyed her thoughts as clearly as if she'd said them aloud. She wasn't interested. Oh, sure, he was good for a few drinks, especially since he was buying. Good for an hour of conversation. But that was all.

"I really do have to go," Cherry said as she reached for her shopping bags. "My nails are a mess. Thanks for the, uh, company and the wine, though."

"Don't mention it," Greg muttered, watching her leave. He was still reeling from the blow to his pride.

Soon afterward, he left, too. He'd never been one to take rejection well, mainly because he'd had so little experience of it.

After two martinis he knew he wasn't in any condition to drive. So he left his car in the lot and started to walk. With no destination in mind, he wandered down the crowded street, trying to keep his distance from all those happy little shoppers. His stomach growled and his head hurt, but not nearly as much as his ego. Every time he thought about the look on Cherry's face, he cringed. Okay, okay, she'd been too young. At a guess he'd say she was no more than thirty.

However, Greg knew a dozen women her age who would leap at the opportunity to spend a day and a night with him. He was suave, sophisticated and rich. Not as rich as he'd once been—would be again, as soon as he got this latest mess straightened out. *If* he got it straightened out. The truth was, he stood on the brink of losing everything.

Desperate to escape his dark thoughts, he began to walk at a brisker pace. He made an effort not to think, not to acknowledge his fears and worries, concentrating, instead, on the movement of his feet, the rhythm of his breath. He turned corner after corner and eventually found himself on a side street dominated by an imposing brick church.

He paused in front of it. A church. Now that was a laugh. He remembered how his mother had dragged him and his brother, Phil, to service every Sunday. He'd even attended services while he was in college. But he hadn't darkened the door of a church since... Catherine.

She'd been his sweetheart, his *lover,* during college—until he'd broken it off. No, abandoned her. That was a more honest description of what he'd done. The years had numbed his guilt, and he rarely thought of her anymore. Funny how a relationship that had ended more than thirty-five years ago could suddenly rise up to haunt him. He'd been a senior the last time he'd seen Catherine. They'd been madly in love. Then she'd told him she was pregnant and Greg had panicked. About to graduate, about to start his life, he'd done what had seemed sensible at the time; he'd fled.

Unable to face her, he'd written Catherine a letter and told her he was leaving. She should do whatever she wanted about the baby. It'd been cowardly of him, but he was just a kid back then; he'd long since stopped berating himself over it. He'd never heard from her again. He didn't know what she'd done about the baby. Didn't want to know. Abortions hadn't been legal at the time, but there were ways of getting rid of an unwanted pregnancy even then. His mother hadn't ever learned why his relationship with Catherine had ended, but Phil knew. That was the beginning of the estrangement between Greg and his brother.

Almost without realizing it, Greg began to move up the church steps. He blamed it on the throng of shoppers crowding in around him. All he wanted was a few moments of peace and quiet. A chance to think.

He hesitated on the top step. He didn't belong in a church, not the way he'd lived. And yet...

His life was empty and he was old enough to recognize that. But at sixty, it was a bit late. For most of his adult life, he'd followed the path of least resistance, put his own interests above those of other people. He'd believed that was the basis of prosperity, of success. Deserting Catherine was where it had started.

She'd been the first of his regrets. Matthias was the second. And then his mother...

Matthias Jamison was his father's cousin and an employee at the winery. Greg's parents had divorced when he was in high school, and he and Phil had spent summers with their father at the vineyard. Although the younger of the two, Greg was the one who'd been drawn to the family business. He'd spent hour after hour there, learning everything he could about wine and wine making.

Ten years his senior, Matthias had taken Greg under his wing. What John Bennett didn't teach Greg about wine making, Matthias did. His father had also insisted Greg get a business degree, and he'd been right. Several years later, when he died, Greg bought out Phil's half to become sole owner and worked with Matthias operating the winery.

The wine had always been good. What the business needed was an aggressive advertising campaign. People couldn't order the Bennett label if they'd never heard of it. The difficulty with Greg's ideas was the huge financial investment they demanded. Commissioning sophisticated full-page ads and placing them in upscale food magazines, attending wine expositions throughout the world—it had all cost money. He'd taken a gamble, which was just starting to pay off when Matthias came to him, needing a loan.

Mary, Matthias's wife of many years, had developed a rare form of blood cancer. The experimental drug that might save her life wasn't covered by their health insurance. The cost of the medication was threatening to bankrupt Matthias; his savings were gone and no bank would lend him money. He'd asked Greg for help. After everything the older man had done for him and for his family, Greg knew he owed Matthias that and more.

The decision had been agonizing. Bennett Wines was just beginning to gain recognition; sales had doubled and tripled. But Greg's plans were bigger than that. He'd wanted to help Matthias, but there was no guarantee the treatment would be effective. So he'd turned Matthias down. Mary had died a few months later, when conventional treatments failed, and a bitter Matthias had left Bennett Wines and moved to Washington state.

Generally Greg didn't encourage friendships. He tended to believe that friends took advantage of you, that they resented your success. It was every man for himself, in Greg's view. Still, Matthias had been the best friend he'd ever had. Because of what happened, the two men hadn't spoken in fifteen years.

Greg could have used Matthias's expertise in dealing with the blight that had struck his vines, but he was too proud to give him the opportunity to slam the door in his face. To refuse him the way he'd refused Matthias all those years ago.

No, Greg definitely wasn't church material. Whatever had possessed him to think he should go into this place, seek solace here, he couldn't fathom.

He was about to turn away when he noticed that the church doors were wide open. Had they been open all this time? He supposed they must have been. It was almost as if he was being invited inside…. He shook his head, wondering where *that* ridiculous thought had come from. Nevertheless, he slowly walked in.

The interior was dim and his eyes took a moment to adjust. He saw that the sanctuary was huge, with two rows of pews facing a wide altar. Even the church was decorated for the holidays. Pots of red and white poinsettias were arranged on the altar, and a row of gaily decorated Christmas trees stood behind it. A large cross hung suspended from the ceiling.

An organ sat off to one side, along with a sectioned space for the choir. Greg hadn't stopped to notice which denomination this church was. Nor did he care.

Although his mother had been an ardent church-goer, Greg had hated it, found it meaningless. But Phil seemed to eat this religious stuff up, just like their mother had.

"Okay," Greg said aloud. None of this whispering business for him. "The door was open. I came inside. You want me to tell you I made a mess of my life? Fine, I screwed up. I could've done better. Is that what you were waiting to hear? Is that what you wanted me to say? I said it. Are you happy now?"

His words reverberated, causing him to retreat a step.

And as he did, his life suddenly overwhelmed him. His failures, his shortcomings, his mistakes came roaring at him like an avalanche, jerking him off his feet. He seemed to tumble backward through the years. The force of it was too much and he slumped into a pew, the weight of his past impossible to bear. He leaned forward and buried his face in his hands.

"Can you forgive me, Mama?" he whispered brokenly. "Is there any way I can make up for what I did—not being there for you? When you needed me…"

He deserved every rotten thing that was happening to him. If he couldn't get a loan, if he lost the winery, it would be what he deserved. All of it.

Greg wouldn't have recognized his words as a prayer. But, they wove their way upward, past the church altar, past the suspended crucifix, toward the bell tower and church steeple. Once free of the building, they flew heavenward, through the clouds and beyond the sky, landing with a crash on the cluttered desk of the Archangel Gabriel.

"Well, well," the archangel said, a little surprised and more than a little pleased. "What do we have here?"

Chapter Two

The Archangel Gabriel arched his white brows as he reviewed Greg Bennett's file. A very thick file. "Well, it's about time," he muttered, and dutifully recorded the prayer request.

"I certainly agree with you there," a soft female voice murmured in response.

Gabriel didn't have to look up to see who'd joined him. That angelic voice was all too familiar. Shirley was visiting, and where Shirley was, Goodness and Mercy were sure to follow. His three favorite trouble-makers—heaven help him. Without having to ask, he knew what she wanted. The trio had been pestering him for three years about a return trip to earth.

"Hello, Shirley," Gabriel said without much enthusiasm. The truth was, he'd always been partial to Shirley, Goodness and Mercy, although he dared not let it show. Their escapades on earth were notorious in the corridors of paradise and had created an uproar on more than one occasion.

"We've decided you seem frazzled," Goodness said, popping up next to her friend. She rested her arms on Gabriel's desk, studying him avidly.

"Overworked," Mercy agreed, appearing beside the other two.

"And we're here to help." Shirley walked around the front of his desk and gave him a pitying look.

"We feel your pain," Goodness told him.

If she hadn't sounded so sincere, Gabriel would have laughed outright. He was still tempted to tell her to cut the psychobabble, but knew that wouldn't do any good. As it was, he sighed and leaned back in his chair.

"So—what *can* we do to help?" Mercy inquired with a serenity few would question.

"Help?" he asked. "You can help me most by participating in the heavenly host again this year."

"We've already done that for three years," Goodness complained with a slight pout, crossing her arms. "It's just no fun to be one in a cast of thousands."

"We want to go back to earth," Shirley explained. Of the three, she was the most plainspoken. Gabriel knew he could count on her to tell him the truth. She did her utmost to keep the other two in line, but could only hold out for so long before she succumbed to temptation herself.

"I love humans," Goodness said, hands clasped as she gazed longingly toward earth.

"Me, too," Mercy was quick to add. "Where else in the universe would anyone assume God is dead and Elvis is alive?"

Gabriel successfully hid a smile. "Even with the best of intentions, you three have never been able to keep your wings to yourselves."

"True." Shirley nodded in agreement. "But remember we're angels, not saints."

"All the more reason to make you stay in heaven where you belong," Gabriel argued.

The objections came fast and furious.

"But you need us this year!"

"More than ever, Gabriel. You've got far more work than you can handle!"

"You're overburdened!"

True enough. As always, Christmas was his busiest time of year, and Gabriel's desk was flooded with thousands upon thousands of prayer requests. No denying it, human beings were the most difficult of God's subjects. Obtuse, demanding and contrary. Many of them flung prayer requests at heaven without once considering that humans played a role in solving their own problems. The hard part was getting them to recognize that they had lessons to learn before their prayer requests could be granted. God-directed solutions often came from within themselves. Gabriel's task, with the help of his other prayer ambassadors, was to show these proud stubborn creatures the way.

"Do you have any requests from children?" Shirley asked. As a former guardian angel, she enjoyed working with youngsters the most.

"Anyone in need of a little Mercy?" Mercy prodded.

"Any good faithful souls who could use a bit of angelic guidance?" Goodness asked.

"Here," Gabriel said abruptly as he shoved Greg Bennett's prayer request at them.

Gabriel didn't know what had possessed him. Frustration, perhaps. Then again, it could have been something far more powerful. It could have been the very hand of God. "This request will require all three of you. Read it over, do your homework and get back to me. You might decide that singing with the heavenly host doesn't sound so bad, after all."

He grinned sheepishly as they fluttered away, eager to discover everything they could about this sad human and the sorry mess he'd made of his life.

In truth Gabriel half expected they'd choose to return to the heavenly choir; if they did he wouldn't blame them. Greg Bennett's case would be a challenge for the most experienced prayer ambassadors—let alone these three. Once Shirley, Goodness and Mercy had the opportunity to read his file, they were bound to see that.

★ ★ ★

The trio gathered around the file detailing the life of Greg Bennett. Shirley noted that their excited chatter had quickly died down as they read. The oldest and most mature, she could see through Gabriel's ploy. The archangel expected them to give up before they started. To tell him how right he was and scurry back to choir practice. In light of what she'd learned about Greg Bennett, perhaps that would be for the best.

"Oh, my," Goodness whispered. "He abandoned his college sweetheart when she was pregnant."

"Deserted his best friend in his hour of need."

"Look what he did to his own *mother!*"

"To his mother?"

Shirley nodded. "Greg Bennett is a—"

"Scumbag," Mercy supplied.

"He's arrogant."

"Selfish."

"And conceited."

"It's going to take a whole bunch of miracles to whip this poor boy into shape."

Shirley had no argument there. "I'm afraid Greg Bennett is more than any of us could handle," she said sadly.

Goodness and Mercy glanced at each other. "She's joking, isn't she?"

"No, I'm not," Shirley said on a disparaging note. "You read for yourself what kind of man he is. Frankly,

I feel someone else, someone who's got more experience with humans and their frailties, would be better equipped to deal with the likes of Mr. Bennett."

"Oh, fiddlesticks!" Goodness cried.

"We can do it," Mercy contended with considerably more confidence than the success of her earlier exploits might have warranted.

"We all know Gabriel did this on purpose," Goodness said. Apparently she hadn't been fooled, either. "He assumed that once we see what a mess Greg's made of his life, we'll figure it's hopeless and slink back to the choir. Well, I, for one, have no intention of spending another Christmas singing my lungs out over the fields of Bethlehem. To be so close to earth and yet so far…"

Mercy giggled but appeared to be in full agreement. "Come on, Shirley, this is our one and only chance to return to earth. Okay, so you're right. Greg Bennett isn't exactly a believer in God's love, but God does love him. Heaven knows he needs help."

Shirley was adamant. "More than we can give him."

"Don't be such a pessimist," Goodness chided. "If nothing else, we can steer him in the right direction."

"San Francisco," Mercy said, tapping her cheek. "There are ships in San Francisco, aren't there?"

Shirley could already see trouble brewing. "You've got to promise to stay away from the shipyard," she said heatedly. It'd taken them years to live down what had happened at the Bremerton Naval Shipyard in Washington state. The news crew that covered the repositioning of two aircraft carriers might as well have been reporting directly to heaven, what with all the attention the incident had received.

"Okay, I promise, no shipyard," Mercy said. Shirley was appeased until she thought she saw her fellow angel wink at Goodness. Oh, my, if they took the Bennett case, then this was going to be some Christmas. On the other hand...

"Where are you headed?" Goodness called out when Shirley broke away.

"I'm going back to tell Gabriel we'll take the job. Just don't make me sorry I agreed to this."

"Would we do that?" Mercy asked, the picture of angelic innocence.

Shirley had a very good reason for feeling skeptical, but an even better reason for tackling this stint on earth. She wanted out of the choir as much as her two friends did. A human, even one who happened to have more than his share of frailties, wasn't going to stop her.

"Hi, Dad!" Michael Thorpe bounded enthusiastically into the hospital clinic, his eyes sparkling.

Dr. Edward Thorpe looked up from the chart he was reading and smiled at the sight of his son. His wife, Janice, five months pregnant, hurried to keep up with the energetic boy.

The six-year-old raced into his arms and Edward lifted him high above his head. Seeing his own healthy happy son was exactly what he needed. Much of his morning had been spent with another youngster, Tanner Westley, who was ten and suffering from a rare form of leukemia. Edward was an oncologist who specialized in childhood cancers; his work had recently garnered the interest of the *San Francisco Herald*. Just today, a reporter had interviewed him for a piece the paper was running on the urgent need for bone-marrow donors. The story would include a photograph of Tanner. Most members of the public didn't seem to understand that they had the opportunity to save lives by testing to become donors. The only thing required at this stage was a simple blood test. The article would make a strongly worded plea for bone-marrow donors to help children such as Tanner.

The reporter felt the timing was good. People seemed more generous with their time and money over the Christmas period. Edward hoped they'd be equally giving about submitting to a blood test.

"Hello, darling," his wife said.

"Is it lunchtime already?" With the interview and Tanner Westley's additional tests, his morning had flown.

Janice glanced at her watch. "Actually, we're late."

"Mom and I were shopping." Michael rolled his eyes as if to say how much that had bored him. Edward hid a smile. An intolerance for shopping was something he had in common with his son.

"Can you still join us for lunch?" Janice asked.

Now it was Edward's turn to glance at his watch. "If you don't mind eating in the cafeteria." He needed to be within a few minutes of Tanner, who was starting a new chemotherapy session today.

"We can eat in the cafeteria, can't we, Mom?" Michael tugged at his mother's arm. "Their ice-cream machine is way cool."

"Okay—I'm convinced," Janice responded good-naturedly as the three of them headed toward the elevator.

"Why are we here?" Goodness demanded, her voice unnaturally high. "You *know* I don't like hospitals."

"I didn't bring us here. Shirley did."

"Would you two stop it?" Shirley sighed in exasperation. Goodness and Mercy were enough to try the patience of a saint, let alone another angel. "That's Greg Bennett's son."

"Which one?"

"The cancer specialist," Shirley said, thinking it should have been obvious.

"You mean he's Catherine's child?"

"Right." It was Gabriel who'd directed her to the hospital, but she hadn't told the others that. As far as she was concerned, they would receive information strictly on a need-to-know basis. It was safer that way.

"But he's wonderful!"

"Unlike his birth father," Goodness said under her breath.

Shirley agreed completely. "Greg Bennett broke Catherine's heart, you know." The file had told her that, and ever since, she'd found it a struggle to care in the slightest about Greg and his vineyard.

"She loved him deeply," Mercy added, shaking her head. "When Greg turned his back on her, she was devastated."

"Then she gave birth to Edward and raised him on her own, and had trouble trusting men again for a very long time."

"She didn't marry until Edward was nearly eight." Shirley recounted the facts as she remembered them. "But she's very happy now...."

"Does she have other children?"

"A daughter, who's a child psychologist," Shirley supplied. "They meet every Friday for lunch on Fisherman's Wharf."

"That's on the waterfront, isn't it?" Mercy brightened.

Shirley cast her fellow angel a quelling look. She didn't want to say it, but Mercy's obsession with ships was beginning to bother her. Oh, my, she didn't know how she was going to get through this holiday season with Goodness and Mercy and still have any kind of effect on Greg Bennett. As much fun as it was to enjoy the things of this earth, they were on an important mission and didn't have time to get sidetracked.

"Meanwhile, Greg has had three wives and each one of them looks exactly like Catherine," Goodness pointed out.

Shirley hadn't recognized that, but as soon as Goodness made the observation, she knew it was true. "Only he doesn't see there's a pattern here," she murmured.

"He hasn't opened his eyes wide enough to see it," Goodness said.

"Yet." Mercy crossed her arms in a determined way that seemed to suggest she'd take great delight in telling him.

"Yet?" Shirley raised her eyebrows in warning, but continued her summary of Greg's failings. "His only child, a son he deserted before he was born, grew up to become a noted cancer specialist, while Greg has squandered his life on wine and women."

"Yes, and while he was trying to pick up some blond babe in a fancy bar, Edward was treating a ten-year-old leukemia patient," Mercy said in a scornful voice.

Goodness grew quiet, which was always a dangerous sign.

"What are you thinking?" Shirley asked her.

"I'm thinking about Catherine," Goodness confessed.

"He hasn't seen her since college," Shirley put in.

"But it seems to me that Greg's been searching for

her in every woman he's met," Goodness said thought-fully.

"Certainly every woman he marries," Mercy added, not concealing her disgust.

"And?" Shirley prodded. "What's your point, Good-ness?"

"Well...perhaps we should do something to help make it happen."

"What do you mean?"

"Well, if he's looking for Catherine, which he *seems* to be doing, we can make sure he finds her. He should see what she's done with her life, how happy she is..."

"Goodness, I don't think that's such a good idea," Shirley protested. "You know the rules as well as I do, and we're not supposed to interfere in human lives."

"Who said anything about interfering?"

"There isn't any rule against sending humans in a particular direction, is there?" Mercy asked.

"No, but..." Shirley began. Goodness and Mercy, however, had disappeared before the words left her lips.

Oh, dear. Already it was starting. Already she'd lost control.

Shirley raced after the other two, hoping she could stop them in time.

Chapter Three

Greg had remained in the church longer than he'd intended. He felt a little foolish sitting there in that quiet darkened place all alone. It was almost as if...as if he was waiting for something to happen. Or for someone to appear and speak to him—which, of course, was ridiculous. God was hardly going to drop down and have a heart-to-heart with someone like him.

Other than that unaccountable feeling of anticipation, nothing out of the ordinary had occurred during the time he'd been in this church. Nevertheless, the experience had calmed him. For that half hour, Greg was able to set his troubles aside. He'd never been one to dwell on the negatives; it was far easier to push his regrets and worries from his mind, pretend they didn't exist. Anyway, he'd always managed to surmount his business problems, even when the vineyard had suffered from other disasters—flooding or frost or even fire.

Only this time he had a gut feeling that there wasn't going to be any last-minute rescue. This one was different. If some kind of solution didn't turn up soon, he was going to lose everything.

At sixty he was too old to start over.

After he left the church, he began walking again, his thoughts heavy. It probably wasn't a good idea to drive yet, so he aimlessly wandered the streets. He considered the few options he had. He could declare bankruptcy. Or he could throw himself on his brother's mercy. Phil had become a vice president of Pacific Union, one of the largest banks in the state. He could certainly pull strings to help Greg secure a loan.

But they hadn't spoken since their mother's death. Greg didn't blame Phil for hating him, especially after what he'd done. Another regret. Another person who'd needed him—another person he'd failed. His own mother.

A sick feeling settled over him. He increased his pace as if he could outdistance his guilt. His mother might have forgiven him, but his brother hadn't. Their quarrel following the funeral had ended any chance Greg might have had of receiving Phil's help now.

Although he wasn't hungry, Greg decided to find some lunch. With food in his stomach to cut the effects of the alcohol, he could safely drive, and empty though it was, home had begun to seem mighty appealing.

He could buy a cup of chowder or a seafood sandwich along Fisherman's Wharf, so he hurried downhill toward the waterfront, his pace filled with sudden purpose. The wind was cold and brisk, and he gathered his coat around him as he neared the wharf. What on earth were all these people doing here? No doubt spending their money on useless junk for Christmas. Grumbling, he wove his way through the crowds toward the closest fish bar.

"There she is," Goodness whispered, pressing her face against the restaurant window.

"You found her?" Mercy sounded incredulous as she peered in the window, too. "Oh, my, Catherine really is lovely."

Shirley couldn't resist. She cupped her hands about her face and gazed through the smudged glass, too.

"Her daughter looks exactly like her," Mercy said.

Her friends were right, Shirley thought. Catherine was a classic beauty who carried herself with grace and elegance. Her daughter, whose name was Carrie, if she remembered correctly, strongly resembled her mother. It was like turning back the clock and seeing Catherine as the young college student who had loved and trusted Greg Bennett.

Shirley pinched her lips, disliking Greg Bennett more than ever. She wasn't one to suffer fools gladly.

"Greg Bennett needs a lot of help," she said, disheartened that their angelic talents were being wasted on a man who would neither acknowledge nor appreciate their endeavors.

Shirley figured that if the three of them stood directly in front of him in a full display of God's glory, Greg would turn around and head in the opposite direction.

"I bet Catherine didn't think so at the time, but the fact that Greg Bennett walked out on her was probably the best thing that could've happened. He's been a rotten husband to all three of his wives." Goodness shook her head in disgust. Apparently, she, too, was having difficulty finding him worthy of their assistance.

"What I don't understand," Mercy said, her expression thoughtful, "is why Gabriel would assign us someone who's so..." She floundered.

Goodness finished the sentence for her. "Impossible," she said. "Greg Bennett's *impossible*. And he doesn't care about God."

"But as we've discussed before, God cares about him, and so does Gabriel. Greg Bennett is the reason we're here," Shirley said. "The reason we had an opportunity to return to earth. It's our duty to make sure this is a Christmas he'll remember."

Both Goodness and Mercy stepped aside as Catherine and her daughter walked out of the restaurant, laughing and talking animatedly.

"You're right," Goodness agreed once mother and

daughter had passed. "I don't like Greg Bennett any more than either of you, but God loves him." She began to say something else, then stopped abruptly. Her deep blue eyes grew huge. "Oh—look at that!"

"At what?" Shirley demanded.

"You'll never guess who's here," Goodness said excitedly. "Right now!"

Shirley whirled about, almost afraid to look. It couldn't be—but she knew it had to be. "Greg Bennett."

"We've got to *do* something," Mercy insisted. "Think, everyone. We can't let an opportunity like this pass."

"No...no!" Shirley cried, but Goodness and Mercy were already moving toward a table covered with steaming cooked crabs. "Not the crabs," but it was too late.

These Friday luncheon dates with her daughter were a delightful part of Catherine Thorpe's week. The hour with Carrie always went by in a flash. Meeting her daughter gave her an excuse to linger in the downtown area, as well. San Francisco in December was a sight to behold, and she planned to finish up her afternoon with some holiday shopping. She loved spoiling her grandson, and with another grandchild due in April, her world was full.

"I'll see you and Dad on Sunday, then," Carrie said as they strolled toward her office building.

"Bring Jason with you," Catherine urged. She knew her daughter well enough to recognize that her current boyfriend was someone special.

"Mother," Carrie chided, "I don't—"

She was interrupted by a terrible clang. For no apparent reason, a table full of freshly cooked crabs toppled over, scattering them in every direction. Most of the contents slid across the pavement toward a strikingly attractive older man who leaped out of the way with enviable dexterity.

Catherine recognized Greg instantly, but she soon discovered that his gaze was focused on Carrie. He frowned, as if confused.

"Catherine?"

Carrie turned toward her mother and Greg's gaze followed. Catherine looked him full in the face, was looking at him for the first time in thirty-five years. Her lungs felt frozen and for a moment she couldn't breathe.

So this was Greg.

During the past decades Catherine had sometimes wondered how she'd react if she ever saw him again. Now she knew. Her mouth went dry, and the remembered pain of what he'd done made it difficult to swallow.

"Mom?"

Carrie's voice sounded as if it was coming from a great distance.

Catherine had to make a concerted effort to pull her attention back to her daughter.

"You look like you've seen a ghost," Carrie said worriedly.

"I'm fine," Catherine assured her daughter, but in fact, she *was* seeing a ghost. The ghost of a man who had destroyed her ability to love and trust. Time had dulled her bitterness toward Greg Bennett, had changed her feelings, but even all these years couldn't minimize the shock of seeing him so unexpectedly.

Before she could decide if she should approach Greg or ignore him, he took a step toward her, then hesitated. Catherine remained still. He slowly came closer until they stood face-to-face.

A flurry of activity went on about them as several people scurried to pick up the spilled crabs, but Catherine barely noticed.

"Catherine." Greg's voice was low, a little shaky.

"You know my mother?" Carrie asked, taking Catherine's arm protectively.

"Greg's an old friend," Catherine explained when it became apparent that Greg wasn't answering. She saw the way he stared at her daughter, and then she understood why. "Greg, this is my twenty-five-year-old daughter, Carrie Thorpe."

He picked up her message quickly. This wasn't his child, his daughter, and to his credit his recovery was smooth. "You're just as beautiful as your mother. When I first saw you I thought you *were* your mother."

Carrie blushed at the praise. "People tell me that all the time." She suddenly glanced at her watch. "Oh, no. I hope you'll forgive me, but I have to rush back to work."

"Of course," Greg said as Carrie turned away.

"Goodbye, darling," Catherine called after her. "We'll see you and Jason Sunday for dinner."

When she was gone, Catherine looked at Greg. She'd always known this might happen, that she'd encounter Greg again, but now that she had, she wasn't sure what to do or what to say.

Greg seemed equally flustered. "It's been…a lot of years."

She gave a quick nod.

"Would you care to sit down?" he asked, then offered her a shaky smile. "Frankly, my knees feel like they're about to give out on me."

Catherine didn't feel much steadier herself. "That sounds like a good idea."

Greg led her to a sidewalk café, and when the waiter appeared, he ordered coffee for both of them. Although she normally drank her coffee black, Catherine added sugar to help her recover from the shock.

"Does Carrie have any older siblings?" Greg asked after a moment of stilted silence.

"A brother... I...had a boy seven months after you left," she said.

"You kept the baby?"

"Yes."

"You raised him?"

"Yes."

"Alone?"

She merely nodded this time, her throat thickening with the memory of the hardships she'd endured in those early years—the long hours, the hard work, the sleepless nights. "I...married when Edward was eight," she managed after a while, "and a year later Larry adopted him."

"So I have a son."

"No," Catherine told him, but without malice. "You are the biological father of a child. A wonderful young man who matured without the opportunity of ever knowing you. Without your ever knowing him."

Greg stared down at his coffee. "I was young. Stupid."

"Afraid," Catherine added softly. "We both were."

"But you weren't the one who ran away."

Catherine's laugh was wry. "I couldn't. I was the one carrying the baby."

Greg briefly closed his eyes. "I regret what I did, Catherine. I wanted to know what happened, but was afraid to find out."

"I know."

He looked at her then, as if he found it difficult to believe what she was saying.

Catherine glanced away. "It happened a very long time ago."

"I'm so sorry." He choked out the words, his voice raw with emotion.

"Don't say it," she whispered.

His face revealed his doubt, his confusion.

"You don't need to apologize, Greg. I forgave you years ago. You didn't realize it at the time and neither did I, but you gave me a beautiful gift in Edward. He was a wonderful child and a joy to my parents, who helped me raise him those first few years."

"You moved back home?"

"Until the baby was born. Then Mom watched him for me during the day while I finished college."

"It must have been difficult for you."

"It was." Catherine wasn't going to minimize the sacrifices demanded of her as a single mother. Those years had been bleak.

"Edward," Greg said. "After your father."

Catherine nodded, surprised he'd remembered her father's name.

"How could you forgive me?" Greg asked, sounding almost angry that she didn't harbor some deep resentment toward him. It was as if he expected her to punish him, to mete out her own form of justice right then and there.

"I had to forgive you, Greg, before I could get on with my life. After a while, the bitterness was more than I could endure. I had to leave it behind, and once I did, I discovered a true freedom. Soon afterward, I met Larry. We've been married for twenty-seven years now."

"But I don't deserve your forgiveness."

"That's not for me to say. But don't think forgiving you was easy, because it wasn't. When I first heard you'd left, I refused to accept it. I read your letter over and over—even though I couldn't take it in. I was convinced you'd be back. All you needed was time to sort everything out. I told myself you'd return to me and everything would be all right…but I had a rude awakening."

"I…wasn't ready to be a father. I guess I never was."

Catherine wondered if she'd misunderstood him. "You mean to say you never had children?"

"None," he said. "Three wives, but not one of them was interested in a family. For that matter, neither was I." He hesitated and his gaze skirted hers. "I was a selfish bastard when I left you. Unfortunately that hasn't changed."

She couldn't confirm or deny his words, for she no longer knew him.

"Would you mind telling me about Edward?" he asked.

Catherine leaned back and sipped her coffee. "In

many ways he's very like you. The physical resemblance is there, anyway."

Greg looked up and smiled faintly.

"He's six-two and muscular."

"How old? Thirty-four?"

"Thirty-five," she told him. "His birthday was last month on the twenty-ninth."

"Is he married?"

"Yes, and he has a son himself and another baby on the way. Next spring."

Greg's smile grew wider.

"He's a doctor."

"Really?" Greg seemed to have trouble believing it.

"My husband is, too." Perhaps it was time to remind Greg who Edward's father was. "Larry raised Edward, helped make him the kind of man he is. Larry's his father."

Greg shook his head. "I wouldn't interfere in his life."

It took a moment for his words to sink in—and then it occurred to her what he'd meant. "Are you asking to meet Edward?"

Greg didn't respond for a long time. His face pale and intent, he finally said, "Yes. Could I?"

Chapter Four

Matthias Jamison enjoyed puttering around in his greenhouse before breakfast. The mornings—that was when he missed Mary the most. She'd been gone fifteen years now, and not a day passed that he didn't think about the woman he'd loved for more than thirty years. Some men he'd known were quick to remarry after losing their wives. Not him. Mary had been the only woman for him, and no one else would ever fill the void left by her death.

The sunrise over the Cascade Mountains was glorious, the light creeping up over the horizon, then spilling across his western-Washington vineyard like the promise it was. The morning sun was a reassurance, the pledge of another day, another opportunity. Mary had been the one to teach him that, but he'd never fully appreciated her enthusiasm for mornings until it was too late. He wished he'd shared more sunrises with his beloved wife.

Their only grandson now suffered from the same rare form of leukemia that had claimed her prematurely. It looked as if Tanner, too, would die. Matthias's jaw tensed and he closed his eyes. How could a loving God let an innocent child suffer like this?

What made an untenable situation even worse was the fact that his daughter bore the burden alone. Her ex had done nothing for her or the boy, making Matthias feel doubly responsible, but beyond phone calls and the occasional visit, there was little he could do to help her from where he lived.

The phone rang and Matthias hurried back to the house, hoping for good news. "Hello," he answered in his usual gruff voice.

"It's Harry."

A longtime friend and vineyard owner from the Napa Valley. "A little early for you to be phoning, don't you think?" Matthias couldn't prevent his disappointment from showing. He'd been hoping it was his daughter, Gloria, on the phone. He sighed heavily. It damn near killed Matthias that he was as powerless to help the boy as he'd been with Mary.

"I've got news that'll cheer you right up," Harry said.

"I could use some good news."

"It's about Greg Bennett."

Matthias stiffened at the sound of the name. He hated Greg Bennett with an intensity that had grown through the years. Bennett owed him. The success of the winery was largely due to Matthias's guiding hand. If it hadn't been for him, especially in those early years, Greg would have lost the vineyard ten times over.

The younger of the two Bennett boys had shown a talent for the business, but Matthias had been the one to teach him about grapes, about wine making, about operating an estate winery. Greg's father, John Bennett, had lived for the vineyard, to the point that it had destroyed his marriage. But he'd been impatient with the boy, an ineffective teacher.

A few years after Greg had joined Bennett Wines, John had died, and Greg had taken over. From that point on, Matthias had advised Greg, guided him and helped him expand enough to buy out his brother's share. Matthias had treated Greg as he would have treated his own son, if he'd had one. He'd shared everything with Greg Bennett, his skills and ideas, his enthusiasm for viticulture and wine making, his friendship. That was what made the betrayal so painful, so devastating. Mary's illness was an almost intolerable blow, but Greg's refusal to help them—that had been, in a way, an even greater blow.

Mary had loved Greg, too. Many nights she'd insisted Greg join them for dinner. She'd opened her home and her heart to Greg, and when she needed him, he'd said no. Neither bonds of family nor friendship, neither obligation nor gratitude, had influenced his decision.

"What about Greg?" Matthias asked now.

"He was in San Francisco looking for a loan."

So Greg's vineyard had been hit by fan leaf disease. Matthias had suspected as much, but hadn't heard. "Did he get one?"

Harry paused for effect. "Not a dime."

"Good."

"I thought you'd like hearing that."

Matthias did, but not nearly as much as he'd hoped. All his energy was focused on doing what he could to help his daughter and grandson. For fifteen years his hatred of Greg Bennett had simmered, until it'd burned a hole straight through his heart. He couldn't forgive or forget, but his hatred no longer dominated every waking moment.

"You always said time wounds all heels."

Matthias grinned. Actually, Mary had been the one to say that.

"He's going to lose everything."

"It's what he deserves," Matthias said without emotion. The younger man had laid the foundation of his own troubles. If anything, Matthias was grateful he'd lived long enough to witness Bennett's downfall.

"I bet you think he should rot in hell," Harry said, and when Matthias didn't comment, his friend spoke again. "Hey, I hate the guy, too. Everyone does—although not as much as you do." He chuckled. "Well, I better get back to my morning coffee."

"Thanks for the call."

"Talk to you later," Harry said. A moment later, the line was disconnected.

Matthias appreciated knowing of Greg's financial problems. Fan leaf, a virus, had indiscriminately infected a number of vineyards in both the Sonoma and Napa valleys. Owners had been forced to tear out formerly productive vines and start anew, a prospect that was both time-consuming and expensive. Many of the small and medium-sized wineries in the two valleys were in danger of going under, Greg's included.

Mostly retired, Matthias needed something to occupy his time. In recent years he'd been working with local vineyard owners who were trying to grow vines resistant to the fan leaf virus before it had the same devastating results in Washington as in California.

Standing next to the phone, Matthias realized he should be dancing at the news about the disaster at Bennett Wines. A year ago, even six months ago, he would have been thrilled at the thought of Greg's troubles. Revenge was said to be a dish best eaten cold, and he'd certainly waited long enough to have it served to him. But he experienced damn little of the pleasure he'd anticipated. He'd wanted Greg to suffer the same agony that had tormented him as he stood by his wife's bedside.

The vineyard was everything to Greg, just as Matthias's only grandchild had become everything to him. And this time, they were both going to lose what they loved most.

"That is so sad," Mercy said, sitting on the edge of the counter in Matthias's kitchen. "Just look at him."

"He's worried sick about his grandson."

"What's going to happen to the boy?" Both Goodness and Mercy turned to Shirley.

"Do I look like I have a crystal ball?" Shirley asked irritably.

"I don't know about you two—" Goodness reclined on the long counter "—but I was hoping for something a little less stressful during this visit to earth. We're assigned to a guy who's a real jerk. Someone who couldn't care less about anyone except himself."

"Yeah, but we're here on earth, aren't we?"

"Well, yes, but—"

"I agree with you," Shirley said, cutting in while the opportunity presented itself, "but we *can* help."

"Where's the fun? We got a human with his head so far up his—"

"Mercy!"

"A self-centered human," she revised. "You know,

I think I'd feel better if Catherine had torn him to shreds. She should never have forgiven him."

"Mercy! Just listen to yourself."

"Right, right," she muttered, but Shirley could see that Greg was taking a toll on her friend's compassion.

"He's got too many problems for us to deal with," Goodness complained.

Shirley wasn't accustomed to such a defeatist attitude. "There's always his brother."

"What's this about a brother?" Goodness asked, suddenly attentive.

"Don't you remember?" Shirley did a double take. At their blank stares she sighed and reminded them. "Phil. You remember reading about Philip Bennett, don't you? He's a big muck-a-muck with Pacific Union Bank. Greg considered going to him for a loan, but couldn't bring himself to do it."

"Why not?"

Shirley sighed again. It would help considerably if Goodness and Mercy had finished their research.

"Refresh my memory, would you?" Goodness asked.

Shirley felt the burden of responsibility. "You didn't read the whole file, did you?" she asked wearily.

"Ah...no."

"That's what I thought." It would do no good to lecture them now. "Greg's mother was dying while he was in the middle of his second divorce."

"I remember reading about Bobbi," Mercy said triumphantly. "His second trophy wife."

"His second attempt to find another Catherine, you mean," Goodness muttered.

"Yeah, yeah. What does Bobbi and their divorce have to do with Greg's mother?" Mercy asked. Both angels were lying on their stomachs now, chins propped on their hands.

"You didn't finish reading the file, either?" Shirley was dismayed.

Anything that was going to get accomplished on this mission would obviously be up to her.

"It was too depressing."

"I don't have the patience to cope with men like him," Goodness said.

"Go on about his mother," Mercy urged, motioning with her hand for Shirley to continue.

"Greg hid as much of his wealth as he could from Bobbi, mostly in stocks and bonds. Otherwise she'd want her share in a divorce settlement."

"Were they married long enough for her to get much?"

Like most angelic beings, neither Goodness nor Mercy fully understood the way such matters were handled on earth. "Didn't matter," Shirley said. "She had a good attorney."

"Oh." Apparently Goodness and Mercy were knowledgeable enough to know what that meant.

"Lydia Bennett was dying and asked to see Greg," Shirley continued. "Unfortunately her request came the morning of his settlement hearing. Greg chose to go to court. I'm sure that if he'd known his mother would die before he got to the hospital, he would've canceled the court date."

"Oh, my," Goodness whispered.

"Phil never forgave him?"

"Never. They haven't spoken in ten years."

Goodness sat up and looked around. "I don't know if I can take much more of this. You two do what you want, but I need a break."

"Where are you going?" Shirley demanded. If her fellow angel got into any mischief, *she'd* be the one held accountable. As usual.

"Outside," Goodness called over her shoulder.

Without a word, Mercy followed Goodness.

"Mercy!" Shirley shouted.

Flustered now, she raced after the pair and came to an abrupt halt when she saw the hot-air balloons. Their huge parachutes with the bright rainbow-colored panels brightened the sky. There must have been a dozen balloons in the lower Kent Valley. She knew that conditions in the early-morning hours were often ideal for ballooning.

"Goodness! Mercy! Don't even think—" She was too late. Shirley caught sight of them as they hopped into a wicker carriage already filled to capacity. The ground crew was about to release the giant balloon from its tether line.

"Goodness!" Shirley called, exasperated beyond measure. "Mercy! Get out of there!"

Both pretended not to hear her. Shirley had to be careful. It wasn't uncommon for humans, especially young ones between the ages of one and five, to hear angels speak. Some older people possessed the ability, too. Inside the basket was an eighty-year-old grandmother who was taking the flight as a birthday gift from her grandchildren.

"For the love of heaven, will you two kindly—" Shirley froze, certain she was seeing things. The hot-air balloon had risen only about six feet off the ground, where it remained, hovering, even though the ropes that had bound the craft to earth had been set free.

"What's happening?" the old woman called to the ground crew, who'd stepped aside, obviously waiting for the balloon to glide upward. "Shouldn't we be going up?"

Shirley groaned when she saw the problem. Just as she'd ordered, Goodness and Mercy had indeed left the wicker basket, but had taken positions outside it, securing the dangling tether lines to the ground.

"Let go," Shirley yelled.

"Are you sure that's what you really want us to do?" Goodness asked.

Without waiting for a response, both Goodness and

Mercy released their tether lines at the same time. The balloon shot into the sky like a rocket. A few seconds later, its speed became more sedate.

"Wow!" Shirley heard the grandmother shout, holding on to her protective helmet with one hand and gripping the basket with the other. "Can we do that again?"

Goodness stood next to Shirley, looking extremely pleased with herself.

"That felt wonderful."

"You've risked the entire mission," Shirley said coldly. "Gabriel is sure to hear about this."

"Look at this," Mercy called as she joined them. She held a bottle of sparkling wine in one hand and dangled a trio of champagne flutes in the other.

"Where'd you get that?" Shirley asked.

"They fell from the sky." She grinned broadly as she said it.

"Come on, Shirl," Goodness cajoled, "humans aren't the only ones who enjoy a glass of bubbly now and then."

Chapter Five

Greg had barely slept or eaten in five days. He hadn't recognized the gaunt beleaguered man who'd stared back at him in the bathroom mirror that morning. For a long time he'd studied his reflection, shocked into numbness. Anyone seeing him would assume his condition was due to either the stress of his vineyard being wiped out or the failure of his third marriage. Neither was true.

He had a son. Catherine had given birth to a boy, raised that child, loved him, guided him into adulthood. Now this child, the son Greg had rejected, was a doctor. His son was a father himself, which made Greg a grandfather. A grandfather! That knowledge was heady stuff for a man who'd never...never been a real father and never would be. When he'd abandoned

Catherine and the child, Greg had assumed there'd be plenty of time for a wife and family. He hadn't realized back then that this child of Catherine's was his only chance. In his cowardice he'd thrown away the very life he'd always expected to have.

The first emotion he'd felt when Catherine told him about Edward had been undiluted joy. He had no right to feel anything—he knew that without her having to say it—but it'd been impossible to hide his reaction. Catherine always did possess the uncanny ability to see through him. It was one reason he hadn't been able to face her after she'd told him about the pregnancy. Evading responsibility, he'd run and hadn't looked back— but he'd been looking back plenty these past five days. Every waking minute, to be precise.

Greg wouldn't have blamed Catherine if she'd ranted at him, called him every ugly name her vocabulary would allow. But she hadn't. Instead, she'd offered him a gracious forgiveness, of which he felt completely un- deserving.

He could have accepted her anger far more eas- ily than her generosity of spirit. As unbelievable as it seemed, *she* was the one who'd made excuses for the shabby way he'd treated her.

All Greg could do was torment himself by thinking of the opportunities he'd missed when he walked out on Catherine. Since their meeting Friday afternoon, the sick feeling in the pit of his stomach had refused to go away. He didn't know what to do next, but one thing was clear: he had to do *something*.

Catherine had said she'd get in touch with him about his meeting Edward. He could tell she wasn't keen on the idea; her pointed remark that Edward already had a father had hit its mark. She'd said the decision would come after she'd had a chance to talk it over with her husband, Larry, and with Edward himself. They'd parted then, with Catherine promising to call soon.

He hadn't heard from her since, and the waiting was killing him.

By five that evening Greg had lost patience and decided to call Catherine. He hurried into his office and reached for the telephone, intent on dialing directory assistance. As he lifted the receiver, a week's worth of mail slipped off his desk and onto the carpet.

With money pressures the way they were, Greg had been ignoring the mail, which consisted mainly of past-due notices and dunning letters from his attorneys. He stooped to pick up the envelopes, and that was when he saw it.

A letter addressed to him in Catherine's flowing penmanship. Thirty-five years, and he still recognized her beautiful handwriting.

Without conscious thought, he replaced the receiver. He studied the envelope carefully, noting the postmark. She'd mailed it the day after their meeting. He held it for a couple of minutes before he had the courage to open it.

The letter was brief.

> Saturday, December 4
>
> Dear Greg,
>
> I'm sure you were as shocked to see me yesterday as I was to see you. As I said, I always thought we'd meet again one day, but I was still unprepared for actually running into you.
>
> I should have anticipated that you'd want to meet the son you fathered. It was shortsighted of me not to consider that before. I discussed it with Larry. My husband is both wise and generous, and he felt neither of us should be involved in making such an important decision. He thought I should leave it entirely up to Edward.
>
> I was able to reach Edward yesterday evening. It wasn't an easy conversation. He had a number of questions—ones I'd been able to avoid until now. I answered him truthfully; perhaps because I did, he's decided against meeting you.
>
> I'm sorry, Greg. I know this disappoints you.
>
> Catherine

Greg read the letter a second time, then slumped in his chair, eyes closed, while sharp pangs of disappointment stabbed him. It didn't escape his notice that Catherine had used the same form of communication he'd used when he deserted her. When he'd seen her the previous week, he'd given her his business card with his personal phone number. She could have put him out of his agony days earlier; instead, she'd chosen to torment him. She'd probably derived a great deal of satisfaction from turning him down, letting him know he wasn't wanted. No doubt, she'd waited thirty-five years for the privilege.

In an outburst of anger he crumpled the letter and tossed it in the wastebasket. Still not satisfied, he swept his arm across the desktop, knocking everything onto the carpet. His chest heaving, he buried his face in both hands.

The Christmas spirit had infected Phil Bennett. He hummed along to "Silent Night," which played on the bedroom radio, as he changed out of his business suit on Wednesday evening. Some people liked secular Christmas music the best, but Phil preferred the carols.

"You certainly seem to be in a good mood this evening," his wife remarked when he joined her in the kitchen for dinner. Sandy had grown a little thick through the waist over the past decade, but then, so had he. They'd been married for more than thirty years and raised three daughters and now they were both looking forward to retiring. The previous year, Phil and Sandy had purchased property in Arizona and planned to build in a retirement community, together with their best friends. It wouldn't be long now before the only real commuting he'd do would be on a par-three golf course.

"What makes you so happy?" Sandy asked as she brought a platter of meat loaf to the small kitchen table. With the children grown and on their own, Phil and Sandy had taken to eating their meals in the kitchen, instead of the dining room.

"I don't know," Phil said, carrying over the tossed green salad. When she wasn't looking, he removed a sliced cucumber and munched on it.

"Well, then, I'm glad to see you've got the spirit of the season," Sandy said absently as she placed a bowl of steaming scalloped potatoes on a trivet.

"I do indeed," Phil murmured, even though it wasn't Christmas that had made him so cheerful. Actually, Christmas had very little to do with it, but he wasn't telling his wife that.

Once Sandy found out that his glee was entirely because of what he'd learned about his brother's financial woes, she was sure to lecture him. And Phil was in too fine a mood to be chastised.

Word had reached him that afternoon of Greg's numerous attempts to obtain financing for Bennett Wines. It did his heart good to learn that his ungrateful arrogant younger brother was about to receive the justice he so amply deserved.

"You're going to choir practice tonight, aren't you?"

Sandy asked as she pulled out the chair across from him and sat down.

Caught up in his own thoughts, Phil didn't hear her right away. "Choir practice?" he repeated as he helped himself to a warm-from-the-oven biscuit.

"Phil!"

"Of course I'm going."

She relaxed. "Good. We need all the practice we can get."

Phil had recently joined the choir. It was his way of being part of the church community and contributing to the service.

So far, he knew only a few of the other choir members by name, but he'd know them all soon enough, especially now that they were meeting three nights a week to prepare for the Christmas cantata.

Unlike his brother, Phil was personable and generous—if he did say so himself. Plus, he had a reasonably pleasant singing voice. Greg didn't. Oh, his younger brother had certain talents, no question. He'd made Bennett Wines a respected label, well-known to wine cognoscenti. He had a single-minded focus that had led to his success. He could be charming when it was to his advantage.

And he was a ruthless bastard.

Phil had been waiting years for his brother to get what was coming to him. Years. The troubles currently plaguing California's wine industry had dominated the

local news channels for weeks. Fan leaf virus was causing the ruin of many vineyards, and of course, Phil had
wondered about Greg. But he hadn't heard anything
definite until that very day. What he'd learned made
him eager to sing.

After all these years, it was payback time. Greg had
deserted a woman in need; Phil hadn't known Catherine well, but he'd liked her...and he'd heard rumors
about a pregnancy. Then, perhaps worst of all, Greg
had ignored his own mother on her deathbed, and
when Phil had confronted him, he hadn't shown any
genuine remorse.

Naturally, because of his religious beliefs, Phil tried
not to hate his brother. He was willing to admit,
though, that he felt strongly antagonistic toward Greg,
not to mention gleeful about his financial woes.

He hadn't missed the fact that the one place Greg
hadn't come to apply for a loan was Pacific Union.
A wise decision. Given the opportunity, Phil would
have relished personally refusing his brother's application. More than that, he'd done everything he could to
make sure Greg didn't obtain funding. Actually, he'd
handled that situation in a pretty clever way. He'd sent
word through the banking community that when an
application came to them from Bennett Wines, no one
was to accept it. He'd given the impression that he'd
be the one helping his brother.

If Sandy learned about this, she'd be furious. She'd

accuse him of sabotaging Greg's business, but that wasn't how Phil viewed it. All he'd done was make sure Greg didn't get anything he didn't deserve. It'd probably be the first time, too. From childhood on, Greg had been the favored son. His fascination with that damned vineyard had guaranteed his special position with their father. And perhaps because he was the youngest, Greg had been coddled by their mother.

Even when she was dying, she'd made excuses for him. It was now ten years since they'd buried their mother, and every time Phil thought about the funeral, the fury he still felt toward his brother threatened to consume him.

The grief Greg had shown was as phoney as a three-dollar bill. If he'd cared even a little about their mother, he would have come to the hospital when she asked for him. They'd known her illness was terminal! Nothing could have been more important; nothing should have kept him away. When Phil found out that Greg had chosen to attend the settlement hearing on his divorce case instead, he'd completely lost his temper.

The two brothers had nearly come to blows at the wake. What irked Phil the most was the grieving-son act Greg had put on for family and friends.

Grieving? Yeah, right.

Phil had been appalled by the number of people who seemed to fall for Greg's act. Phil had been hurting, too, but he'd disciplined himself not to show his emotions. Grief was private, after all. He'd also grown accustomed to the reality of her death, because he'd been there. His mother's illness had lasted several months, and Phil had been the one to sit at her bedside, to read to her and comfort her.

Sure, his brother had come to visit on occasion, but he always had a convenient excuse for not staying long. In the beginning it was because he was harvesting the grapes. That was followed by the wine-production period, which he said demanded constant supervision. During the last months of their mother's life, Greg had been involved in his divorce, too. His *second* divorce.

As far as Phil was concerned, his brother's marital problems were exactly what he deserved. The first wife, who'd lasted ten years, was bad enough. The second one, who looked shockingly like the first, had stayed around three years, possibly four, he couldn't remember. Phil had heard that there was a third Mrs. Greg Bennett, and he couldn't help wondering if she'd go the way of her predecessors.

"Phil, hurry, or we're going to be late," Sandy called from the kitchen.

They'd finished dinner and washed their few dishes, and while Sandy was collecting the sheet music, Phil watched the last of the national news.

"I'm ready," he called back, turning off the TV. Preoccupied with thoughts of his brother, Phil hadn't heard a word of the newscast.

The church parking lot was only partially filled when they arrived. The choir director smiled in greeting, but didn't allow anyone to waste time. The Christmas cantata was only two weeks away, and there remained plenty of room for improvement.

The choir members gathered on the bleachers; as a tenor, Phil stood in the back row behind the women singing first soprano. It wasn't until they started the first song that he noticed the blonde standing directly in front of him. He'd never heard anyone with a more spectacular voice. It was hard to remember his own part. The woman's clear strong voice was so stunning he was completely distracted.

"I don't believe we've met," he said during the break.

She turned around and smiled. "We haven't."

"Phil Bennett," he said.

"I know."

"You do?"

"Oh, yes. I know quite a bit about you, Mr. Bennett."

This was something. Phil squared his shoulders a bit, feeling downright flattered by this lovely woman's interest.

The director was pleased with their performance and after an hour and a half, dismissed them for the night.

"We sounded quite good, didn't we?" Sandy said on the drive home.

"I thought so, too. By the way, who was the woman standing in front of me?"

"Mrs. Hansen?"

"No, the blonde."

His wife cast him a curious look. "There wasn't any blonde standing in front of you."

"Yes, there was. We spoke. You couldn't have missed her, Sandy. She had the most angelic voice. Really gifted."

Sandy laughed softly. "And what was her name?"

Phil hesitated, trying to remember. "I don't believe she gave it to me."

"I see." Although Sandy wasn't actually smiling, he heard the amusement in her voice.

"I'm telling you there was a blond woman standing in front of me, and she sang like no one I've ever heard."

"If you say so, darling."

Women! If Sandy hadn't seen the blonde for herself, Phil couldn't make her believe she'd been there. Next practice, he'd be sure to introduce the woman to his wife. Then he'd see what Sandy had to say.

Chapter Six

"Goodness!" Shirley waited until the church had emptied before chastising her fellow angel. She just didn't know how to handle Goodness and Mercy. Their antics were going to get them permanently expelled from earth. "You had to do it, didn't you?"

At least Goodness had the decency to look properly repentant. "You're right, I know you're right, but I couldn't stand the smug way Phil Bennett was acting. From the moment he heard about his brother's problems, he was beside himself with pleasure. All his talk about being a good Christian, too!"

"We aren't here to deal with Phil Bennett."

"But he's part and parcel of what's happening to Greg."

"Well, yes, and no..."

"I don't think we need to worry," Mercy told her. "If Gabriel's going to be upset with us, it'll be because of what happened with the hot-air balloon. Goodness singing in a church choir is minor compared to that."

Shirley had done her utmost to put the balloon episode out of her mind, and Mercy's reference did nothing to calm her already tattered nerves. "Please, don't remind me."

"If Gabriel didn't hear about *that*, then we don't need to—" Mercy stopped midsentence. A panic-stricken look came over her face, and she blinked several times before she said, "Oh…hello, Gabriel."

"Hello, Gabriel," Goodness repeated, wide-eyed and subservient.

"The Archangel Gabriel to you," their boss said sternly.

Feeling slightly light-headed, Shirley turned around and swallowed nervously. She opened her mouth to offer a multitude of excuses and saw that it would do no good. Their chances of putting something over on the archangel were virtually nil.

"I'm here for a progress report," he announced in the same controlled voice.

Goodness and Mercy both gazed pleadingly at Shirley, silently begging her to respond. She glared at them. When she tried to speak, her tongue seemed glued to the roof of her mouth.

"Well?" Gabriel muttered. "I'm waiting."

"Greg talked to Catherine and he knows he fathered a son," Shirley blurted out.

"Are you telling me that after thirty-five years, Greg just *happened* to stumble upon Catherine?" Gabriel demanded.

Shirley was never sure how much Gabriel knew of their antics, but suspected he was aware of it all. The questions were most likely a test to see how much they'd learned….

All three nodded in unison.

The archangel's frown darkened. "Thanks to a tableful of spilled crab, as I understand it."

"Yes, but that was only a means—"

"To an end," Gabriel completed for Mercy.

"Yes, and it worked very nicely, in my humble opinion," Goodness said in a bold rush. "It seemed a shame for the two of them to be in the same place after all those years and not know it. Really, all I did was point Greg out to Catherine. It was up to her to ignore or confront him."

"Yes," Mercy agreed. "Greg never did appreciate Catherine's strength."

"In other words, you're telling me," Gabriel said thoughtfully, "that Catherine chose to face him?"

Again all three nodded as one.

Gabriel's smile seemed involuntary. "The truth is, Catherine has Greg to thank for that inner strength. She gained it when he deserted her."

"They might never have met again if it hadn't been for those spilled crabs." Goodness made her foolishness sound like an act of genius.

Gabriel didn't look pleased—nor should he, Shirley reasoned. But that one antic *had* worked beautifully. She'd admit it now, even though she hadn't approved at the time.

"Do you have anything else to report?" Gabriel asked.

The three glanced at one another and shrugged.

"We've been to visit Matthias in the Seattle area," Mercy told him in an offhand manner meant to suggest that Gabriel probably already knew about it. "He still hates Greg, but he's more concerned about his grandson's condition just now."

"Ah, yes," Gabriel said, frowning again. "I've heard something about that. Cancer, is it?"

Shirley nodded. "The same form of leukemia that killed the boy's grandmother." Then, because she wanted to impress upon the archangel that their time on earth had been well spent, she said, "We've been to see Greg's brother, as well. Phil Bennett. You remember him, don't you?"

"Of course," Gabriel assured them. "I didn't realize Goodness enjoyed singing in choirs as much as she does. I'm sure she'll volunteer to be part of the heavenly host next year—is that correct?"

"Ah…" Goodness waited desperately for Shirley to

rescue her, but Shirley was in no mood to offer assistance. She might have leaped in to save her friend, if not for that escapade with the hot-air balloon. She felt mortified every time she thought about it. True, the sparkling wine had gone a long way toward tempering her anger, but...

"I'll be happy to serve wherever assigned," Goodness stated with a woeful look in Shirley's direction.

Gabriel arched his brows as if to say her willingness surprised him. "I find your attitude a refreshing change from when we last spoke."

"Singing with the heavenly host isn't my favorite Christmas duty," Goodness was quick to add, "but I'll serve wherever you feel I'd do best."

Once again Gabriel's expression implied that he was having trouble believing her. "Anything else you'd like to report?" he finally asked.

"Not a thing," Shirley said, eager for him to be on his way.

"None."

"Nothing I can think of."

He stared at the three of them. "All right, then, carry on. Just remember there are less than three weeks until Christmas."

"Oh, yes," they said in unison. They'd made a lucky escape, Shirley felt. Gabriel hadn't even mentioned the hot-air balloon.

"It was very good of you to check up on us," Goodness said.

That was overdoing it, in Shirley's opinion. She resisted the urge to step on the other angel's foot.

"Oh, yes," Mercy chimed in. "Stop by again any time." For good measure, she added a small wave.

Shirley sent both Goodness and Mercy looks potent enough to perm their hair.

Gabriel turned away, then abruptly turned back. "I had no idea you three enjoyed wine."

Not one of them uttered a word. Shirley swallowed hard, certain they were going to be plucking harp strings on some cloud for the remainder of their careers.

"I don't suppose you happened to notice the label, did you?" he asked.

No one answered.

"That's what I thought," Gabriel said. "It was the Bennett label. Greg Bennett is a talented wine maker. It would be a pity for him to go out of business, don't you think?" Not giving them the opportunity to respond, Gabriel whisked back to the realms of glory.

Greg Bennett had an aversion to the antiseptic smell that permeated hospitals. It nearly overpowered him the minute he walked through the large glass doors of San Francisco General. His dislike of hospitals was linked to his mother's long stay before her death, he supposed. That, and his own revulsion to needles and blood.

He paused at the information center.

"Can I help you?" a much-too-perky candy striper asked him.

"Where might I find Dr. Edward Thorpe?"

"Oh, you're here about the article. That's wonderful!"

Article? What article? Greg hadn't a clue, but he played along as if he did. His son had decided he didn't want to meet him, and that was his choice, but Greg wanted to see Edward. *Needed* to see him. He wasn't going to make an issue of it, wasn't going to announce who he was. He didn't plan to cause a scene or even call attention to himself. It was just that his curiosity had gotten the better of him....

Greg realized he'd given up his parental rights years ago, but he couldn't leave matters as they were. Not now that he knew Catherine had borne the child.

Catherine had mentioned the physical resemblance between them, and Greg felt an urge to simply see his son. He doubted they'd exchange a word. Without ever knowing him, without *wanting* to know him, Edward had rejected Greg.

Like father, like son.

"Take the elevator to the fifth floor." The young woman at the information desk pointed toward the row of elevators on the opposite side of the lobby. "Tell the nurse at the desk that you're here for the blood test."

"Ah." Greg hesitated. Did she say *blood?* He was most definitely not interested in anything to do with blood.

"I think it's wonderful of you," she added with a sweetness that made him want to cringe.

Greg didn't feel wonderful. Furthermore, he had no intention of giving anyone a drop of his blood. Not without one hell of a fight first.

"Dr. Edward Thorpe—you're sure he's there?"

"He's on the fifth floor," the woman assured him. "Just ask for him at the nurses' station."

"Thank you," he said, turning toward the bank of elevators.

"No, thank *you*," she called after him.

Greg got off the elevator at the fifth floor and to his surprise walked into a corridor filled with people. As instructed, he headed for the nurses' station, but before he could say a word, he was handed a clipboard.

"Complete the form, sign the bottom of the page and bring this back to me when you're finished."

Greg stared at the woman. "What's it for?"

"We need you to fill out the questionnaire and sign the release if we're going to take your blood." Unlike the perky candy striper, this one looked harassed and overworked.

"I realize that, but—"

"Just read the form. If you have any questions after that, I'll be happy to answer them."

That sounded fair enough. Greg joined the others,

sat down and read the page. It was exactly what the nurse had said. Basically, San Francisco General was requesting permission to draw blood. Not that he'd give it. Not in this lifetime.

As soon as he finished reading the form, he knew it was time to leave. He was about to pick himself up and discreetly disappear when a physician entered the room.

Conversation stopped as the man stood before the group and started to speak. Greg glanced up and froze. It was Edward. He recognized him immediately, long before he looked at the identification badge that hung around his neck.

"Has everyone finished signing the waiver?" Dr. Thorpe asked. "If you've decided this isn't something that interests you, you can leave now. We appreciate your time. For those of you who wish to continue, we promise to make this as quick and painless as possible. Before you know it, you'll be on your way."

Three or four people left the room.

Greg could follow them or proceed with this. Swallowing his natural aversion, he quickly signed his name. Okay, so he had to give a little of his blood. No big deal. He'd give a lot more if it meant he could spend a few minutes getting to know his son.

Catherine was right about one thing. Edward was tall and distinguished-looking, but as far as family resemblance went, Greg didn't see it. Still, he couldn't stop staring. This was *his* son. Edward looked good. Damn good. One glance had told Greg that his son was everything he wasn't. Dedicated. Compassionate. Smart.

"I'll need that," the nurse said as Greg shuffled past.

He gave her the clipboard and walked down the corridor, along with the others.

"Before we go any further," Edward said, "I want to personally thank each of you for your generous response to the recent newspaper article. We didn't have this many volunteers in the entire month of November. I'd like to think the Christmas spirit has touched us all. Does anyone have any questions?"

A man with prematurely white hair raised his hand. "What will happen if we're a match?"

While Edward talked about obscure-sounding medical procedures, Greg leaned toward the woman standing ahead of him. "A match for what?"

"Bone marrow," she muttered out of the corner of her mouth, then turned to eye him. "Are you sure you're supposed to be here?"

If ever a question needed answering, this was it.

"No," he said more to himself than to her. He wasn't sure of anything. Curiosity had brought him to the hospital. A curiosity so deep it had consumed him for days. After thirty-five years of not knowing, not caring, he now felt an overwhelming desire to see his son.

"Who'd like to go first?"

Before Greg could stop himself, he shot his hand into the air.

"Great. Follow me." Greg stepped out of the line and followed his son down the corridor to a cubicle.

"The nurse will be right in to draw blood."

"Aren't you going to take it yourself?" Greg asked. Already he could feel his panic level rise.

Edward shrugged lightly. "Well...the nurse usually does this."

"I'd prefer if you did it yourself. In fact, I insist on it."

Surprise showing in his eyes, Edward turned to face him. It seemed he was about to refuse, but for reasons Greg wouldn't question, silently led him to a chair and instructed him to sit down.

Greg sat, unbuttoned his shirtsleeve and rolled it up.

"Do I know you?" Edward asked, studying him carefully.

"No," Greg responded. "Do I remind you of anyone?" He was well aware that this was an unfair question.

"No, but I thought you might be a friend of my father's, Dr. Larry Thorpe."

"No, I've never met him."

Edward took a short piece of what looked like rubber tubing and tied it around Greg's upper arm. Next he gingerly tested the skin. "Nice blood vessels. We shouldn't have any problem."

"Good." Greg's mouth went dry at the sight of the needle, and closing his eyes, he looked away. This was even worse than the last time he'd had blood tests. He felt the needle against his skin and braced himself for the small prick of pain. As a kid he'd fainted in the doctor's office every time he received a shot or had blood drawn; he wasn't keen to relive the experience. That was years ago, but even now, as an adult, he generally avoided annual checkups if he could and— The needle was the last thing he noticed until he heard Edward's voice, which seemed to boom at him like a foghorn.

"Are you awake?"

Greg blinked and realized he was lying on the floor. Edward knelt beside him.

Their eyes met, and embarrassed, Greg glanced away. "What happened?" he asked, still in a daze.

"You passed out."

"I did?" Abruptly Greg sat upright. He would have fled, but the room had started to swim in the most disturbing fashion.

"Take it slowly," Edward advised, then helped him stand up. "I've asked one of the nurses to take your blood pressure. Tell me, when was the last time you had anything to eat?"

"I'm fine. I had breakfast this morning." It was a lie. He wasn't fine and he hadn't eaten breakfast. "I just don't happen to like needles."

"Then it's a brave thing you did, coming in here like this."

"Brave?" Greg repeated with a short laugh. "I'm the biggest coward who ever lived."

Chapter Seven

On Monday morning Greg recognized that he had no other options left to him. It wouldn't be easy to apply for a loan at Pacific Union Bank, but he had nowhere else to go. He'd never been a person to beg. Never *needed* to beg until now, but if begging would help him hold on to Bennett Wines, he'd do that and more.

The worst of it was that he'd have to go begging to his own brother. Phil, who'd like nothing better than to call him a failure. He wouldn't be far from wrong; Greg *felt* like a failure.

Despite his mood, Greg prepared carefully for the interview, wearing his best suit. He was about to head out the door when his phone rang. Caller ID told him it wasn't a creditor.

"Hello," he snapped.

"Hello, Greg."

It was Tess, his almost ex-wife. Ex-wife number three. "What's the matter? Are you after another pound of flesh?" he sneered. The last thing he needed right now was to deal with spoiled selfish Tess.

"I heard about your money problems."

"I'll bet you're gloating, too."

He heard her intake of breath. "I don't wish you ill, Greg."

He didn't believe her for a moment. "What do you want?" He was facing an unpleasant task that demanded all his attention, and he didn't want to be waylaid by an even more unpleasant one.

"I called because I didn't realize the extent of your money problems until now and, well...I'm sorry."

He said nothing.

"I wish you'd told me earlier. If I'd known, per-haps—"

"Would it have made any difference?" Their troubles had started long before the fan leaf virus had destroyed his vines. Long before he'd been confronted with one financial crisis after another. He knew when he and Tess got married that they were probably making a mistake. Still, that hadn't stopped him. He'd wanted her, and she'd wanted the prestige of being married to him. True, they looked good together, but at the moment it seemed that was *all* they'd had going for them.

He didn't like living alone, but he figured he'd get used to it eventually.

She didn't answer his probing question right away. "If I'd known about your troubles, I like to think it would have changed things."

All women preferred to believe the best about themselves, he thought cynically. "Think what you like," he muttered.

"Oh, Greg, do you hate me that much?"

Her words caught him up short. "I don't hate you at all," he said, and realized it was true. He was sorry to see the marriage end, but he hadn't been surprised and, in fact, had anticipated their divorce long before Tess moved out.

"You don't?" She sounded surprised, but recovered quickly. "Good, because I was thinking we should both do away with these attorneys and settle matters on our own. I can't afford three-hundred dollars an hour, and neither can you."

Greg wasn't sure he should put too much faith in this sudden change of heart. "Do you mean it?"

"Of course I do."

"All right, name a date and a time, and I'll be there." Greg hated the eagerness that crept into his voice, but he wanted the attorneys out of these divorce proceedings as much as Tess did. Without them—stirring up animosities, asking for unreasonable concessions—he and Tess had a chance of making this separation amicable.

"How about next Tuesday night?" she suggested.

Greg noted the time and place and, with a farewell that verged on friendly, they ended the call.

Well, well. Life was full of surprises, and not all of them unpleasant.

The drive into the city, however, could only be called unpleasant. Traffic was heavy and Greg soon lost his patience, particularly when it took him nearly an hour to find parking, and that wasn't even close to the financial district. The cost of parking in San Francisco should be illegal, he grumbled to himself. This was his third trip into the city within ten days; he hadn't been to San Francisco three times in the entire previous year. Greg preferred his role as lord of the manor—a role that was about to be permanently canceled if he couldn't secure a loan.

The sidewalks were crowded, since it was almost lunchtime. A brisk wind blew off the bay and he hunched his shoulders against it, ignoring the expensive-looking decorations on the bank buildings and the tasteful Christmas music floating out from well-appointed lobbies as doors were opened.

He sincerely hoped he wouldn't be forced to see Phil this early in the process, if at all. Knowing Phil as he did, Greg was keenly aware that his brother would take real pleasure in personally rejecting his application. Then again, he might exercise some modicum

of mercy and leave it to someone else, a junior offi
cer. But that wasn't something Greg needed to worry
about just yet. Today was only the first step—meeting
with a loan officer and completing the lengthy application. Once he'd finished the paperwork, he could
leave. Walk out the doors of yet another bank, wait for
yet another rejection.

He hated his own pessimistic attitude, but nothing
had happened in the past week to give him any hope.
His brother hated him—it was that simple—and Phil
wasn't the kind of man to put their argument behind
him. If he hadn't forgiven Greg in ten years, he wasn't
likely to do it now.

Phil had always been somewhat jealous of him, Greg
knew, something he'd never really understood. Greg
supposed his greatest sin was the fact that he'd been
born last. That, and sharing a passion for wine making with his father. Despite what Phil believed, Greg
had loved their mother. Her death, although expected,
had hit him hard.

He'd had no way of knowing how critical her condition was. They'd spoken briefly the night before, and
while she'd sounded weak, she'd encouraged him to
take care of his own business, to keep his appointment
at court. So he'd felt there was still plenty of time. She
hadn't seemed that close to death.

His fight with Phil after the funeral had been the

lowest point in his life. The truth was, Phil hadn't called him any name he hadn't called himself in the years since.

When Greg had finished with the loan application at Pacific Union, he walked back to the parking lot and paid the attendant what amounted to a ransom. But instead of heading for the St. Francis for a good stiff drink as was his custom, Greg drove to Viewcrest, the cemetery where his mother was buried.

He spent more than an hour wandering down long grassy rows in the biting wind before he located his mother's grave. He stood there, gazing down at the marker. *Lydia Smith Bennett, 1930-1989 Beloved Mother.* Phil had arranged for that stone. Phil had made all the arrangements.

This was Greg's first visit since they'd buried her. He shook his head, brushing away tears, overwhelmed by all the things he'd left unsaid. *I loved you, Mom. I did. I do. I'm sorry...*

Eventually he squatted down, touched his fingers to his lips and pressed them to the marble gravestone. A long moment passed before he stood up again, shoulders bent, head bowed, and silently walked away.

"Has anyone got a tissue?" Mercy wailed, and when no one responded, she threw herself against Goodness, wiping her face on her friend's soft sleeve.

"Would you kindly *stop?*"

But Goodness sounded suspiciously tearful. Shirley, too, was having a hard time holding back her emotions. Seeing Greg like this, broken and defeated, was painful. She barely recognized him anymore. She didn't know when it had happened or how, but she'd started to care about this man. Obviously Goodness and Mercy had also revised their feelings toward him.

"We've got to do something to help Greg!"

"We're trying," Shirley said.

"But he's in bad shape."

"I have a feeling it's going to get worse," Shirley whispered, fearing the future.

"Say it isn't so." Mercy wailed all the louder.

"His brother's going to reject the loan, isn't he?"

Shirley couldn't imagine Phil making any other decision and said as much.

"Not if I have anything to say about it," Goodness cried. "I think it's time I got ready for choir practice again, don't you?"

"Goodness, no!"

"I don't care if Gabriel sends me back to singing with the heavenly host or even gatekeeping. Phil Bennett is about to get a piece of my mind."

"Goodness." Mercy gasped.

"What?"

"Goodness," Shirley began. "You—"

"I'm going, too." Mercy glanced at Shirley.

Shirley could see she had no choice. "Oh, all right, but we can't all three join the choir."

"Why not?" Mercy asked, rushing to catch up with Goodness.

Shirley shook her head in wonder, sure they'd be facing the wrath of Gabriel once again. She just hoped the sacrifice they were prepared to make on Greg Bennett's behalf would turn out to be worth it.

"Phil, I swear you haven't heard a word I've said all evening."

Phil lowered the evening newspaper and looked at his wife. "What gives you that impression?"

Sandy threw back her head with a frustrated groan and returned to the kitchen.

Reluctantly Phil followed her. He should have known better than to try bluffing his way out of this. After all these years of marriage, there wasn't much he could hide from Sandy. He *was* preoccupied, true. It had to do with his brother. His shiftless irresponsible no-good brother who'd once been everyone's golden boy. Well, not anymore.

"Greg was in the bank this afternoon," Phil told Sandy in a nonchalant voice, pouring himself a cup of coffee.

He had Sandy's full attention now. "Did you talk to him?" She knew as well as he did that they hadn't spoken since their mother's funeral.

"No-o-o." He shrugged and tried to look regret-ful. "Dave Hilaire was the one who dealt with him."

"Greg's applying for a loan?"

Phil replied with a somber nod, but he felt like jump-ing up and clicking his heels.

"I've been reading for weeks about the problems the wineries have been experiencing," Sandy said thought-fully. "It must be terrible to have some virus wipe out generations of work. From what I read, some vineyards were more badly hurt than others."

"Greg's vineyard is one of the worst hit," Phil ex-plained in the same grave voice.

"I wondered about Bennett Wines…."

"Me, too." He did his best to sound sympathetic.

Sandy studied him, her eyes narrowed, and Phil struggled to hide his true sentiments. This virus, or something like it, was exactly what he'd been waiting for. *Justice. Retribution. Revenge. Call it what you will.* Phil had suspected that sometime or other, Greg would come crawling to him, asking for help. He'd antici-pated that day, longed for it.

"Are you going to be able to get him the loan?"

"I…I don't know," Phil hedged. He could hardly admit that he'd wear thong underwear in public before he'd sign off on the money Greg needed.

"But you'll do what you can?" Sandy gave him a hard look, and it was all he could do to meet her eyes.

"Of course," he said, sounding as sincere as he could.

She sighed, then walked over to him and kissed him

on the cheek. "Good. I've always hoped you two would put aside your differences."

Phil hugged her rather than look her in the face. "I know."

"You're all Greg has in the way of close family."

True, but that hadn't made any difference to his brother, and Phil didn't see why it should to him. Greg would come to him when he needed help and only because he needed help. So, any apology, any effort toward reconciliation, was tainted as far as Phil was concerned. Not that he intended to forgive his brother or had any interest in reconciling with him. It was too late for that. A just God would surely understand that some things were unforgivable. Wouldn't He?

"Poor Greg," Sandy whispered.

Oh, yes, and Greg wouldn't know how truly poor he was until Phil had finished with him.

"No wonder you weren't listening earlier," Sandy said, freeing herself from his embrace. "You had other things on your mind."

"I'm sorry, honey."

"You *are* going to help him, right?" Sandy was obviously seeking reassurance.

He nodded, still without looking at her.

"Fine. You'll be busy with that, so let's skip the practice. I'll tell Evelyn we can't do it."

Evelyn was the choir director. "Can't do what?"

"Go caroling Christmas Eve."

"Just a minute," Phil said. "Why not? We don't have

anything on the schedule, do we? None of the girls can come until Christmas morning."

"You're sure you still want to?" Sandy asked, sounding pleased.

"Very sure."

"You're just hoping to see that blonde again, aren't you?" she teased.

The blonde he'd spoken with earlier in the week hadn't shown up for practice the last two times, and Phil was growing discouraged. She hadn't been a figment of his imagination, despite what Sandy claimed.

"Maybe I did just imagine her," he said to appease Sandy. "I have to keep you on your toes, don't I?"

"We're going to be singing at the hospital Christmas Eve. San Francisco General." Sandy eyed him as though expecting Phil to change his mind.

"That's all right." Not exactly his favorite place, but he could live with it.

Besides, singing carols for the sick was what Christmas was all about. This was the season of love and goodwill, and he had an abundant supply. Not for his brother, but that was Greg's own fault. "As a man sows, so shall he reap." That was somewhere in the Bible, and if anyone questioned his actions, Phil would happily quote it.

Oh, yes, his brother was getting exactly what he deserved.

Chapter Eight

Matthias stepped off the plane and walked through the long jetway to the terminal at San Francisco International Airport. He'd come to spend Christmas with his grandson, fearing it would be the boy's last.

He spotted his daughter in the crowd and rushed toward her. "Gloria," he whispered, hugging her close. She'd lost weight and looked pale and fragile. This was destroying her—to watch her son dying, one day at a time. Matthias remembered how emotionally drained he'd become when Mary had been so terribly ill. Gloria had suffered then, too—and now she had to go through all this grief and pain again…. How could she bear it?

"Oh, Daddy, I have wonderful news!" his daughter exclaimed. "A donor's been found."

The unexpected relief, the gratitude Matthias suddenly felt made him go weak. "Where?" he asked hoarsely. "Who is it?"

"I don't know his name. He's a stranger, someone who responded to the article in last week's newspaper about the need for volunteers. Dr. Thorpe says he's making the phone call this afternoon and the whole process should start before Christmas. Isn't that *wonderful?* Oh, Daddy, I can't tell you how happy I am!"

"It's the best Christmas gift anyone could have given me."

"Me, too." Gloria's eyes shone with unshed tears. "Dr. Thorpe says the match is an especially good one. He sounded really hopeful, Dad. He didn't come right out and tell me this was going to save Tanner's life, but it is, I know it is. My heart tells me everything's going to be all right now." No longer did she struggle to hold back the tears. They fell unrestrained down her cheeks.

"When can I see this grandson of mine?" Matthias asked, eager now to reach the hospital.

They chatted nonstop on the drive into the city. When they got to the hospital, they hurried to the eighth floor. Weak as he was, ten-year-old Tanner was sitting up in bed waiting for Matthias.

"Merry Christmas, Grandpa." His pale face was wreathed in an extra-wide grin, although his eyes were sunken and shadowed.

"Merry Christmas, Tanner." Matthias hugged his

grandson, careful not to hurt the fragile little body. Seeing him like this was hard. So hard.

"Grandpa, are you crying?"

"It's only because I'm happy." Matthias glanced up and smiled apologetically at his daughter and the young nurse who stood beside her.

"Everything's going to be all right now," Gloria assured him again, and Matthias believed her. Everything *was* going to be better.

"Hello," Greg snapped into the small cellular phone. He'd never enjoyed talking on the telephone and was particularly annoyed by these newfangled cell things.

"Is this Greg Bennett?"

"Yes." Again his voice was as sharp and short-tempered as he could make it. He was walking between the rows of dead and dying grapevines, recognizing with final certainty that nothing was salvageable. No one could save what had taken fifty years to build.

"This is Dr. Edward Thorpe from San Francisco General."

Greg was so shocked he nearly dropped the phone. "Yes...Dr. Thorpe."

"I was wondering if you'd be willing to come back to the hospital later this afternoon?" His voice was pleasant, smooth, and if Greg wasn't mistaken, there was a hint of relief, too.

"I'll be there," Greg told him immediately.

"I realize it's short notice and this is the Christmas season, but—"

"I'll be there," Greg interrupted. "What time?"

"Is three o'clock convenient?"

"Sure." Then he couldn't resist asking, "Can you tell me what this is about?"

"I'd prefer we discuss it once you get here." He ended the conversation by giving Greg detailed instructions on where and how to reach him at the hospital.

"I'll see you at three," Greg said, then slipped the phone back into his shirt pocket. He drew in a deep breath, releasing it slowly.

Somehow, some way, Edward had discovered the truth about their relationship. Apparently his son had experienced a change of heart and decided to meet his biological father, after all.

Although Greg could offer no excuse for what he'd done to Catherine, he was grateful for Edward's decision. He did want Edward to know that he was proud to have fathered him, proud of the man he'd become. Greg could claim no credit; Edward owed him nothing. He only hoped that one day his son would be able to forgive him. He'd like a relationship with him, but wouldn't ask. That, like everything else, was up to Edward.

The drive into the city was becoming almost routine by now. Greg found he was nervous and at the same time excited. He parked where Edward had suggested and followed the directions he'd been given. Not until he was in the elevator did he realize the hospital's antiseptic smell hadn't overpowered him. That, he decided, was a good sign.

Edward was waiting when he arrived and personally escorted him into his office. Greg noted with some satisfaction that Edward was as tidy and organized as he was himself. The physician's desktop held a pen-and-pencil set, a clock and a computer monitor. On the credenza behind him was a small collection of framed photographs. He recognized Catherine in one, beside a tall gray-haired man, obviously her husband.

"Your wife?" Greg asked, looking past him to the gold-framed photograph of a younger woman.

Edward nodded.

"I've been married three times," Greg blurted out, then wanted to kick himself.

His son had the good grace to ignore that comment. "I suppose you've guessed why I asked you to stop by the hospital."

Greg liked the fact that Edward was forthright enough to get to the point immediately. "I have an idea."

"Good," he said, and seemed to relax. "That being the case, I'd like to introduce you to someone very special."

Greg hesitated. "Now?" To his mind, there were several things they should discuss before he met anyone important in Edward's life, but he was willing to let his son chart their course.

"If you don't mind, that is?"

"All right." Greg was simply grateful for this unexpected opportunity. His miserable attempt to see Edward earlier in the week had failed and humiliated him. Thankfully, Edward hadn't seen fit to remind him of what had happened at their last meeting.

Edward led him to the elevators and together they rode silently up several floors. They stopped at what appeared to be a children's ward. Greg frowned. Without asking any questions, he followed Edward to a room at the end of the corridor.

"This is Tanner Westley," Edward whispered, nodding toward the sleeping youngster.

From the tubes and other medical equipment linked to the emaciated body, Greg could tell the boy was gravely ill.

"Should I know him?" Greg asked, also in a whisper.

Edward shook his head. "Let's return to my office and I'll explain the procedure."

Procedure? Greg wasn't sure he understood, but he accompanied Edward back to his office.

When they entered the room and resumed their seats, Edward said, "I can't tell you how delighted I was that you proved to be a match for Tanner."

"Match?"

"Bone-marrow match," he said, eyeing Greg closely. "I assumed you understood the reason for my call."

"No. No way." Before he knew it, Greg was on his feet, emphatically shaking his head. "You want me to be a bone-marrow donor? This is a joke, right? You saw for yourself what happens any time I have blood taken."

"But you did come into the hospital for the test. Surely you realized—"

"There's no way in hell you're going to get me to agree to this!"

"Please, sit down." Edward motioned calmly to the chair.

He made an effort to fight back his disappointment. This meeting had nothing to do with Edward wanting to know his birth father—it was all about what he could do to help some *stranger*. Greg continued to shake his head. No amount of talk, even from his son, would convince him to let someone stick another needle in his arm. Or anyplace else, for that matter.

"Before you refuse, let me explain the procedure."

"You have a snowball's chance in hell of talking me into this," Greg felt obliged to tell him. He sat down, crossing his arms defensively.

"Two weeks from now, Tanner will be placed in an aseptic room where all his bone-marrow cells, both the good ones and the bad ones, will be destroyed by high doses of chemicals and radiation. This is the only way we have of completely eradicating the malignant cells."

"Doc, listen—"

"Let me finish, please, and if you still feel the same way after that, then…well, then we can talk."

Greg groaned silently and saw that he had no choice but to listen. Once Edward was finished, he would make some excuse and leave by the fastest route possible.

"This will be a dangerous time for Tanner, when he's most susceptible to infection.

"On the day of the transplant, the bone marrow will be extracted from you and stored in a blood bag, then intravenously transfused into Tanner over the course of several hours." He paused and studied Greg, who sat quietly, without moving. "Do you want to ask me about the pain or how the marrow is extracted?"

"Not particularly." He didn't need to know, didn't care to know, seeing that it wasn't going to happen.

"Most people are curious about the pain, and rightly so. I won't deny that there is some discomfort involved in this process, but I like to tell my donors that it never hurts to save a life."

Apparently Edward hadn't heard him correctly the first time. Greg wasn't doing this. *Couldn't* do this.

"I want to schedule the procedure as quickly as possible. As you can see, Tanner's health is failing."

Greg stared at him, wondering why Edward refused to understand. "Don't schedule anything for me. You'll just have to find another donor."

Now it was Edward's turn to wear a shocked disbelieving look. "You really won't do it?"

"Not on your life."

"It isn't *my* life or *your* life you're sacrificing. It's that young boy's. He'll die without a bone-marrow transplant."

"You'll find another donor." Greg stood, desperate to escape.

"No, we won't." Edward stood, too. "Do you think just anyone can supply the bone marrow for Tanner? If that was the case, I'd give him my own—but it's not. There has to be a match. You're that match."

"Don't see how I can be," Greg said stubbornly. He wasn't any relation to the boy.

"Why did you sign the release and agree to have your blood tested if you weren't willing to be a donor?" Edward raised his voice.

Greg dared not tell him the truth, dared not announce the real reason he'd come to the hospital.

"Did you take a good look at Tanner?" Edward asked. "He's only ten. He could be your son or even mine, and he's only got a very small chance of living without your bone marrow."

"And *with* my marrow?" Greg couldn't believe he'd even asked.

"There's a much greater likelihood that he'll see another Christmas."

Greg slumped back in the chair and covered his eyes with the heels of his hands. He didn't know what to do.

"Is he going to do it?" Mercy cried, pacing the area directly behind Edward's desk. "I can't stand not knowing."

"Shush! I can't hear." Goodness waved a quieting arm at Mercy.

"Shirley, do *you* know?" Mercy asked.

Shirley shook her head.

"He's going to refuse?" Mercy collapsed against a bookcase. "Has the man no heart?"

"Would you kindly stop that noise?" Goodness warned a second time. "I can't hear a thing."

"They're arguing," Shirley said. "And poor Greg has no way of knowing—"

"That Tanner is Matthias's grandson?"

"No, not just that," Shirley said sadly. The irony here had God's fingerprints all over it.

"No?" Goodness paused to look in Shirley's direction, clearly puzzled.

"What Greg doesn't know," Shirley told her two friends, "is that the boy is more than Matthias's grandson. He's Greg's chance for redemption."

Chapter Nine

Phil and Sandy Bennett arrived five minutes late for choir practice. Weaving his way between choir members, Phil climbed into his position on the riser, frazzled and irritated with his wife. Sandy might not have intended to make him feel guilty about Greg—but somehow he did. Well, not guilty exactly. A little uncomfortable, perhaps.

It wasn't until he opened the sheet music and started singing along with the others that he heard her. The blonde who sang first soprano was back! Gradually the tension between his shoulder blades relaxed. He knew it; she hadn't been imaginary at all. He waited until the last notes had died down, then casually leaned forward to speak to her.

"Where have you been?" he asked her, unable to disguise his excitement. Before she could answer, he asked another question. "What's your name?" It would have helped if he'd had a name to give Sandy. She knew a lot more of the choir members than he did.

"I've been busy," she told him.

"You're a member of the choir, though, aren't you?"

"I'm here."

Her hair was so blond it was almost white, and her singing voice... Phil had never known anyone who could sing quite like this woman. Her voice had a power and beauty that was almost unearthly.

"I've got to introduce you to my wife," he said while they shuffled through their sheet music, preparing for the next carol.

"What about your brother?" she asked. "Don't you want to introduce me to him, too?"

The music started before Phil had a chance to recover. "You know my brother?" he asked as soon as the last notes had died away.

"Oh, yes. I know a lot about you both."

"Who are you?" He didn't like the turn their conversation was taking.

"A friend."

Phil was beginning to wonder about that.

"You have Greg's loan application on your desk, don't you?"

How she knew that, he wouldn't ask. He'd been reading it that very afternoon just before he'd left the office, but only one person in the entire loans department was aware of it. He narrowed his gaze and studied this woman, who seemed to know more about him than she should.

"You haven't forgiven him for what he did to your mother, have you?"

"Damn straight I haven't."

"Then it might surprise you to learn that he hasn't forgiven himself, either."

"Pigs will fly before I believe he has one iota of remorse."

Frieda Barney turned around and glared at Phil. Someone else indicated her displeasure with his talking by pressing her finger to her lips. From the opposite end of the riser he could feel his wife's look burn right through him.

The music started again and Phil did his best to remain focused on it. The warmth he'd felt toward the beautiful willowy blonde had evaporated. By some corrupt means, his brother had finagled this...this spy into the church choir one week before Christmas. Greg always had been a good manipulator.

"You haven't spoken to him in all these years." A second voice came from beside him. This woman was slightly taller than the other. A second blonde? And one who sang? That didn't make sense. He closed his eyes, then opened them again, thinking he was losing his mind.

"Who are you?" he demanded in an angry whisper.

"The more appropriate question would be who are *you*."

"I know who I am."

"Do you?" the second woman asked. "Do you really?"

"You've always thought of yourself as the good brother," the first soprano chided.

"The churchgoer."

"The choir member."

"Yet all the while you've been plotting your brother's downfall, relishing it. You can hardly wait to see him suffer."

Female voices were coming at him from every direction. Not one voice, not even two, but three distinct voices. He thought he'd go mad if he heard another word. "Would you kindly *shut up*."

The room abruptly went silent. Everyone turned to stare at him. "I'm sorry," Phil mumbled. He could feel the heat rush into his face as he returned his attention to his music. He didn't know what had come over him.

Evelyn, the choir director, looked at him sternly. "Is everything all right?"

"Yes, I'm sorry. It won't happen again."

The director asked the altos to go over a particularly tricky piece of music while the others waited. They'd just sung the first line when the blondes started in on him again. "It's the season of brotherly love," the one beside him said. "I'm beginning to wonder if you know what that means."

Phil ignored her, refusing to let his gaze waver from Evelyn. At last the choir director motioned for the other sections to join in. These spies of Greg's could say and do what they wished, Phil thought, but he wasn't going to listen.

"You hide behind a cloak of decency all the while plotting your brother's downfall," the first blonde sang, the words fitting the music perfectly.

Phil's breath caught. He sincerely hoped no one else could hear these ridiculous lyrics.

"The good brother."

"The churchgoer."

"The choir member."

These three lines were sung as solos. The words seemed to linger in the air long after they'd been sung. Phil was convinced everyone knew the taunts were meant for him. Angry and embarrassed, he was about to get down off the riser and escape when he noticed the blonde beside him had vanished. He looked toward the row of first sopranos and saw that the other one was gone, as well. He'd never even seen where the third one had stood. How they'd left he didn't know. Didn't care. Good riddance. His relief was almost palpable.

Sandy began to berate him the minute they were in the car. "Your behavior tonight was appalling," she said angrily. "What's wrong with you?"

"Nothing." The car engine roared to life and he drove out of the church parking lot, eager to put the entire episode behind him.

"Telling Evelyn to shut up was probably the rudest thing you've ever done."

"I wasn't talking to Evelyn."

"If not Evelyn, then who?"

Phil exhaled sharply. "The blonde."

Sandy was quiet for a long moment—unfortunately not long enough to suit Phil. "What blonde?"

"The one standing in front of me. Actually, there were two blondes. No, three, only I didn't see the third, only heard her."

Once more his wife grew quiet. "Phil, there wasn't any blonde standing in front of you," she finally said. "No blonde singing first soprano."

"Yes, there was." He didn't know how Sandy could be so blind. Did she honestly think he'd make up something like this? "Greg sent them."

"*Greg?* Your brother?"

"Who else would do anything so underhanded?"

Silence again. Sandy didn't seem to believe him, which irritated Phil even more. Of course Greg was behind this. He'd put those women up to mocking him in front of his wife and all these other people—and then disappearing. This was exactly the type of stunt his brother would pull, but Phil wasn't going to stand for it. Oh, no. If Greg was planning to make trouble for him, he'd be ready.

"What does Greg have to do with any of this?" Sandy asked.

"He's paid them to spy on me."

"Oh, Phil, that's crazy."

"They had to be spies to know the things they did. Only someone who's been watching me would know I have Greg's loan application on my desk. Furthermore these women seemed to know how much I'm looking forward to turning him down." He hadn't meant to say all of that, but it was too late now.

"You're rejecting Greg's loan application." The accusation in his wife's voice stung.

"He's a bad credit risk."

"Phil, this is your *brother.*"

"My selfish arrogant brother." Apparently his wife needed to be reminded of that. "Even at the end of her life, Mom was making excuses for him. Don't *you* start."

"You're jealous, aren't you? Both your parents are long dead, and you still think they loved your brother more than you."

"They did." It was a fact he'd lived with his entire life.

"Greg has come to you looking for help. It couldn't have been easy for him."

"It's not going to get any easier, either," Phil snapped.

"You sound…happy about it."

Phil entered the ramp leading to the freeway with a burst of speed, pushing the accelerator all the way to the floor.

Sandy waited until they were moving smoothly along with the traffic. "Greg's your brother," she said again. "And you have the power to help him."

Phil tightened his hands on the steering wheel. "You're beginning to sound just like those blondes, singing their solos, humiliating me in front of every-one."

"The blondes sang?" Sandy sounded worried.

"You mean to say you didn't *hear* them, either?"

"No," Sandy said. "Should I have?"

"Yes…no." Maybe it wasn't as bad as he'd first thought. "You're not just saying that, are you?"

"Saying what?"

"That you didn't hear them."

"I didn't," Sandy assured him. "But I still want to know what they said."

He sighed. "According to them, I like to think of myself as the good son and I wear a cloak of decency while plotting against my brother. Something like that." Phil checked the speedometer and realized he was speeding. As he slowed the car, he glanced at his wife, only to discover that she was staring intently at him. "Don't tell me my own wife agrees with them!"

Sandy didn't answer, but her silence said it all.

"Go ahead and be angry," he said, and noted he was speeding again. He seemed in an all-fired hurry to get home and he wasn't sure why. If anything, this argument was bound to escalate once they got there.

"I can only imagine how difficult it must have been for Greg to come to Pacific Union," Sandy said not for the first time. "Especially when he knew that you'd be the one who'd ultimately accept or reject his loan application."

Phil refused to dignify her comments with a response.

"Greg is coming to you for help."

Despite himself, Phil snorted with laughter.

"Oh, Phil, how could you?"

"Easy."

Right after Christmas he intended to call Greg into the bank. He'd leave him to wait and wonder during the holidays. When his brother arrived at the bank, Phil would have him escorted into his office. It would be the first time they'd been face-to-face since their mother's funeral.

Then he was going to personally deliver the news.

Chapter Ten

Christmas Eve Matthias stopped at the hospital following his grandson's bone-marrow procedure. Gloria had spent the day with Tanner and called to tell Matthias that the transplant had gone well. Tanner was in an aseptic room Matthias couldn't enter. Only Tanner's mother was allowed to visit, and even then the boy was kept behind a protective plastic barrier. Despite that, Matthias couldn't think of anyplace in the world he'd rather celebrate Christmas.

Because of the unknown bone-marrow donor, they actually had something to celebrate. The change in Gloria since the donor had been located was dramatic. The edge of fear was gone from her voice, and color had returned to her cheeks.

"Dad!" Gloria waved to attract his attention when he walked into the hospital lobby.

"Merry Christmas, sweetheart." He kissed her cheek.

"Dad, Tanner's donor is still here. Everything went as expected, but when he stood up to leave, he blacked out and fell against the hospital bed. He's got quite a gash on his head."

The donor had asked to remain anonymous and had given up today—Christmas Eve—for Tanner's sake. "I'm sorry to hear that. Is he okay?"

"He's fine. Said he felt foolish for causing all this fuss. He's in the emergency room, waiting for his wife to pick him up now."

"I'd like to thank him personally," Matthias said. "Do you think he'd mind?" This stranger, who'd responded to a newspaper article, had given his grandson a second chance at life. The only reward he'd received for his effort had been a cut on the head—and the grateful appreciation of Tanner's family. The least Matthias could do was sit with him until his wife got there.

"Well, I'll go and talk to him."

"If you don't mind, I'll go up to Tanner again."

"Good idea," Matthias said. He followed the sign that pointed to the emergency room; it led him to a large waiting area. Groups of people were scattered about. A lone man sat in a shadowy corner, his forehead bandaged. That had to be him.

He walked over. "Hello, I'm Matthias Jamison, Tanner Westley's grandfather, and I—" Matthias didn't finish. He couldn't finish. All he could do was gape at the man he'd hated for fifteen years.

"Matthias, is that you?"

"Greg?"

In shock, they stared at each other for the better part of a minute.

"You're Tanner's grandfather?" Greg finally asked.

Matthias nodded.

Apparently Greg hadn't known of the connection between him and Tanner. The anger and hatred Matthias had lived with all these years flared back to life, racing through his blood like a shot of adrenaline. But to his surprise, it died a quick and sudden death.

Matthias claimed the chair across from Greg, astonished that he couldn't think of a single word to say.

"That explains it," Greg said, slowly shaking his head.

Matthias had no idea what he was talking about.

"Now I understand why I was a match for Tanner. It's because you and I are second cousins."

"You mean you really didn't know? That Tanner's my grandson?" Matthias had to ask.

Greg smiled wryly. "Not a clue. You're telling me that was Gloria I talked to a few minutes ago? Your Gloria...and Mary's?" As soon as he spoke, he seemed to regret bringing up Mary's name. "She's certainly changed from the little girl who used to race up and down the vineyard rows."

"It's been a long time."

Greg nodded. He splayed his fingers through his hair and winced when he touched the bandaged gash.

His hair was almost completely gray now, but it looked good on him. "She isn't the only one who's changed."

"We've both changed," Matthias murmured, and leaned forward to rest his elbows on his knees.

"About Mary," Greg whispered. "I...I was wrong. I've thought of Mary, of you, so often..." He seemed unable to continue.

Emotion blocked Matthias's throat. It'd been so long since he'd cried that when the tears filled his eyes, they burned and stung like acid. Embarrassed, he blinked hard and looked away. "She died fifteen years ago and I still miss her. Doesn't seem right not having Mary."

"Can you forgive me?" Greg's voice was raw with pain.

"The Lord takes away, but He also gives. Mary's gone, but because of you, young Tanner's got a real chance at beating the same cancer that killed his grandmother."

"Mr. Bennett." Tanner's doctor joined them. Judging by the way he was dressed, he was about to leave. Not that Matthias begrudged him that, seeing as it was Christmas Eve. Edward, like everyone else, wanted to be with his family. "I just heard about your accident and I came to tell you how sorry I am."

Matthias, for one, was grateful for the distraction. It gave him a moment to compose himself.

"Not to worry," Greg said, as if the stitches in his head were of little significance. "It'll be healed in no time. Besides, I should've known better than to stand up without the nurse there."

"I did warn you not to be in too much of a hurry." The doctor smiled, then glanced at Matthias. "I see you two have met."

"We're old friends."

"Cousins, actually," Greg added, and because they needed an excuse to laugh they both did.

"I see..." the doctor said. "You have a ride coming for you?" he asked Greg next.

"Yes. My wife will be here any minute."

"If there's anything else I can do for you, don't hesitate to let me know."

"I won't," Greg promised.

Dr. Thorpe nodded. "I probably won't be seeing you again, Mr. Bennett, but I want you to know that I think you did a brave thing. A selfless thing. Thank you." With that he held out his hand. Greg stood and clasped it firmly.

"Thank you," he returned.

Greg slumped back into his chair, eyes on the retreating physician. "He's a fine young man, isn't he?"

Matthias heard a catch in his voice. "One of the best cancer specialists around." Gloria had repeatedly told him of the wonderful caring physician who'd been so good to Tanner and to her.

Greg's gaze lingered on Dr. Thorpe and his expression was oddly pained.

"You okay?" Matthias asked.

Greg's nod was slow in coming. "I will be."

Not understanding, Matthias frowned. "You want to tell me about it?"

"Perhaps someday," Greg mumbled.

The tension was broken by the sound of carolers. "Joy to the World" drifted toward them, the music festive and lively, a dramatic contrast to their current mood.

"Is it close to Christmas?" Greg asked, seemingly unaware.

"It's Christmas Eve," Matthias told him.

Greg's eyes widened with surprise. "I didn't realize..."

The music made for a pleasant background as the two men continued to talk, mostly about Tanner and Gloria. Several minutes later Matthias brought up the subject of the vineyard. "I read about the fan leaf problems in your area."

"It wiped me out," Greg said.

That accounted for his cousin's haggardness and his beleaguered look, Matthias thought.

"A lifetime of work destroyed in a single season," Greg murmured.

"You're replanting of course."

Greg shook his head. "Takes capital, more capital than I can muster."

"Get a loan. That's what banks are for."

"You think I haven't tried?" Greg's voice rose. "I'm not a poor risk, at least not on paper, but money's tight.

Tighter than I realized. Despite everything, I haven't been able to convince a single bank to give me a loan."

"I've been working with Columbia Wines up in Washington. The vines there are stronger, more resilient. Say the word and I can arrange for you to replant with those."

Greg shook his head again. "Hell, I'm sixty. Too damn old to start over now. Lately I've been thinking of selling out completely and hiring on with one of the other wineries."

That wasn't the answer, as Matthias was well aware. "You never could tolerate working for others. You like being your own boss too much. Besides, you're still young. I'm damn near seventy and I don't think of myself as old."

"Well, I can't get the financing."

"What about Phil? He works for a bank, doesn't he? He should be able to help you."

Greg shook his head. "He has as much reason to hate me as you do."

The carolers drew closer, drowning out any chance of further conversation. Matthias could only imagine what had caused such a rift between the two brothers.

Memory told him that Phil had always resented Greg's good looks, his social skills and sense of purpose. Whatever happened had been building for years. Matthias didn't doubt that Greg had played a role—but Phil had already been holding a grudge. Looking for a reason to justify his resentment.

Then, without warning, Greg rose slowly to his feet, almost as if he was being drawn upward against his will.

Matthias looked up and then he knew.

Phil saw his brother and Matthias at the same time as Greg saw him. His first reaction was shock, followed by unexpected compassion. Greg—head bandaged, features pale and drawn—stood beside Matthias Jamison, of all people.

Hardly conscious of what he was doing, Phil stopped singing. Sandy did, too. Slowly, involuntarily, he separated himself from the band of carolers. Almost before he realized his intent, he stood silently before his brother. They stared at each other, eye to eye.

Neither man spoke. For his part Phil couldn't find the words. This was what he'd wanted, what he'd dreamed about—seeing his brother, his sophisticated suave rich brother, broken and humbled. Greg was certainly humbled, but to his own amazement, Phil experienced no glee at the sight.

He was incapable of speaking. His mind had emptied, but his heart had grown suddenly full. His eyes filled with tears, and he struggled to hold everything inside.

Then, wordlessly, compulsively, the two brothers strained toward each other and hugged.

"What happened?" Phil asked when they broke apart. He was looking at his brother's bandage.

As if he'd forgotten, Greg touched his head. "Nothing much. It's nothing to worry about."

"Matthias," Phil said, glancing toward his cousin, "I didn't know you still lived in California."

"I don't. I came to see my family—and to thank Greg. He was the bone-marrow donor for my grandson."

Greg had voluntarily given his bone marrow? Phil remembered his brother's aversion to needles—the way he'd always fainted in the doctor's office whenever he had to get a shot.

"I…" Clearly Greg was flustered. "I was a match for the boy. Matthias is our dad's cousin, remember?"

Phil nodded.

"How are you?" Matthias asked.

"Good," Phil told him, and the two exchanged hearty handshakes.

"You still work for Pacific Union, don't you?" Matthias asked him.

"Yes." Phil already knew what his cousin was about to ask.

"Can't you help Greg get the financing he needs to replant?"

"How are you going to answer him?" Sandy whispered, slipping her hand into the crook of his arm. Phil was sure the two men hadn't heard. He was reminded of other voices he'd heard that apparently no one else had. *You hide behind a cloak of decency… The good brother…*

"I'll see to it that you get your loan," Phil said, looking directly at Greg. "Drop in after the holidays to sign the paperwork, and I'll arrange for the transfer of funds."

Greg just stared at him. "Phil," he began hesitantly, "you'd do that for me after..." Words failed him.

"It seems we both had a lot of growing up to do."

"Thank you," Greg said, his voice choked and low.

"Greg!" cried a female voice from across the room.

Phil turned and saw a stunningly beautiful woman at least twenty years his brother's junior come racing across the emergency-room waiting area. "Oh, darling, just look at you."

Greg smiled as the woman ran one hand down the side of his face and inspected the damage to his head. "How did this happen? Omigosh, you can't imagine what I thought when the nurse phoned."

Not answering, Greg placed his arm around the woman and turned to Matthias, Phil and Sandy. "This is Tess, my wife," he said matter-of-factly.

"Hello, Tess," Sandy said, and in that warm welcoming way of hers, extended an invitation to Christmas dinner. Matthias and Gloria were included, too; Gloria would be with Tanner for part of the day, but Matthias thought she could join them for a few hours.

"Can we, darling?" Tess opened her eyes wide. "You know how much I hate to cook. Besides, it's time I met your family, don't you think?"

Greg nodded, still smiling.

The women started talking, and soon it was impossible to get a word in, but Phil didn't mind. And from the looks of it, neither did Greg or Matthias.

"Isn't that the most incredible sight you've ever seen?" Goodness said from her perch atop the hospital light fixture. Shirley and Mercy sat with her, nudging each other as they jostled for space.

Seeing Greg with his brother, his cousin and his wife was heady stuff, indeed. Shirley couldn't have wished for more. Despite their antics, everything had worked out beautifully, and this hadn't been an easy case. Gabriel had made sure of that.

"I see you three are mighty pleased with yourselves," the archangel said as he appeared beside them.

"We did it," Mercy told him with more than a hint of pride.

"And all without involving the FBI or the National Guard," Goodness was pleased to report.

"There was that one minor incident with a hot-air balloon, though," Gabriel reminded her. "The Federal Aviation Administration is still looking into it."

Shirley noticed that her friends had suddenly gone quiet. "All in all, it's been a challenge." They'd brought the case to a successful conclusion, but Shirley was convinced it had taken more than a little heavenly intervention. "What's going to happen to Greg?" she asked, curious to learn what the future held for the man she'd once thought of as despicable. In time she'd actually come to like him and wish him well. He wasn't as bad as he'd seemed at first glance, and she wondered if this was the real lesson Gabriel had been hoping to teach them.

"Well, as you can see he's mending fences with Tess," Gabriel said. Greg had his arm around his wife as they stood and talked to Matthias, Phil and Sandy.

"So their settlement meeting went well," Shirley murmured.

"Really well," Mercy said, grinning widely. "Okay, okay, so I joined them for a few minutes. Trust me, the meeting went better than either of them expected."

"They're getting back together," Gabriel continued, "and are determined to make a real effort to give their marriage another chance."

"Do they last?"

"With ups and downs over the next few years, but they always manage to work things out. They both decide that love, like most everything else in life, is a decision and they've decided to stay together."

"What about the winery?" Shirley asked.

"Greg does replant with the vines Matthias sells him, and in a few years Bennett Wines will once again be known as some of the area's best."

"Matthias and his grandson?"

"The boy makes a full recovery and Matthias takes frequent trips to California. When the grapes mature, Greg gives Matthias a percentage of the profits as a means of thanking him for his forgiveness and for his help through the early years. That small percentage is enough for Matthias to retire completely. And Gloria meets a good man, a new assistant winemaker hired by Greg. They eventually get married."

"I'm glad," Mercy said. "For all of them."

"What about Greg and Edward?" Goodness asked. "Does he ever find out that Greg's his biological father?"

Gabriel shook his head. "Edward doesn't change his mind about not wanting to know him, and Greg respects his decision. However, he is deeply grateful for the opportunity to have met the son he fathered."

Mercy smiled sadly as the carolers began singing "What Child Is This?" Shirley nodded in understanding.

"Now, are you three ready to return to heaven?" Gabriel asked.

Goodness and Mercy agreed, but with obvious reluctance.

"Can we come back next year?" Goodness asked as they drifted upward.

"We'll have to wait and see," Gabriel told her.

"Yes." Shirley linked hands with her two friends. "We'll just have to see who needs our help most," she whispered to Goodness and Mercy.

★ ★ ★ ★ ★

Loved this book?

Visit Debbie Macomber's fantastic website at
www.debbiemacomber.com for information
about Debbie, her latest books, news,
competitions, knitting tips, recipes,
Debbie's blog and much more…

You can also follow Debbie online
f facebook.com/DebbieMacomberWorld
🐦 twitter.com/debbiemacomber
📷 instagram.com/debbiemacomber